Black Ops: Red Alert

Book 1 of the Natasha Black series

Richard Benham & James Barrington

PostScript Editions Limited

First publication in Great Britain 2021 by PostScript Editions Limited

Richard Benham and James Barrington have asserted their rights under the Copyright, Designs and Patents Act 1988 to be identified as the authors of this work.

To receive a free copy of Manhunt by James Barrington, go to:

www.JamesBarrington.com

Contents

PART ONE – THE SECRET

Prologue

5 May 1945: Berlin, Germany

Captain Nick Fletcher MC stared at his badly scuffed and battered leather army boots, now deeply stained with human blood and, not for the first time, wondered just what the hell he was doing there. 'There' being at that moment a small but elegant office in one of the few remaining buildings still standing in the centre of Berlin. The bombing campaign and the relentless artillery barrage mounted by the Russian Army, a barrage that would later be described as the biggest bombardment in history, had flattened almost everything else in that district.

When they'd reached Berlin, well ahead of the American and British troops, the Soviet forces had employed a line of heavy weapons some 18 miles long containing over 9,000 artillery pieces and *Katyusha* rocket launchers to utterly destroy the German forces and open the road to the city. The attack had begun on 20 April 1945, coincidentally Adolf Hitler's fifty-sixth birthday, and the weight of ordnance fired into Berlin in that short final assault greatly exceeded the entire tonnage of bombs dropped on the city by the Western Allies during the whole conflict.

The pivotal moment of the offensive had been the capture of the Reichstag, the German parliament building, because of its obvious symbolic significance. The Soviets had captured the building on the evening of 30 April, the same day that Hitler had committed suicide, and early the following morning a Russian soldier had raised the flag of the 150th Rifle Division, later known as the Banner of Victory, on the roof.

The Russian bombardment had only stopped when the Germans finally surrendered on 2 May and two days after that Fletcher and the handful of men under his command – a dozen survivors from two of the Rifle Sections in his Platoon – had walked into the ruined city. Fletcher's field promotion to captain and his orders had been delivered at the same ad hoc briefing by a major who looked either bemused or possibly confused. His unit was to enter Berlin, avoid all contact with the Soviet forces and simply observe and record anything of interest. Clarification of what was meant by the word 'interest' was not forthcoming. Once they had completed this task they were to travel by train and boat back to Britain to be demobbed.

Those orders had led Fletcher to the room and the seat he was then occupying, an over-stuffed easy chair that was the sole remaining piece of furniture.

His gaze rested on the highly polished wooden panelling on the opposite wall, panelling that was entirely undamaged, a rare sight after the utter devastation in the streets outside. The room was grand in style but not in size, and its position in the centre of the city, with two big windows overlooking the square, meant it had probably belonged to, or more likely had been commandeered by, someone very senior in the German command, possibly within the notorious *Schutzstaffel*, better known as the SS.

Something caught his eye on the panelling, something that wasn't quite right. He stared at it for a few moments and concluded that three of the panels were not precisely aligned and each had a slight indentation only noticeable from a certain, very precise angle. It was probably where a desk had been placed against the wall. Fletcher was interested but simply too tired to bother to walk over and look at it.

He closed his eyes, feeling completely drained. His shoulders slumped and his mind drifted into a state of utter exhaustion.

Like many others, he had signed up for the war in 1940, believing it would be over in a few months once the Americans had become involved. Unusually he had come from the clergy and had decided his belief in God would be a force for good in the war, at least from his standpoint. The bishop had raised an eyebrow when Fletcher's papers had come through from the army, but he had been released without fuss after a somewhat stilted interview when the bishop and two other senior members of the clergy had done their best to dissuade him.Now, nearly five years on, the captain was a broken man. Devoid of emotion, he'd killed so many men he'd genuinely lost count and he'd long ago abandoned whatever final scraps of his former faith had survived his initial forays into combat.

The war was over and he'd survived, but was this a world he wanted to be part of or could even face after what he had experienced? Good had ultimately won over evil but at what price, he wondered. The financial cost to all the nations involved would be staggering, but he was more concerned about the moral and spiritual price that would have to be paid. Other people would decide that while he faced the ghosts of his own empty future.

Fletcher knew he would not be going back to the Church and, while he had done well enough in school, he had entered the clergy at seventeen with no university education. With no other skills or vocation, apart from how to lead troops across battlefields and kill Germans, neither ability having much obvious value in civilian life, he concluded with a sense of irony he was almost certainly completely unemployable now that the war had ended.

He had led his small unit in a search of the now empty and deserted remaining buildings of Berlin, looking for anything that might be of military interest. All the furniture, paintings and anything else of any value had already been taken, most probably looted by servants, fleeing Germans or even by Russian soldiers.

The door of the room suddenly opened with a crash that had Fletcher instinctively reaching for his non-official sidearm. Rather than the Enfield revolver he had been issued, his belt holster now contained a Browning FN-Inglis nine-millimetre semi-automatic pistol he'd 'recovered' from a Waffen-SS soldier who no longer needed it because Fletcher had just shot him. The automatic was a far better close-quarter weapon than the Enfield. Not quite as accurate as the revolver, but the much larger magazine capacity more than made up for it.

Then he relaxed as he saw who it was.

'Sir, come quick, they've found a Nazi hiding in a cupboard, with a false back like and he's got a bloody grenade.'

Corporal Jack Mitchell, a Geordie by birth, had been with Fletcher as his number two for over two years, his previous senior NCO – a sergeant – having been killed by a sniper with no replacement sent. He trusted Mitchell totally and owed the man his life – twice over, in fact – and concluded that their relationship went beyond friendship as he would forever be in his debt.

But even as he stood up from the chair to investigate there was a huge flash and an explosion that shook the room. The blast threw both Fletcher and Mitchell to the floor in a shower of dust and debris.

Fletcher winced as the back of head throbbed and his eyes began to sting. To be killed after the German surrender would be both ridiculous and rotten bad luck, he mused. Mitchell was now swearing fluently and rapidly in a thick Geordie accent. Fletcher had to smile as he opened his eyes and saw his corporal standing up and surrounded by a hazy cloud of dust. He was clearly unhurt but equally clearly as mad as hell.

The two men walked out of the room to inspect the damage.

Rather than be captured, or possibly even by mistake, the hiding German soldier had detonated the grenade, making an extremely nasty mess within the cupboard cavity where he had been crouched, and which had been lined with concrete. The roof above had caved in as the explosion had been channelled upwards and outwards like a funnel.

Fletcher and Mitchell had been barely ten feet from the back of the reinforced cupboard and the concrete lining had clearly saved them from injury. What it had also done, however, was to rip apart the panelling, tearing a jagged hole in the wood, and from this opening a small book and several gold coins had spilled out onto the dusty floor. Behind the broken panels the two men could see the door of a steel safe that for some reason appeared to have been left unlocked.

Mitchell bent down and instinctively reached out for the gold coins. To Fletcher, they looked about the size of the old eighteenth century George III two-penny piece he had at home in a box of curios. Commonly known as a 'cartwheel,' it was a large, thick and heavy coin, and what they'd found resembled it only in size and in having a raised rim around the circumference. The coins were bright and shining, the Nazi swastika symbol on one side and Hitler's profile on the other. Fletcher had heard somewhere that Hitler only wanted his profile on coinage once he'd won the war as he believed it to be bad luck, so these were certainly unusual.

As Mitchell put them in his pocket, something stopped Fletcher from reprimanding him and he helped him pick them up. There were about half a dozen coins in total, all apparently identical and each about double the thickness of a normal coin and looking more like a medal with an inscription around the rim. Whatever they were, they would certainly be worth something even if they weren't solid gold, which Fletcher doubted because he didn't think they were heavy enough. Maybe they were gilded silver.

'Good luck, Jack,' Fletcher said, 'you deserve these. I hope they'll help you make a good life for yourself after all you've been through.'

'Thank you, sir. Normally I wouldn't, but everyone else in here is stuffing their pockets and I feel like I deserve it, if that makes sense?'

'It does. The truck should be here soon to take us back. Get the men ready to move and I'll be down in a few minutes.'

For what they both knew might be the last time, the two men shook hands, then Mitchell turned and disappeared through the dust.

Fletcher picked up the small, tatty burgundy book embossed with a swastika and a single coin that Mitchell had overlooked. He shoved them into his outer pocket, looked around and then headed for the staircase.

Discipline had all but vanished amongst the allied men around him in the euphoria of victory, and whilst he should have tried to maintain order as a British officer, he simply walked quietly down the dirty carpet on the wide grand staircase and out into the square below to wait for the lorry that would take him back to the British lines and from there on to the French Channel coast and Britain.

Chapter One

Present day: GCHQ Cheltenham, Gloucestershire, England

A very slight flicker of government-issue lighting stalked Natasha Black as she walked below the hallowed buildings of GCHQ in Cheltenham. It intruded on her consciousness like the irritating buzz of a mosquito.

She distracted herself by focussing on the curved corridor and how it mirrored the building above. The locals called it 'The Doughnut,' an architectural spying confectionary opened in 2003 and designed to resist a rocket-based attack and, at least according to some sources, in theory able to withstand a nuclear explosion. Natasha suspected the nuclear angle was a probably fictitious afterthought, just a bit of optimistic PR to help justify the huge cost and overspend that had run into hundreds of millions of pounds.

Not for the first time Natasha found her mind wandering, thinking about random ideas, how the world actually worked and her own personal place in it. Her life story to date had neem somewhat fractured. A religious upbringing had shaped her views during early childhood, but then she had ended up in a children's home when both her parents had simply disappeared. The feeling of being abandoned and constantly challenged by the world around her had never really left her and she'd found that some of the more troubling aspects of her job compounded her drive to do good and try to fill that void.

She was, she had decided many years earlier, really an angel, albeit well disguised. But then she'd recalled that angels or similar spiritual beings were believed by some religions to be evil. Perhaps she was some kind of an avenger then. Yes, that had sounded right but angel seemed cooler and more moralistic somehow.

What she was driven by, however, was helping people and in her work she had a gift for seeing situations and outcomes that others simply didn't. That was the reason she had been snapped up by the Intelligence Services. She had a reputation not just for challenging both the status quo and those above her but for being consistently and annoyingly right in what she said, an ability that her superiors found particularly difficult to accept. Or to cope with. But her autism diagnosis also meant that when she insisted and simply wouldn't be ignored she was always granted a certain amount of leeway and space, where others might have been sanctioned or disciplined for insubordination.

She reached the grey steel door with the number 23 stencilled on it in faded yellow paint that looked retro, even old fashioned. Whether this was deliberate or just because these sorts of places followed the same book of military rules and building standards she wasn't sure. What she did know was that the door marked 23 either led to somewhere very special or contained something very secret. She also knew she had been asked by the man who ran GCHQ to go inside and bring back a specific object that was in the room.

At odds with its retro look and out-of-place character was the sophisticated black box attached to the wall on the right-hand side of the door. Placing her left eye in front of the small camera to allow the retina scan to function, three simultaneous clicks echoed around her and the door opened slightly with a small gasp of air.

Natasha immediately knew something wasn't right. The sixth sense she possessed was sending alarms to her brain which then converted them into hard fact. She remembered there were always four clicks when all the other doors down here in the underground tunnels were opened. Why was this one different?

She took a step back and felt a surge of irrational fear as she stared into the darkness revealed by the partially opened door. Everywhere was silent. No one came down into these corridors without both purpose and permission and there were deliberately no security cameras. The area was sterile and, like everything else at GCHQ, top secret.

Natasha knew there was a secret passage connecting the corridor with a secure building at Gloucestershire airport. This allowed all manner of politicians, military personnel, spies and other undesirables to enter and exit GCHQ discreetly. No recordings of meetings or discussions in these basement rooms were permitted and all recording devices, including mobile phones, were forbidden. Records could and would raise questions and expose inconvenient facts and possible compromises that no one, least of all Her Majesty's Government, would want to either acknowledge or address.

That knowledge gave her no comfort at all in the subterranean passage.

'This is silly,' she said out aloud. That remark had the effect of slicing through the silence and scaring her slightly.

She slowly put her hand around the door frame expecting to find the switch that would activate the lighting inside. It wasn't there but her hand touched some electric cables so at least she knew there should be lights in the room, even if her probing fingers couldn't find the switch. Natasha snatched her hand back sharply and, now totally spooked, she turned to run back upstairs to safety.

As she turned, she literally bumped into one of her least favourite people on the planet: her manager, David Hargreaves. He was a middle-aged, odious and malodorous man who not only apparently didn't use deodorant but detested woman in the workplace, and especially those with any opinion or authority. Natasha spoke to him only when she absolutely had to. His smirk, showing both rows of his yellow and appalling teeth, was slightly more alarming to her than the unseen contents of Room 23.

'Natasha, I was worried you were lost and came down to check that you were all right,' Hargreaves said in his usual offensively condescending manner. 'What's the matter, my dear? You look terrified.'

Natasha's mind was working overtime. She was sure that his sudden and unexpected appearance in the deserted underground corridor and the peculiar task she'd been given were connected. Something was amiss. It was almost as if she'd been deliberately isolated in the corridor to give Hargreaves the chance to be alone with her. She would need to bluff this out.

'Sorry, David, you scared me. I was just about to go into Room 23 as Sir Charles told me to, but the door seems to be slightly jammed. Could you take a look at it?'

'Of course, my dear,' he said patronisingly. He leaned into the doorway and murmured 'Nothing wrong here.'

Then he gave a shout of alarm as Natasha used both hands to shove him into the darkness of the room and then forced the door closed behind him.

Immediately she froze. What had she done? She could lose her job over this, she realised. Assaulting a superior officer, false imprisonment, maybe even attempted murder if she didn't open the door and let him out almost immediately: her mental list of the potential charges she could face was lengthening by the second.

But even as those thoughts raced through her mind, she also coolly, albeit subconsciously, rationalised that there was something very, very wrong with Room 23. Why had her creepy boss followed her down here, into this almost permanently deserted corridor at least fifty feet underground? She would never admit it to anyone, but she felt scared and extremely vulnerable at that moment.

What she definitely wasn't going to do was open the door and let Hargreaves out. She found him unpleasant enough in the normal office environment and pushing him into a dark room and slamming the door was never going to improve either his personality or his temper.

Her best option, she realised, would be to call security and claim it was all an accident and she had unintentionally shut her boss in the room. They had passkeys and codes for everywhere and getting a burly security guard down there would ensure Hargreaves couldn't lay a finger on her when he got out. That would work. And even if she was disciplined for what had happened she might even get transferred away from him, a move that would be long overdue and a definite bonus.

Feeling better with her self-justification and decision, she took a deep breath and turned away.

The thin spray she immediately inhaled smelt of lemons. As Natasha fell to the floor her last memory, for absolutely no reason, was of bright yellow daffodils.

'Nice try, Ms Black,' a tall man wearing a dark suit said, holding a small canister in his palm. 'You really should have played along. You could have been so useful.'

He looked down at her to make sure the spray had worked.

'Take her away to the Farm and get her ready to answer a few questions tomorrow,' he said politely to the three shadowy figures silently emerging from the open door of another room a few yards along the corridor. 'When I've finished with her you can dispose of her in the usual way, please, without trace.'

The apparent leader of the men, all of whom were wearing black battledress and balaclavas, nodded but didn't respond, simply picked up the unconscious woman between them and strode away.

The current director of GCHQ, Sir Charles Martin, rubbed his hands as he watched them headed down the corridor. Then he sighed, perhaps with resignation, and as he walked towards the stairs and what passed for normality at GCHQ he turned his thoughts away from the imminent interrogation and subsequent death of Natasha Black and to more pleasant matters. He decided he would order the lobster tonight at his club back in London. He was never a man to be kept away from the pleasures of the dining table for very long.

While the loss of Natasha Black was irritating, her disappearance could quite easily be explained away as a secret posting abroad from which she had never returned. He knew she had no family left to start asking awkward questions. That sort of thing happened only rarely, but it did happen.

And if any journalists got wind of anything, he could arrange to have them slapped down by the two most effective blunt instruments in his arsenal: the Official Secrets Act and a D Notice.

Natasha Black, he'd decided, was going to disappear permanently, and nobody would ever know how. Or why.

Chapter Two

GCHQ Cheltenham, Gloucestershire, England

Sir Charles Martin leaned back in his comfortable leather seat in his office at GCHQ and glanced through the panoramic arched window towards the town of Cheltenham. It was a view he always enjoyed and the elevated position always reminded him of the power he held over the lives of so many people.

The 'Farm' that he had mentioned in the underground tunnel was a euphemism for an industrial unit covering about two acres and situated deep in the countryside between Woodstock and Chipping Norton. Originally part of the Ditchley Estate used by Winston Churchill and his military advisers in World War Two, the unit was advertised publicly as a helicopter repair station and from the outside that was exactly what it looked like. This cover allowed helicopter flights in and out without raising the suspicions of any local residents and was ideal for the conduct of various covert activities by the intelligence services and other secret squirrel outfits.

The highlight, if it could be called that, of the Farm was hidden behind some trees in a man-made opening. At the rear of the buildings was a pathway that led through these trees to a large and very deep slurry pit. Originally part of one of the estate farms it had been modified to be a lot deeper and almost impossible, even with machinery, to access or examine.

Nobody was actually counting, but those few, those very few, people with the necessary level of security clearance were aware that at least seventy-five souls had been consigned to the pit over the last five decades or so. All had been confirmed – or at the very least had been strongly suspected – to have been enemies of the state, whose fate had been decided without trial or jury, or people who had proved themselves too troublesome to either ignore or to be permitted to live. It was even rumoured that some of the particularly undesirable human victims had been gagged to prevent them screaming and then thrown alive into the pit to suffocate from the fumes or drown and sink to the bottom and join the other rotting corpses.

Over the centuries, slurry pits had been used as a dumping ground for anything undesirable on a farm including dead animals, the bacteria and chemical mix putrefying everything over time into a dark and extremely unpleasant liquid. The fumes from any size slurry pit were highly toxic and extremely flammable.

Natasha Black wouldn't yet know she was scheduled to be number seventy-six in the slurry pit at the Farm and that it was his judgement alone that had condemned her, simply for asking too many questions and not taking a hint to stop. Indeed, she had infuriated him with her unrelenting questions about Room 23 and what was inside it, not respecting his authority in any way at all, and of course not disclosing her own knowledge of that wretched gold coin.

He'd hoped her visit to Room 23 would have allowed him to see for himself her reaction to the sight of the other coins, which would have confirmed to him her knowledge of their existence and that she owned the last one. He could then have persuaded her to tell him where it was and he could have sent a covert team into her house to recover it. And if they couldn't, then he'd planned a long slow torture session as a very last resort to persuade Ms Black to tell him where it was.

Instead she'd not even entered the bloody room and his plan had immediately gone south. It hadn't been his intention to kill her but having shut David Hargreaves in Room 23 and obviously intending to raise the alarm it had all gone horribly wrong.

His personal small team of ex-SAS soldiers – in reality mercenaries – were officially assigned to him and paid for by the taxpayer to deal discreetly with any matters of national security. The top-ups he made to their wages also meant they looked after his personal wellbeing as well as the odd extra, unacknowledged, job.

They had coincidently been on their way out of GCHQ on a special task for him and that had indeed been fortunate. That moron Hargreaves had failed in the simplest of instructions and had decided to follow Natasha down into the basement. Martin suspected he held unprofessional – even weird, possibly sexual – feelings for her but he didn't really want to hold onto that thought.

What was it with these people, he thought, that they simply wouldn't do as they were told?

Sir Charles had decided that David Hargreaves would commit suicide that evening with enough incriminating pornographic evidence on his home computer to make even the most hardened police officer wince. Both his death and the existence of those images and videos would then be automatically covered up by all parties, given his current government role, to save embarrassment all round and he would soon be conveniently forgotten. Forever.

Fortuitously his personnel file said he lived alone, and his vetting data noted that he was thought of as slightly peculiar by his neighbours. Even better, just like Natasha Black, no relatives would ever be likely to pop out of the woodwork and start asking awkward questions.

Thinking back to Natasha Black and having read both her personnel and vetting files he knew she had been orphaned and had few close friends who would actually miss her. She had been quite brilliant as an analyst, perhaps in part due to being autistic, and had been completely dedicated to her work almost every minute of the day. She had been rated by Human Resources as a loyal and valuable GCHQ asset, and her entrance exam scores remained some of the highest on record.

Her demise would reduce the risk to Sir Charles at that moment and the option of simply searching her home and grounds without hindrance from her or anyone else had become a better solution now his attempt to be subtle in his approach using Room 23 had failed. The important missing piece of the jigsaw however remained the successful interrogation and torture session of Ms Black at the Farm, which he would direct the following morning. Once she'd revealed the hiding place of the remaining gold coin – and she would, his men would make sure of that – its recovery would, he hoped, bring matters to a speedy conclusion.

With that thought he rose and put on his overcoat, locked his office door, bade farewell to his night secretary, and set off for his club in London.

As he left the building, his armoured black Range Rover and driver were already waiting for him for the long trip down the A40 which, as usual, would be congested with traffic.

Sir Charles quickly climbed into the leather rear seats, flung his briefcase on the seat next to him, clipped on his seat belt, sighed and closed his eyes.

Chapter Three

Gloucestershire, England

The grey single rotor helicopter was parked inconspicuously among the light aircraft and other helicopters outside the hangars on Staverton airfield, just under a mile from the United Kingdom's distinctive spy station at Cheltenham, better known as GCHQ. A privately owned airfield, it had opened as Down Hatherley airfield in 1931 and was used in the Second World War as a training base for RAF pilots. In the post-war years several aircraft firms had constructed buildings there and it became established as an aircraft test centre before opening its facilities in more recent times to commercial flights.

All of which had masked its true current purpose when the new GCHQ building was built: the airfield had become the spy centre's own private airport.

The three bulky men had had no trouble putting Natasha – she wasn't particularly heavy – into a zipped plastic body bag and carrying her down the underground passageway not far from Room 23 to the inside of one of the hangars on the airfield. The operation was conducted in silence and the trip to the helicopter via the hangar took a little over thirty minutes.

In the helicopter, Natasha stirred and woke slowly. She was not scared by the darkness nor by the plastic loosely covering her face because her brain had always worked in a different way, tending to look inwards instead of outwards. By the time she had fully awoken and focussed on her surroundings she had analysed the situation rationally and calmly.

She remembered nothing after standing outside Room 23, but the rotor noise and vibrations told her she was then in a helicopter and the smell of plastic indicated she was inside a body bag of some sort but had not been restrained as she could still move her arms and legs.

Because she hadn't been tied up or gagged, she assumed that whoever had taken her either believed she was still unconscious or, worse, that she was no threat to them. Her head was throbbing slightly, and her tongue appeared to have swollen so it was filling her mouth in an unpleasant fashion, like a large lump of indigestible meat.

Having grown up without parents from a young age, Natasha was independent of mind and very resilient. She had not panicked and would not do so. She already knew she had to extricate herself from the situation because nobody else was going to rescue her.

She had always had a fascination with James Bond-style gadgets, everything from pens that shot bullets to the latest nano-drones, and she'd stumbled across a set of titanium claw nails online which clamped securely around the ends of her fingers. Not only did the colour last for weeks without cracking, but because the claws were flesh-coloured they looked completely natural and the sides, which Natasha had carefully sharpened, could be used to cut many things. She had fantasied about using them as a sort of weapon. It looked as if she was going to get the chance to see if she was right.

The plastic body bag offered little resistance to her gentle, slow slice and she carefully eased the slit apart to see what was there.

Without warning a large face suddenly appeared, unsmiling, hard and with eyes as empty as black granite.

'Bugger. She's awake and she's just seen my face.'

Without even thinking about it, and relying purely upon her survival instinct, Natasha stabbed her right hand, fingers spread, into the man's face which was barely twelve inches away. The titanium nails sliced deeply into one of his eyes and gouged flesh from his cheeks.

His scream was audible even over the engine and rotor noise of the helicopter. Bellowing in pain and instantly half-blinded, he clutched at his eyes and stumbled away, tripping up and crashing to the floor.

Natasha ripped the rest of the body bag open and stood erect, clinging onto the inside of the cabin as the aircraft manoeuvred.

Apart from the man she had attacked there was just a pilot at the front in a semi-enclosed cabin. The area she was standing in had two seats and a loading space where she had obviously been dumped. She knew this because her hip hurt badly and for some reason this, more than being drugged and kidnapped, absolutely infuriated her.

Natasha had a hair-trigger temper – she thought she might even have psychopathic tendencies as well as all the other diagnoses she'd been given over the years – and at that moment she guessed that losing her temper was probably a good thing, because she acted immediately and without thought for the consequences.

Silently grateful she'd chosen to wear her dark green Doc Martens that day she stamped her foot at the man's ankle but missed and scraped his shin instead.

Unfortunately, her attacker had recovered slightly from the loss of one eye and had stopped screaming. He lurched to his feet and threw a heavy punch at Natasha. The blow hit her left shoulder which exploded in a cocktail of pain, numbness and then immobility.

She knew then that she was in real trouble. She knew some basic martial arts and a load of dirty tricks, but the man in front of her was a professional soldier, trained to kill quickly and silently and without remorse. He was also very, very angry.

He stepped forward and grabbed her by the throat so quickly she hadn't even seen it coming. Then he leaned in close to her face, blood and fluid from his ruined eye dripping down his cheek.

'Bitch, I'm going to kill you. Look at me. You're going to feel the pain as I pull *your* eyes out.'

He might have been highly trained, but right then the man wasn't thinking straight. In particular, he hadn't stopped to think how Natasha had opened the body bag or stabbed him in the eye. If he had, he would certainly not have made the error of leaning in towards her.

She knew she only had once chance, so she took it.

With a sideways slash of her hand held rigid like a blade the titanium nails ripped into his throat, opening deep multiple wounds. As the blood spurted out his grip on her throat loosened and she stepped backwards.

The man stared at her, his tortured expression showing his incredulity and disbelief at what had just happened.

'Bitch,' he gurgled as he slumped onto his knees, head bowed. Blood started to rapidly pool around him.

Hearing a voice shouting from the man's headset, Natasha yanked this off his head and stamped on it in fury, a release of sorts as she took deep breaths. Her attacker had been so keen on taking his revenge slowly that he hadn't actually crushed her windpipe, but it had been close.

Turning to the front she saw that the pilot was trying to both fly the helicopter away from the tarmac and at the same time extract a small handgun from a pocket of his flying overalls. And that was never going to work. Flying a chopper requires both hands and both feet and a lot of coordination.

The pilot apparently realised this at the same time as Natasha, forgot about his pistol and concentrated on just landing the aircraft.

Looking through the windscreen Natasha was amazed to see that they were barely airborne and that the aircraft was still at the airfield. She had wrongly assumed they were already en route to somewhere she definitely didn't think she wanted to go.

She saw what the pilot was doing and knew that once the helicopter was back on the ground she'd be at his mercy. He'd grab his pistol and shoot her down.

But he couldn't do that until he'd landed the chopper.

And that gave her the chance she needed.

Without further thought she stepped to the side door of the cabin. She grabbed and twisted the emergency door release lever, which was clearly marked in red lettering and more helpfully with a big arrow. Pushing hard with her good arm it sprang open and she jumped just over five feet down onto the tarmac. The Doc Martens provided enough support on impact to prevent a twisted ankle and she again praised her luck in wearing them.

It was dusk, the sun setting in the west, but Natasha had no real idea of the time. All she knew was she was in deep trouble. She had to lose herself to avoid capture and try to work out what was going on. Her arm, hip and throat all hurt badly but an adrenaline rush was taking over as she sprinted away from the aircraft.

-o0o-

As Natasha Black disappeared rapidly from view into the fading light, the helicopter pilot was waiting for the rotor disc to stop and was already frantically explaining to his incredulous superior via his secure comms what had just happened.

How, exactly, a young female GCHQ analyst had not only fought and killed the highly trained ex-SAS soldier guarding her but had then escaped from the helicopter and was now at large somewhere near Cheltenham.

Chapter Four

White's Club, London, England

White's is a gentlemen's club based in St James's Street in London and is not simply arguably the most exclusive such establishment in the capital, but also the oldest, having been founded in 1693. Unusually, its members have been known over the years for being somewhat exuberant in their behaviour.

As he took his seat in the dining room, Sir Charles reflected that this reputation had been born of its members' impeccable breeding and class and that he himself fell into this category. Apparently. The truth, however, fell somewhat short of this assumption.

Sir Charles Martin was, and in fact always had been, an imposter and the fortuitous lie that underpinned his adult life was so big he had been amazed when it had worked. Admittedly there had been nothing to lose, but lady luck had certainly been smiling on him.

His life had changed irrevocably, and entirely accidentally, in the summer of his seventeenth year, an event that still never failed to astonish him every time he recalled what had happened.

Named Paul Scott at birth and an orphan from early childhood – he had never known either of his parents – he had been sent by his temporary foster parents to a large country estate in Buckinghamshire to act as a companion and playmate for the owner's disabled son. He had never found out the real reason for being chosen but he guessed it had been a mixture of charity towards the poor and finding someone aged about seventeen who wasn't either prejudiced against the boy's disability or very obviously reluctant to help him.

He had been dropped off by his entirely disinterested foster father along with a bag of what passed for his best clothes and been introduced to Charles Martin, the only son of Sir Francis Martin, Bart, and owner of, it appeared, about half of Buckinghamshire. The country seat was immense with farms, cottages, follies, lakes and outbuildings galore in addition to the mandatory grand old manor house approached along a sweeping driveway.

At that time Sir Francis had been sixty-eight years old, widowed, and apart from his son had no living relatives and virtually no friends or visitors. The only staff in the huge old house had been a cook, a cleaner and a team of gardeners, and the baronet and his son had lived in the Manor House as virtual recluses. The management of the estate had been undertaken by a national firm of solicitors who had held considerable sums in trust that were barely spent apart from basic maintenance costs and payment of their generously padded annual fees.

Charles Martin's mother had died giving birth to her first and only child, and Charles had only just survived the experience, the trauma he had suffered consigning him to a wheelchair for life. Sending him to school had seemed inappropriate because of his condition as well as his status, and so Charles's education, such as it was, had been the responsibility of a succession of private tutors who had wrestled with the boy's frustration and bitterness at his physical condition coupled with his utter lack of interest in learning anything at all. At seventeen, Charles had been both literally and figuratively bitter and twisted.

On the only occasion Paul had actually met Sir Francis, the man had simply glanced at him without comment and shuffled himself away to some distant wing of the property, leaving the cook to introduce him to his son. Charles Martin was clearly not loved by his father and Paul knew exactly how that felt.

Charles obviously had problems, not just being lonely but also backward because of his lack of proper education and the circumstances of his life. He had an enduring anger based, Paul had suspected, on deep-rooted frustration and a lack of love. The two boys had been alike in many ways, including physically. Seen together, you could almost have mistaken them for brothers because they were about the same build and shared the same complexion, hair and eye colour.

For his part, Paul didn't like Charles at all and could find no redeeming qualities in him. He had tolerated the constant moaning, criticism and mood swings as he'd pushed him around the house and estate in a wheelchair, slightly heartened by knowing there was someone in the world who was in a more of a shit state than he was. After all, Paul had possessed nothing of value and had nowhere else to go but his body was whole and healthy. Charles was simply trapped in his crippled body and permanently angry despite his father's wealth.

Fate can be defined as inevitability, but this is not completely true. It's always the reaction to an opportunity that defines its outcome and many people never recognise or take what is placed before them. Despite Paul Scott's circumstances – without a family, with no money and absolutely no prospects – he was suddenly handed a unique opportunity that could only have been described as fate.

One evening that summer Charles had thrown yet another tantrum as Paul went to leave the estate and walk the two miles to his home, or to be precise the house where he was currently staying for two nights every week, an arrangement that his present foster parents – a couple named Buck and Sheila – had insisted on to allow them to continue claiming payments for him from the local council. He had known they didn't care for him in any way at all and were quite happy when he was staying at the manor house. They had a regular supply of misfits and troubled teenagers passing through their home, many of whom were returned to the council for another foster family to try to cope with or who simply ran away. The local council was grateful, the money was good for the foster carers – using that last word in the loosest possible way – and even if a child did run away, both parties knew there were plenty more of them in the pipeline.

Paul had just reached the end of the long gravelled drive with its impressive pillars and black wrought iron gates and was stepping over the old cattle grid but before he stepped out onto the road, something made him glance back. When he did so he'd noticed a plume of thick black smoke rising from the basement window to the right of the front door of the manor, appearing almost to cling to the ivy and ancient brickwork like a stain. And as he'd watched, the black smoke had suddenly turned to crimson as flames erupted from it.

He'd run as fast as he could back up the drive to the house and had come to a stop about twenty feet away, unable to approach any closer because of the intense heat. There was nothing he could have done. The property was well on the way to being engulfed, bright red and yellow flames leaping from blown-out windows and curling around the walls. A sudden explosion from inside the house had blown smoke and debris all over him, and he'd had to move back a few yards.

Paul had simply stood and stared. Transfixed by the fire's ferocity and the destruction of the house he had felt, of all things, a simple wave of pleasure pass through him. Whether this was driven by jealousy, resentment of other people's wealth or simply his experiences at the hands of the obnoxious Charles Martin he wasn't sure.

As he had stood there, the sound of sirens filled the air as two fire engines roared between the pillars and skidded slightly as they swung round in the turning area, avoiding the historic statue in the centre.

The fire crews had efficiently started to douse the flames, but it was obvious that they were too late. The late mediaeval-period manor, largely timber framed and full of generations of combustible furnishings and clutter, simply turned into a massive fireball, roaring its death throes into the blackness of the night sky.

A small crowd had started to assemble and had to quickly move away as two ambulances and three police cars arrived in a flurry of sirens and flashing blue lights.

Paul had a horrible thought that he might be blamed or could find himself under investigation. He'd seen enough in his life to know that the police always wanted a culprit and that young men with his background were an easy solution when they wanted to apportion blame and close a case quickly.

Edging away back across the lawn he bumped into one of Charles's wheelchairs that he used for his outdoor trips, a model equipped with extra grip tyres and bigger handles. Paul had sat down in it and, utterly transfixed, continued to stare at the inferno and surrounding chaos.

And he remembered exactly what had happened next as if it had been yesterday, the one instant that had changed his life forever.

A shrill voice had called out. 'My dear, thank heavens you're safe.'

Paul had turned and seen an elderly but well-dressed woman wearing a tweed skirt and jacket and Wellington boots waving and stumbling towards him.

'Charles, my dear, are you all right?' she'd panted, lightly touching his cheek. 'Your face is covered in soot. And your clothes are as well.'

Paul had flinched slightly and had been about to point out her mistake but in the instant before he spoke a sudden vista of an entirely different life had flashed into his mind. So instead he'd just nodded and replied 'I'm fine, thank you.'

As he'd sat there in the wheelchair, numerous people he didn't know had kept coming up to him, all expressing their concern and sadness. He assumed that his similar build to Charles Martin and the layers of soot covering his face had been enough for people to assume who he was. After all, Charles Martin was a resident of the house, and he was sitting in Charles Martin's wheelchair on the lawn outside what was left of the building. He doubted if most of the people around him had even heard of Paul Scott, the unpaid companion, far less knew anything about him.

By the time a somewhat grumpy senior police officer finally had finally walked over to him, he'd already been playing the role of Charles Martin for thirty minutes and saw no good reason not to continue.

The police officer had simply offered his apologies and regrets and had pushed him, accompanied by the woman in Wellington boots, to an empty cottage on the estate. It obviously hadn't been inhabited for some time and was shabbily furnished with remnants of the previous tenant's possessions.

Paul had managed to convince them both that he would be all right alone, and that he didn't want to go to a hotel or other accommodation. He could navigate his wheelchair on his own and had no one to contact – which was as true for Paul himself as for the now, presumably deceased, Charles Martin. They'd reluctantly agreed, arranged for the bare necessities like a washing kit – clearly essential given his appearance – and food and drink to be provided in the cottage that evening and had then left him to his own devices. The police officer had said he would back in the morning and that he would arrange for social services to be there as well.

The lady with Wellington boots, who Paul had worked out was called Lucinda, had presumably decided her stint as a good Samaritan had ended once the food parcel had arrived and had left quickly to avoid any tasks that might be coming her way.

With the added problems of what he was going to tell the police and hoping that the person from social services didn't recognise him, Paul had spent a restless night in the cottage trying to sleep on the sofa, praying that Charles's body had been utterly consumed by the fire and would never be found.

But then he'd realised that even if the body was found, it would be far too badly damaged to be identifiable, and as Paul spent five nights a week sleeping in the mansion, he could simply claim that he – as Charles – had decided to push himself around the grounds that evening before returning to his room. Then he'd seen the flames and smoke but there had been nothing he'd been able to do to help.

In his mind, Paul Scott would perish in the flames and Charles Martin would arise, phoenix-like, from the ashes.

In fact, nobody had turned up the following day. The estate's lawyers based in central London had quickly acted to say that all matters should go via them and a cheery looking man had arrived the day after and knocked twice on the door. Paul had initially frozen but then, once back in the wheelchair, had let the man in. He'd introduced himself as Frederick Manson from Manson, Manson and Bush, solicitors and commissioners for oaths, whatever that meant.

In a complete whirl of solicitor-speak and condolences Manson had produced lots of papers for Paul to sign and explained that provision had been made under his father's will for a simple memorial ceremony after his death, which his firm would arrange. He had also talked about an inheritance tax liability and a trust fund, none of which Paul even vaguely understood. Mr Manson would be his point of contact for anything he needed, and he had handed him a card with a telephone number on it as he'd left.

Paul had already decided he had no intention of calling him for anything. His best option, very obviously, was to keep as low a profile as he could and hope for the best.

Now thinking of himself as Charles and having done his best to completely adopt his new identity, Paul had also signed numerous papers – he'd seen Charles's signature several times, an almost featureless squiggle that he could easily replicate – sent to him by post, citing his entirely predictable distress and grief to avoid most face-to-face meetings. The postman, used to visiting the estate, had been happy to accept cash to buy the stamps needed to return the documents.

Within a remarkably short time he had found himself, at seventeen years of age, sitting in a cottage on a huge estate that he now legally owned. He also had a bank account that Mr Manson's firm had opened for him, with a very large monthly allowance appearing on the statement, the monies derived from the various investments Sir Francis Martin had made. With no formal schooling outside the house, no documentation or photos that hadn't been destroyed in the fire, and no close relatives to identify him as an imposter, the transition was smooth.

Nobody had had any reason to assume that he wasn't Charles Martin, but out of instinct he continued to keep himself hidden, still expecting the police to arrive at any moment to arrest him, but they never did. The solicitor had continued to visit him infrequently to discuss various estate matters and to get him to sign documents, and on an early visit had explained to him that he'd inherited the baronetcy on his father's death and that he was entitled to be called 'Sir' because of that. Days turned into months and by the time his 'new' birthday had arrived and 'Sir Charles Martin' turned eighteen, he'd inherited everything his 'father' had owned. He even had a passport with his photo in it.

For his own continuing safety, he had decided he needed to start again somewhere else, well away from the area where either the real Charles Martin or Paul Scott might still be known. Buck and Sheila had simply moved onto the next adoption and, in reality, he doubted if either of them could even remember what he had looked like.

Unknown to him at the time, his luck had held better than he could possibly have hoped. While effectively hiding out in the cottage during the first few weeks, the two permanent staff members – either of whom would have recognised him immediately – had been dismissed on the grounds that the property no longer existed so there was nothing for them to do. With the mansion destroyed, there had seemed little point even in retaining the gardeners. One minor complication was that the building hadn't been insured for anything like its real value and so rebuilding it was not an option, not that 'Charles' would have wanted to do that anyway.

Concealing the fact that he was no longer disabled proved easier than he had expected. He invented cutting-edge treatments and expensive operations performed in hospitals abroad that he would not discuss in detail, and by the time he'd turned twenty he was walking normally, his footsteps punctuated by the occasional grimace as his back apparently gave him another twinge. A year later, he'd even given up pretending to have had a disability because nobody seemed to care one way or the other.

The solicitors had charged huge fees and undertook everything on Charles's behalf including running the rest of the estate and ensured that all the paperwork was duly completed. All parties had been entirely satisfied with this arrangement, none more than the new Sir Charles Martin, Bart, and the final act of demolishing and removing the burnt remains of the old manor house had brought a forensic closure. The grounds were sold for a spectacular sum to a property developer as the site for a new and upmarket housing estate, which had swelled Charles's bank balance even more.

The lack of a formal education hadn't held him back, money being a very persuasive lever that could be applied to almost any situation, and in England good breeding and a noble background were almost as useful as education. The young baronet had found that doors opened easily for him and his naturally devious nature, perhaps inevitably, had led him towards a career in the intelligence services, culminating in his present post at GCHQ.

As he always did when he found his mind recalling that traumatic period of his life, Sir Charles smiled to himself, wondering what would have happened to 'Paul Scott' if he hadn't 'died' in the fire. Then he shook his head and dragged his attention back to the present situation and to the pleasures of the table.

It had been a tiring day with the Room 23 matter and Ms Black. He decided to have an indecently expensive bottle of wine with his lobster as a reward to himself.

Chapter Five

1946: Gloucestershire, England

In the years since the Second World War had ended, the former priest and decorated army officer Captain Nick Fletcher had settled into a small cottage in a hamlet just outside Cheltenham.

The journey back from Berlin after the end of hostilities had been uneventful albeit fragmented, the simple rule being to catch a ride on anything heading west. Generosity abounded everywhere and he was offered food and drink on all parts of his journey as the celebrations of the war's end continued.

The other soldiers seemed to fall into two camps: those who were loud and jubilant and those who simply sat in silence with a far-away look in their eyes, an expression christened the 'thousand-yard stare' by somebody. Fletcher felt he lay somewhere in between with a painted-on positive exterior but total despondency and despair raging within him.

When he had finally arrived in Dover by boat, he had caught a train to his mother's house in Norfolk using almost the last of his money. His father had died of tuberculosis when Fletcher had been ten and his mother had raised him well but she herself now needed looking after.

Taking on the immediate role of her carer as her condition quickly deteriorated, Fletcher felt a simple contentment in this act, an antidote to the purgatory of what he had awoken to every day for the last four years. He felt that she had been hanging on, waiting for his return and that this alone may have been the only thing that had kept her alive.

His mother had died peacefully just a few weeks after his return and had been buried locally with only a handful of mourners attending. The house with its small orchard went on the market and Fletcher took what he knew was a low offer even by post-war standards just to settle matters quickly. Living in the house with his mother's belongings had been uncomfortable and he was able to pack all the old photos and other items of sentimental value that he'd wanted to keep in a single suitcase.

He had also started talking to himself and he knew this wasn't a good thing. With the money from the house sale in his bank account, he'd literally put a pin in the map of England and one afternoon shortly afterwards had found himself visiting Cheltenham in the heart of the Cotswold countryside.

Arriving by train from London he had fallen in love with the refined Georgian architecture, the parks, and the graciousness of the inhabitants. With nowhere else he could think of to go he had ended up living in the Queens Hotel on Imperial Square for two months.

With few possessions and dwindling funds he had decided one day that it was the right time to find a home, a sanctuary for himself, somewhere definitely quiet and maybe, just maybe, to look for a job.

The abandoned cottage nobody seemed to want was barely three miles from Cheltenham and overlooked open countryside all the way down to the River Severn. With over an acre of overgrown garden, Fletcher had bought it just days after seeing it and spent the summer simply making it habitable, shifting undergrowth and planting a vegetable plot.

The solitude and fine weather he'd experienced during this time went a long way towards restoring his wellbeing. He was clearly resilient, and the discipline instilled into him by the army gave him the ability to plan each day and follow a routine. Food was still hard to come by, but he had set up snares for rabbits and even started to catch trout on the Severn as well as harvesting the first vegetables from his garden. By post-war standards he had soon been living comparatively well.

The telegram from Room 47 at the Foreign Office had arrived one evening, hand-delivered by a uniformed Post Office employee on a bicycle. The message asked if he would be so kind to attend a meeting at Betchley Park in Buckinghamshire. Despite the somewhat casual language and tone, Fletcher knew the headed notification was in fact a military order as it was addressed to Captain N. G. A. Fletcher MC, even though he had been decommissioned months earlier and was technically a civilian. He was intrigued.

Known as the establishment that housed the Government Code and Cypher School, Bletchley Park was a spacious mansion house set in about fifty acres of grounds that had been pivotal in winning the war thanks to the code-breaking that had been carried out inside the building. Over eight thousand women had worked as cryptanalysts at Bletchley Park and its various outstations, including Fletcher's mother, a fact he'd only discovered when she was on her deathbed. She had been very proud of her role and had talked to her son in general terms about her work there but Fletcher suspected she'd had taken many secrets to her grave.

He had known little more than that as he sat on the steam train the next day from Oxford to Bletchley railway station. The station was situated midway between Oxford and Cambridge on what was commonly known as the varsity line because both universities had supplied a stream of academics, mathematicians and code-breakers to Bletchley Park during the war. This activity was still shrouded in secrecy but Fletcher had learned from his mother that what had been done at the country house had definitely helped to win the war.

Fletcher had enjoyed both train journeys immensely, from Cheltenham to Oxford and then on to Bletchley, the slow and steady thump of the steam engine and the beautiful views from the carriage relaxing him. This, this England, was what he had fought for, he'd reflected. With space for six people in each compartment, he always hoped that people moving down the corridor wouldn't enter his because he was enjoying the journey and didn't want to have to engage in polite conversation.

However, a smartly dressed gentleman did enter shortly after they had left Oxford, but merely nodded, sat down, and engrossed himself in a newspaper as Fletcher stared out of the window.

The journey was uneventful and as Fletcher stepped down onto the platform at Bletchley, he took a deep breath. He had dressed in his only suit and wore his regimental tie, feeling it was probably appropriate in the circumstances. He headed for the exit to find a taxi or bus to his destination. It was a clear warm day and quite pleasant, he thought.

He was in plenty of time, having caught the first train from Oxford for his noon appointment. He was hoping to find a taxi outside the station, but if there wasn't one he thought he had enough time to walk it.

As he strode under the old iron Victorian arch that led out of the station a gentle tap on the shoulder made him turn around.

'Hugh Parker,' the man he'd shared the carriage with said brightly. 'I'm delighted to meet you, Captain Fletcher.' Then he added: 'Shall we?' as he waved a hand towards a black Jaguar parked next to the pavement, the rear door already open.

Taking a closer look at his new companion, Fletcher could see he was possibly in his sixties, clearly military given his pristine attire and grooming, and quite unthreatening, or so the twinkle in his eye suggested.

'Who are you and how do you know my name?' Fletcher blurted out, more than a little taken aback. 'And why are you following me?'

'Pure coincidence, old chap. I work at B.P. and I guessed who you were only when we left the train together.' He waved his hand around. 'No-one else gets off here but us lot, you see.'

Fletcher didn't see and didn't believe a word of it, but he nodded. This Parker chap was clearly important and judging by the luxurious leather seat he now found himself sitting on and that Parker had a driver, who possibly doubled as a bodyguard, Fletcher decided to just stay silent.

Barely a minute later and looking out of the window Fletcher saw a sign for Fenny Stratford as they drove alongside a field studded with what looked like dozens of tall aerials. Turning into the drive towards what he assumed was Bletchley Park, he noted that the car had been waved straight past the guard house and barriers.

He could have walked there in five minutes from the station, he realised. Hugh Parker had not said another word since the short journey had begun, and Fletcher began to wonder what he was becoming involved in.

Chapter Six

Present day: Gloucestershire, England

More by luck than judgement, Natasha had made it as far as the perimeter fence which was about seven feet high with coils of razor wire running along the top. Clutching her side because of the stitch caused by her unaccustomed exertions, and wincing at the pain in her shoulder, she started to stumble her way along the fence trying to find any openings to freedom.

She had no coat or jacket and although her sweatshirt was thick, and despite her desperate flight from the helicopter, she also felt cold and pulled up her hood. The shivering could be either from the cold or just shock, she thought. Or more likely both.

Despite its darker aspects, Gloucester was a local commercial airport rather than an official military site and Natasha soon found herself next to a lowered barrier that would stop a car but which she could easily duck under. This led her out onto a quiet public road where occasional cars and lorries drove past her at speed. The hedges on either side were quite low with ditches dug to collect rainwater and no gates in sight.

She knew about ANPR, the automatic number plate recognition system used by the police, and that GCHQ had a full battle response plan for the area surrounding it in the event of attack or other security breach. Escaping on foot would involve evading everything from drones to roadblocks, while tracker dogs and a full-scale manhunt – or rather woman-hunt in her case – would be her most immediate threats. She wouldn't take bets on her life expectancy. Someone in GCHQ, and by default someone in an official position of power, had wanted her abducted or more likely dead for some reason.

Natasha should have been scared but she wasn't. What she felt, almost to her own astonishment, was exhilaration at the upcoming challenge. She had killed another human being and yet felt nothing. The clear and simple justification of defending herself against the threat to her own life simply nullified any negative emotions or feelings of guilt.

She knew she had to think outside the box, an expression she hated but which focussed her mind on her predicament. She was now, she assumed, and for whatever reason, an enemy of the state. Somebody at GCHQ had decided she needed to die and that threat remained. She couldn't go to the police nor back to GCHQ nor even to the cottage that was her sanctuary and place to escape from the outside world.

And she wasn't what might be called equipped for making her escape. Her mobile phone was in her office inside GCHQ, but even if she had it she couldn't think of anybody she could call for help. And there was also the Smurf problem, which meant that if she had been carrying her mobile she would have had to dump it. The Three Smurfs were part of one of GCHQ's mobile phone tracking and monitoring apps and Natasha had no doubt at all that by now all three would be targeting her smartphone.

At that moment, her only assets – if that really was the right word – were her Pokemon key ring with her house and car keys on it, a couple of credit cards and some cash in a small purse.

But what she did know at that precise moment was exactly what her only option was and what she now had to do.

Chapter Seven

Cheltenham, Gloucestershire, England

The team leader of Sir Charles Martin's mercenary bodyguard group, a soldier named Blake, had gone off for an early evening snack in the small cafe on site at the airport with one of the other soldiers, leaving the third to escort the 'package' onto the helicopter and deliver it to the Farm.

He was surprised but not entirely shocked when his meal was interrupted.

'She did what?' he demanded, seconds after answering the call on his mobile.

'She killed Wallis, your man who was supposed to –'

'I know who you're talking about. Just get on with it.'

'Right,' the helicopter pilot said. 'She must have had a knife or something on her. She half-blinded him with a blade and then cut his throat. The inside of the chopper looks like a butcher's shop, blood everywhere. Who's going to clean it out, that's what I –'

'Your chopper, your problem,' Blake interrupted. 'Just get it sorted. Where is she?'

'Who?'

'That bloody woman, of course,'

'She legged it. Used the emergency handle to open the side door and then ran off. I've no idea where she went.'

'Wonderful,' Blake ground out, and ended the call.

As he frequently remarked, 'Shit happens,' but he really hadn't expected any problems. Their task had seemed simple enough and should have carried almost no risk. But it never paid to under-estimate somebody unknown, and there was clearly far more to the woman than any of them could have anticipated.

Springing into action, the two men immediately returned to their parked black van and released the two autonomous bloodhound drones that were programmed to methodically cover a specific area to detect human bodies. Using a mixture of body heat, predicted direction of travel, facial recognition software and some other clever, real-time, top secret data feeds from – somewhat ironically – GCHQ, the bloodhounds almost always found their man or in this case, they hoped, their woman.

She couldn't have gone far from the airport, Blake rationalised, and she would be looking to cover as much distance as possible to get clear of the area. If she'd secured a lift from a passing car then checking the ANPR system and the surveillance cameras around the airfield would hopefully provide a lead, and Blake sent the necessary high-priority request for that particular search. He knew his authority wouldn't be questioned by the police or security staff at GCHQ as the Director General had authorised all the necessary clearances for him at the very highest level.

He was confident she would be caught within the hour, once again loaded into the helicopter, this time in handcuffs, and ultimately both bodies – her corpse and that of the man she'd killed – would be dumped in that death pit at the Farm, cutting off the two loose ends.

But as well as mounting the search, there was one other thing he needed to do immediately, and that wasn't a task he was looking forward to performing: he had to let Sir Charles Martin know what had happened. He knew that he would be less than impressed.

In fact, he was wrong about that.

'Less than impressed' didn't even come close. His employer was clearly incandescent with rage, almost screaming abuse into his mobile.

As he listened to Sir Charles ranting at him, the team leader knew he had made a bad mistake in not personally ensuring the woman's delivery. Should he fail to find her, he doubted he would be given a second chance. He knew he had the skills to simply disappear but that had consequences. Certainly no more easy money from Her Majesty's Government for doing relatively safe jobs, but more importantly he would be placed on the deniable kill-list that the intelligence services kept. A price would be put on his head for others in the know to locate and eliminate. There would be no time limit and he would be forever looking over his shoulder and waiting for a bullet. He simply had to find the woman. The personal consequences if he failed didn't bear thinking about.

Sir Charles's rage was still palpable as he terminated the call. 'So, you incompetent bloody idiot, you'll need more men, and fast. But you must find her. Call me the moment you have her.'

'I'm confident we'll find her shortly,' Blake replied, then realised he was talking to himself.

Ninety minutes later, he knew his optimism had been premature, to say the least.

The initial ANPR, road-side camera footage and facial recognition searches had returned negative results, suggesting that the woman was on the run somewhere out in the countryside and avoiding the roads. The bloodhound drones were good but had limited range and endurance, and he knew he would now need to introduce some bigger and better long-endurance military drones to cover a much wider area.

He made a few urgent phone calls to secure not only the drones but also more men and a hangar on the airfield that he could use as a proper command centre for the hunt. As he walked across the tarmac towards the building, he noted with some satisfaction that both men and equipment were already visible through its open doors.

With all that he now had at his disposal, the hunt for Natasha Black would be intense but, he sincerely hoped, quite brief.

Chapter Eight

1946: Bletchley Park, Buckinghamshire, England

Fletcher sat across the solid wooden table opposite the man he now knew to be Major General Hugh Parker CVO. The senior officer was exchanging polite pleasantries with his secretary as she poured coffee into two china cups. He couldn't quite work out if Parker was in charge of the establishment, but he sat a bit straighter in his chair anyway, old habits in front of senior officers still being deeply ingrained.

'Well, old chap, I owe you an explanation,' Parker said as his secretary walked briskly out of the room and closed the door behind her. 'Make yourself comfortable and enjoy your coffee. Then I need to explain what's going on before I show you a few things and tell you a somewhat strange story that, quite frankly, we need your help to finish.'

Fletcher stared at him, but with no immediate or obvious response forming in his mind he just nodded.

'Bletchley Park, where we're now sitting, is being closed and what you see around you is the beginning of its decommissioning. Sad, really, as there is no doubt that all the people – including your mother, I believe – who worked here definitely shortened the war and saved thousands of lives. But now the powers that be just want to move on and make a fresh start, according to our new Prime Minister, Mr Attlee.'

Parker sighed and Fletcher saw that with no war to fight, the old man was a bit lost in this new and uncertain world.

'Anyway, when the allied troops started to search the German military factories and all manner of other places, many strange things came to light. It appears our old friend Mr Hitler and his scientific chaps were designing and building weapons and developing technologies that were truly like science fiction. I cannot tell you how appalling some of it was, particularly the human experiments and the mutations we found. Simply disgusting.

'It all made me grateful that the Americans managed to develop the atomic bomb before the Nazis, which was certainly lucky for us. If Hitler's men had managed it first, and they very nearly did, London would now almost certainly be a smoking ruin, there'd be SS and Gestapo offices in every town in Britain and we'd all be learning how to speak German. That said, the Americans have been very much ahead in this post war game and, as you may be aware, have recruited many of the best of the German scientists and taken a lot of this clever Nazi technology back across the Atlantic.'

In fact, Fletcher wasn't aware of any of that because he'd had no contacts with anybody in the military since he'd been decommissioned and had read nothing about it in the newspapers, but he kept quiet because Major General Parker was clearly on a roll.

'We, however, haven't been too far behind and for the last year Bletchley Park has been the home of our own collection of Nazi curios.'

What Fletcher had read in the papers were articles about the concentration camps where so many Jews had been murdered, and about some of the vast treasures that had been discovered but he knew very little more than that. Not for the first time, he wondered where all this was going.

As he finished his coffee, Parker pushed back his chair and stood up. 'Come with me, Captain Fletcher. Let me show you the sort of things I mean.'

Leading the way, Parker walked out of the room and through an open door into a concrete yard surrounded by ten-foot red brick walls and barbed wire.

Fletcher found himself facing a huge set of steel doors situated at the other end of the yard with two armed soldiers on guard. As he and Parker approached, both guards saluted and then pulled open the doors, which appeared to be mounted on small wheels and glided silently sideways along their tracks.

In front of Fletcher was a short tunnel and a set of wide metal stairs that appeared to head down deep into the earth. A string of bright lights on both sides disappeared into the depths as far as his eyes could see.

One of the guards then took down a thick and bulky overcoat with a fur lined hood and handed it to him.

'No heating, I'm afraid, and it gets a bit cold down there,' Parker said as he pulled on an identical coat.

Without another word the two men strolled side by side down the steps as if was the most natural thing in the world to do.

Chapter Nine

Present day: GCHQ Cheltenham, Gloucestershire, England

Natasha's unique brain had worked out quite easily what she had to do. She'd looked at every possible option open to her and deduced how her enemy might react to each course of action. For that reason, she had immediately slipped back onto the airfield and made her way towards the hangar that was directly in line with the GCHQ building that she could just see through the trees.

The one place they wouldn't expect her to go was there. No one would anticipate her covert return to the place from which she had fled, and she hoped that the empty tunnels without cameras below GCHQ would offer her a secure place to hide while she decided on her next move.

She knew there were security cameras around the airfield but by checking carefully, applying a little patience before she moved – and one near miss – she had circumvented them all. The small flashing red light designed to be a deterrent on each one proved extremely helpful for her needs by showing her exactly where they were.

There seemed to be a fair amount of activity taking place on the airfield which made her move cautiously, but she stayed totally focussed on reaching her destination without being detected. If she were to be spotted, she'd decided she would simply run back out onto the road and take her chances there.

She reached the inconspicuous hangar on the eastern side of the airfield without incident and was surprised to see the large doors were slightly ajar. She'd already worked out that this was the building most likely to contain the entrance to the tunnel back to GCHQ, the spy centre being directly behind it and slightly elevated in the distance.

As she approached the structure she realised that the most likely reason for the groups of men and trucks entering and leaving the airfield was her. Or rather the fact that she had managed to escape from the chopper. But there seemed to be no activity in or near her objective, which was a bonus.

'Clearly I'm the most popular girl in town,' she muttered to herself.

She slid slowly though the gap between the doors and into the hangar, keeping her body tight against the back of the door, ready to turn and run if she had to. One row of ceiling lights was switched on, allowing her to see the interior. It looked empty except for several large piles of rubbish in black bin liners and a row of dustbins, making the hangar look like a disused dumping ground for garbage. Which was probably the intention.

But what she saw immediately, because she was looking for it, was an old wide wooden door at the back of the structure. Most people wouldn't even have noticed it, and would probably have ignored it if they had seen it. But the clue was the small black box on the wall next to it. Natasha knew that this was her way out and that whilst no cameras would be present, the tunnel behind it would almost certainly be alarmed and protected against intruders.

She around the perimeter of the hangar towards the wooden door, trying to be both silent and to leave no footprints on the dusty floor, which wasn't easy with her choice of footwear.

But at that moment one of the hangar doors behind her rumbled and opened further, letting in more light.

Natasha immediately dropped to the floor behind the industrial sized rubbish bags to hide. Two large men dressed in black, just like the man she had killed, walked inside and dropped what was very obviously a body bag onto the floor without even the suggestion of any dignity.

'Killed by a kid, by a girl who shuffles paper for a living. What a way to go. What a loser,' one of the men said.

'Come on, let's go. We need to find her quickly or we're all going to be deep in the shit,' the other replied. 'We can pick him up later before we fly out.'

With that they closed the hangar doors, the catches sliding home with a loud double click. She didn't know if they'd locked the doors as well, but she assumed there would be a way of opening one of the doors from the inside, so she was hopefully not trapped inside the building.

She was also a long way from being a kid and no part of her job involved shuffling paper, but Natasha still felt a stirring of anger at how she had just been described.

Looking at the body bag she felt a sense of remorse and sorrow. Not for the man she knew was inside it: he had been like a feral animal intending to inflict pain and certain death on her at the simple behest of another, but for herself. She had crossed a line that most people never would by taking a human life. It felt like the act had taken something from inside her, something she couldn't define or explain.

With a deep breath, she said a silent prayer for what she hoped to find in the body bag as she walked over to it and started to slowly pull down the zip.

Chapter Ten

1946: Beneath Bletchley Park, Buckinghamshire, England

The journey to the centre of the earth, as Fletcher had begun thinking of it, didn't actually last very long. A wide corridor opened up at the foot of the stairs. It was well lit and the air seemed clean and almost sterile, like a hospital. But it was cold.

'These rooms, Captain Fletcher, were built here to house any captured soldiers should we ever be attacked, so technically they're prison cells. It only occurred to the buffoon in charge afterwards that if Bletchley Park were to be overrun it would mean we had been invaded and most likely the staff here would have been the people incarcerated in them. They would have managed to build their own prison.'

Fletcher laughed gently out of politeness, but he had seen enough of bureaucracy, of acts of pointless belligerence and pure incompetence, during the war to know it was no laughing matter. He knew that so many lives had been needlessly lost as a result of decisions made a very, very long way behind the front lines by people who had never even held a rifle or a pistol and who had no idea what armed combat was like.

'There are twenty-four cells or rooms, which have now become our very own temporary museum.'

Parker pulled the three bolts back on the door marked 'Room 1' and slowly opened it.

Whatever Fletcher had been expecting, it wasn't what he found himself looking at.

The room was painted brilliant white on all sides including the floor and ceiling and was brightly lit. It was also large, going back at least twenty-five feet. In its centre was a long white stone block on which was positioned a large but stubby rocket about ten or twelve feet long and painted olive-green. It was fitted with four large fins about a third of the way back from the tip, plus another four much smaller fins at the rear end, set inside a kind of more or less oval metal cage.

Fletcher was very familiar with a huge variety of weapons because of his military service, but he'd never seen anything like that before.

'This is one of the Germans' most secret weapons,' Parker said. 'We've nicknamed it the Fritz X. It's a marvellous piece of design. It's radio guided and can carry up to seven hundred pounds of explosives, according to the manual we captured with it. It's designed to sink ships. Any ships, in fact. Even our battleships would have been vulnerable because although this is a short-range weapon – about three miles – it does nearly eight hundred miles an hour, without an engine.'

That got Fletcher's undivided attention. He stared open-mouthed at the weapon in front of him.

'So it's essentially an armour-piercing glide bomb,' Parker explained. 'The Germans would drop it from a bomber at about twenty thousand feet and then steer it straight onto the target. The thing is, Captain Fletcher, this could have brought us to our knees almost immediately had it been deployed in large numbers against our naval forces.'

Fletcher stared at it in wonder. He had read about the V1 rockets – the 'doodlebugs' – and the much more dangerous V2 rockets and was in no doubt this missile had been the next step forward for the Germans as a ship-killer. Radio guided, he assumed, meant a remote pilot which to him sounded impossible.

'The truly frightening thing is that it does actually work,' Parker said, somehow almost guessing what Fletcher had been thinking. 'You probably don't know this, but back in September 1943 the Italian battleship *Roma* was hit by two of these weapons and sunk. That ship had belt armour well over a foot thick and six-inch thick deck armour and the two Fritz X weapons went straight through it.'

Stepping back out into the corridor, he repeated the exercise for Room 2. Fletcher stepped into a huge room with massive sliding double doors at the rear, which had clearly been necessary to allow the entry of a corroded grey single-seater aircraft, shaped like a grossly-enlarged letter V, flattened and pointed at the front and with what looked like a rocket engine built into the root of the wing on each side. A white distorted swastika was painted on its nose. The fuselage was about 25 feet long but the wingspan was around 60 feet and it was a tight fit, even in that vast space.

'Like something out of a science fiction novel, don't you think?' Parker asked. 'It's called the Horten Ho 229 and yes, it does actually fly. According to the German records is can do six hundred miles an hour and climb as high as 49,000 feet. An incredible feat of engineering.'

Fletcher couldn't help himself but be impressed. The imagination and sheer engineering skill of their former enemy, not only in the designs but in their actual construction and operation was astonishing.

'It's amazing, sir. Truly amazing,' he replied. 'Are those rocket engines?'

'No, but they're the next best thing. They're called turbojets. I don't actually know how they work but they don't need propellers and the thrust, as it's called, comes straight out of the back of each engine. Some people think that's the aircraft engine of the future.'

As they exited the second room Parker turned to Fletcher.

'I'm conscious of the time and I have two rooms in particular I'd like to share with you. I must warn you they will stretch your imagination. Please do take what I say about their contents at face value, because I'll only be repeating what our best boffins have worked out about the objects.'

The next room they entered was dominated by metal racks with hundreds of wires and what looked like a typewriter contained within a wooden cabinet sitting on a large metal box like a safe.

'I need to explain this one carefully as it's all quite complicated,' Parker said. 'This is called a Z3 and it's an electromagnetic computer. What it does is similar to our own code-breaking machines, and it's designed to work out answers to problems quickly and without any errors.'

Fletcher had never heard the phrase 'electromagnetic computer' before but got the gist of what Parker was saying.

'That doesn't sound very exciting if I'm honest,' he said, 'so I'm assuming there's something more to it?'

'Indeed,' Parker nodded 'we played down its capability amongst the staff here at Bletchley Park to keep morale high as breaking the German Enigma machine was always our primary objective. It looks like behind the scenes the Germans were already years ahead of our own Colossus computer with the Z3. One concern is that its design and some of its parts appear to have the hallmarks of American help, though we can't be certain. Sometimes lack of confirmation is better than the reality of knowledge. Clearly neither of these facts would help Mr Attlee and his government's current propaganda machine now we have won the war. That's why it's down here and hidden away.'

'I still don't really understand, sir. Why is this important?'

'I asked you to open your mind. When we examined this Z3 machine it prompted us to ask the same question. In a war of armaments and battlefields and bombers and battleships, why was this machine so important to the enemy and why was it so heavily guarded?'

Parker paused, took a deep breath, and continued. 'So, imagine a machine that you can input a mathematical sum into, for example thirty-four and a half multiplied by one and a quarter plus the square root of six divided by Pi to ten decimal places. Our best mathematicians here can do that in a few minutes with pencil and paper. This machine or computer as they call it produces the answer in under one second. That is a massive number of times faster and with no possibility of a mistake.'

Parker paused again before continuing. 'By applying pure logic, it follows we can now say, as a fact, that this machine is cleverer and more intelligent than our cleverest people for just this one calculation. Wouldn't you agree?'

'Yes, I suppose so.'

'Keep that thought in your head and let me take you into the last room down here in the depths. Then we can go back up to my office where I'll explain how all of this fits together and how you can help.'

Being neither a scientist nor an academic Fletcher was unsure how he could ever possibly help. But all that changed rapidly when he entered Room 23.

Chapter Eleven

Present day: White's Club, London, England

Sir Charles had retired to his regular bedroom suite on one the upper floors of the club and was sitting on the edge of the bed, mentally reviewing the events of the day, events that still caused him surges of anger and irritation. He appeared to be surrounded by incompetent idiots, at least in terms of his unofficial employees.

He was in some respects only a figurehead, the work of GCHQ being conducted in his absence and under delegated authority. He was normally only ever bothered when there was some kind of a crisis. In truth, he spent most of his time doing personal favours for powerful people, networking and building relationships that gave him both power and money under the wide-ranging and unquestionable auspices and authority of national security. It was a fine line to tread with government ministers changing either their minds or their posts, and sometimes both, all the time, and it was not without an element of danger when some politician decided to start asking awkward questions.

He expected to end up sitting in the Upper House and that would suit him fine. His baronetcy was hereditary, but he wanted to add a lordship or barony to his name and getting into the House of Lords, he felt, was nothing more than he was entitled because of his birth-right. Or to be exact, the birth-right he had assumed when the old manor house had gone up in flames in front of him and consumed both the owner of the estate and his heir. After so many years of self-centred self-delusion Sir Charles no longer felt any guilt or irony in these thoughts and desires and continued to carry a huge personal grievance from his childhood, despite his good luck.

He decided he would stay awake for a while to watch the breaking news about Hargreaves on television. Once he'd seen it he would then approve the necessary form of words for the GCHQ media team to release to the press.

He had ordered his team to drag Hargreaves out into the underground corridor to avoid making a mess in Room 23. Then they were to force a fatal cocktail of over-the-counter drugs containing codeine – most likely a mix of Solpadeine and Nurofen Plus but at least a dozen times more than the maximum recommended dose – down his throat, and to wash it down with as much Balkan 176 vodka as they could get him to swallow.

Once he was unconscious, which would probably only take a matter of minutes if they got enough vodka into him, they were to take him to his home and get him inside. Martin had suggested that sequence of events on the grounds that it would be easier to carry the unconscious man into his property – they wouldn't even need to pretend that he was drunk – rather than struggle inside with a clearly alive and frightened man. Or they could just knock him out with a blow to the head, but Martin wanted them to avoid that if at all possible, because suicide victims very rarely hit themselves on the head during the process of dying, especially if their preferred method of ending it all was a massive drink and drugs overdose.

Once in his home they would load Hargreaves's computer with some of the worst and most disturbing and illegal pornography they could find on the Dark Web: 'heavy on snuff films and especially on kiddies,' Martin had ordered. Then they'd write a suicide note on his laptop – something like 'I can't go on living this lie any more' – and shut the doors behind them as they left.

It wouldn't have been the first enforced suicide the team had ever arranged, and Martin knew it probably wouldn't be the last. Because of the team's experience, he knew that that part of his plan, at least, would be conducted properly.

But his other reports worried him more than he wanted to admit. Ms Black was proving to be surprisingly capable and so far his men had been unable to eliminate her simply because they had not the slightest idea where she was. She appeared to have almost literally vanished. His anxiety at their continued failure to even get a sighting of her was clawing at his stomach more and more as time went by.

He took four aspirins washed down with a cup of strong coffee followed by a couple of glasses of straight single malt that he sipped and savoured, and in minutes he fell asleep fully clothed on his bed. Almost immediately he plunged into one of his regular nightmares, involving him running down never-ending streets while being chased by creatures he could not see, though the dark shadows they cast were always clear enough, and always getting closer to him as he fled.

Chapter Twelve

GCHQ Cheltenham, Gloucestershire, England

Natasha closed her eyes and then squinted as stale air and rancid odours rose out of the bag. Without looking at his face, she unzipped the bag completely and started to feel in the dead man's many pockets for the electronic pass she assumed must have been used to open the door to allow him and at least one other person to carry her body from GCHQ through the tunnel.

But the pass wasn't there. She found a combat knife and a small multitool, both of which she took – the knife-blade, pliers, screwdrivers and other stuff should prove more than useful, perhaps even life-saving – and a packet of chewing gum that she didn't.

'Shit,' she muttered, thinking that one of the other men must have taken the pass.

Now she knew she was really in trouble, potentially trapped in the hangar because if she went out of the main door there was a good chance – or perhaps 'bad chance' would be a more appropriate expression – she would be spotted. She really needed to get into the corridor that led under GCHQ because she was sure that she could find somewhere there where she could lose herself for a few hours. Without the pass, she would have to wait in the hangar until somebody opened the door and then try to slip past him and into the tunnel.

And like a lot of things in life, that was something that was an awful lot easier to say than to do.

She ignored the bloody mess that had been his face and checked the rest of the corpse. Almost the first thing she saw was a plain black lanyard around his neck and her heart skipped hopefully as she grabbed it. With any luck at all the pass would be on it. Then she stopped as she realised she would need to remove it over his head and she didn't think she could cope with doing that.

'Double shit,' she thought, then picked up the combat knife and cut through the lanyard.

'One nil, Natasha!' she said to the body as the pass came into view, and then immediately felt bad for doing so. But not for long.

She quickly zipped up the bag again, looking away as she did so, and then walked over to focus on the black box next to the rear door of the hangar. But she could see immediately that the electronic pass didn't open the door, at least not from that side, because the box didn't contain a card reader. Instead, it held only a plastic-coated keyboard for a PIN number, similar to one that a standard bank cash dispenser would use. She stared at it.

'You're joking,' she muttered.

Natasha could hack into basic systems as well as anyone else in GCHQ but with PINs and passwords it was always quicker if she knew something about the individual involved, the administrator's override number or just the manufacturer's codes used for testing and maintenance.

A big mistake made by some organisations when installing high end corporate security systems is that they don't realise it is almost always the same handful of global manufacturers that supply the hardware and equipment for multiple secure sites across the world.

The UK Government procurement rules, as an example, tended to favour those chosen few firms with a solid track record and, by default, they would almost always win the big contracts. That was why Natasha knew that the keypad in front of her was the same make and model that was also used by the Prison Service, the Environment Agency and most police stations to protect their premises. She also knew, thanks to her eidetic memory, the system engineer's default code which she hoped hadn't been changed.

About three years earlier she'd seen a report that had recommended the immediate changing of guessable codes like 1234, 4321 and 0000 after half a dozen police stations had been broken into and the information posted gleefully on the Internet the next day. The days of using simple codes like that, codes that everybody could easily remember and that were almost never altered, were probably over.

Holding her breath and saying her second prayer of the day, she keyed in 7481, hoping that it would still be valid.

She heard no clicks but as she gently pulled the handle towards her, the door silently swung open.

But then she heard voices coming towards her from somewhere in the tunnel beyond and she closed it again as quickly and as quietly as she could.

Who else could possibly be coming down here? she thought. And why now?

She ducked down again, this time behind the row of dirty metal bins, and tried not to make any sound.

The door opened, swinging outwards, and another two men, again dressed in black, appeared carrying a second body bag between them.

Natasha risked a quick glance at the bag and wondered who could be inside that one. Maybe somebody had decided that David Hargreaves had messed up so badly when he'd approached her in the tunnel that he'd outlived his usefulness. And, while she had never liked the man, she didn't think he deserved to be murdered.

Or did he? she thought. So maybe it was him. She couldn't think of anybody else at GCHQ that it might be.

The two men laughed as they carefully lowered the bag next to that of their dead comrade, then went back up the tunnel, the door shutting behind them.

Natasha didn't want to look in the second bag because sometimes ignorance really is bliss, but she forced herself to do so.

She strode across to it, pulled down the zip and for a few seconds just stared at what she'd revealed.

It wasn't a body, but about half a dozen weapons wrapped in a kind of grey blanket. She was no expert, but to her they looked like assault rifles, futuristic-looking devices with large magazines and complicated sights. At least that explained why the two men had lowered it so gently, so as not to cause any damage to them.

A few minutes later, creeping along the tunnel towards the Doughnut, Natasha was being very careful. The two men were long out of sight somewhere ahead of her, but there were no hiding places in that section and the bland and featureless tunnel seemed to go on for ever. She had no choice but to keep moving forward as quickly and quietly as she could.

That worked until she was faced with another solid steel door that looked bombproof and was set in an equally solid steel frame.

For some reason the electronic pass didn't work on its black box and there was no keypad or other buttons or handles to press or pull on the door itself.

'Bugger,' she muttered.

Natasha didn't normally swear, but today she had done so frequently. On the other hand it had been, she decided, a really, really bad day and she was therefore excused.

As she stared at it, the door started to slowly open towards her.

Chapter Thirteen

1946: Bletchley Park, Buckinghamshire, England

The final room Parker showed Fletcher was smaller than the other three. Fletcher had assumed that as prison cells they would all have been about the same size, so they had obviously been modified at some point

There one common feature was that they had all been coated in a clinical white paint on unblemished walls, still meticulously spotless, and he guessed there was some sort of air filtration system in each. Like a museum, as Parker had described it. These artefacts were clearly valuable and were being preserved for many reasons, he suspected, and not just out of historic interest. The British Government had clearly spent a huge amount of money in a short period of time on this.

For the second time that day Fletcher wondered what he had let himself in for.

In the middle of the room was the, by now expected, white block on which sat a metallic bowl, silver in colour with a taut red wire in its side which fed flush into the wall, neither end having any visible join or plug. Floating above the bowl was a gold-coloured sphere about the size of a football.

'Not magic I'm afraid,' said Parker, looking at the expression on Fletcher's face, 'just simple magnetic repulsion. Remember your school days playing with two magnets? This is same thing only big, round and gold.'

Fletcher had to admit it looked like magic and pointed at some small holes on the surface of the gold sphere. 'Those holes have a purpose, I assume?' he asked.

'Not for power in, which we had originally thought. The gold sphere rotates naturally within the magnetic field. We did an x-ray of the golden ball and that's when we became completely stumped.'

Parker paused and looked directly at Fletcher. 'It appears, but we are still not sure about this by a long way, that within that sphere are many, many smaller copies of the Z3 computer you saw next door, with those components forming part of the actual structure itself.'

Fletcher couldn't see how that was even possible in such a small object. 'How would anyone ever do that, sir?' he asked. 'And why?'

'We don't know, and I'm afraid the worst is still to come, Captain Fletcher. Our scientists tested the ball and it isn't gold or even a metallic object. It seems to be an unknown polymer or type of plastic, something a bit like Teflon but about ten times heavier.' He paused. 'Somehow it has magnetic properties, hence its levitation, but we're baffled about what it is or what it's supposed to do. But we do have one clue.'

Taking a gold disc from his pocket he positioned it above the ball where it floated face-up, apparently repelled by the complex magnetic forces being generated so that it appeared to hover.

Fletcher's heart jumped as he recognised the disc as being the same as the gold coins he and his old corporal had found in the abandoned building back in Berlin just before they'd left Germany for the last time. This was obviously why he had been summoned to Bletchley Park. He was there for a gentleman's interrogation, a chat officer to officer, as opposed to the bright lights and pliers and other devices of persuasion they might use in some soundproof basement.

Clearly his mother's previous role and his own impeccable war record, including winning the Military Cross, had most likely saved him from that fate, but he now knew for certain he was in some sort of trouble.

The problem was he didn't have any idea what. Or why.

He noticed that Major General Parker was no longer smiling. A moment later he turned and left the room, waving at Fletcher to join him. Both men walked back up the stairs, Fletcher deep in thought and more than slightly worried, but not just because of what he had been shown.

His extra layer of concern was because, presumably acting on orders previously issued by Parker, two armed guards had suddenly appeared behind him and were obviously escorting the two men back along the tunnel.

Chapter Fourteen

Present day: GCHQ Cheltenham, Gloucestershire, England

Natasha took the only option open to her.

She stepped behind the door as it opened towards her. The door pushed her up against the wall and completely hid her from the view of the same two men she had seen before. Wheeling in what looked like two racks of guns – again she thought they were assault rifles – on a trolley, they positioned it against the door, presumably to keep it open, and they then turned silently and went back up the tunnel, perhaps to go and collect something else.

Recognising that this was most likely her only chance to move, and whilst she would have the advantage of surprise if she needed to make a sudden dash for it, she knew that sneaking in unseen was still her best option. Once they returned and closed the door she would certainly be discovered and, she suspected, shot there and then and stuffed into yet another body bag to join the other corpse ready for disposal in the hangar. She shuddered involuntarily.

She squeezed through the narrow gap between the wall and the trolley and briefly considered taking one of the guns. Looking at them, she thought they looked heavy and because they were on a rack she assumed they were unloaded, so she decided on balance not to do so. Also, a missing gun would alert them to her location in the tunnels under GCHQ and not halfway across Gloucestershire as she hoped they would already believe.

No sooner had she decided this than she heard noises filtering towards her from the hangar end of the tunnel, from behind her.

Someone was heading in her direction. In fact, it sounded like several people. The one thing she knew was that she couldn't ask them for help. Whoever the approaching people were, they were most unlikely to be anything other than actively hostile towards her. Looking at the gun rack that had just been left in the tunnel, she guessed that these were being collected by the new arrivals. In fact, Natasha realised that these guns were most probably intended to be used by some of the people who were hunting for her.

Without any other choice, Natasha walked through the doorway, along a short corridor and straight into the basement of GCHQ, without any further sight or sound of the two men. She found her way to one of the noisy boiler rooms, crept in and then huddled down behind the machinery to hide herself as best she could.

She heard a fair amount of shouting and swearing from outside the room in the passageway and held her breath.

Clutching the combat knife in her good hand, she silently vowed that anyone entering the boiler room would do so at their peril. After a few minutes the noises subsided and, totally relieved, she briefly closed her eyes.

And, without quite realising it, she fell fast asleep.

Chapter Fifteen

GCHQ Cheltenham, Gloucestershire, England

The next morning and unbeknown to either of them, Natasha Black and Sir Charles Martin awoke at almost exactly the same time, both from a deep but troubled sleep.

While Sir Charles had taken a shower and skipped breakfast ready to be taken back to Cheltenham by his driver, Natasha had spent about the same length of time staring at the pipework and valves in front of her and trying again to work out what had happened and how she had managed to find herself in her present predicament.

She concluded it was obvious: it all came back to Room 23, which she knew wasn't very far from where she was now sitting. She wasn't sure if her retina scan would still open it but assuming security hadn't cancelled it, she might be lucky.

Stretching her limbs and rolling her head, she knew she was physically in a bad way with not only a headache, but shoulder ache and numbness in her left hand. Her throat no longer hurt but this was probably because the pain from everything else was more intense. And her teeth definitely felt like they had a coating of fur growing on them.

After listening intently for several minutes, she stepped carefully out of the boiler room and crept down the corridor towards Room 23.

Arriving at the old door she hesitated, knowing that her entry would possibly trigger an alarm somewhere and she would need to get in and out quickly. It was a dilemma but she knew she had to act, to find out what was going on. Living the rest of her life hidden in the boiler room wasn't really a lifestyle choice she was prepared to accept.

'Here goes,' she whispered, and for the second time in twenty-four hours she placed her left eye in front of the black box outside Room 23.

Three clicks later, she was in. The room was now lit, unlike before, and she could see no evidence that David Hargreaves had ever been inside it. She stared at the brilliant white walls and at a silver bowl on top of a white block. In the bowl she could see several gold-coloured fragments that might have formed a sphere or ball if they'd been put together. Or not. It was difficult to tell.

There was a square thick-looking glass covering the bowl with no visible means of access apart from a discreet keyhole on each corner. She presumed undoing the locks would allow the glass to be lifted away.

'Well, that doesn't help at all,' she said, and walked around the exhibit to where a smaller plinth, hidden from immediate view, had been placed. On it was an old wooden tray bearing very ornate carvings and Latin inscriptions and what she knew was a form of the papal insignia of a pair of crossed keys – the keys of Simon Peter. And incongruously at the other end was the Nazi swastika.

What really caught Natasha's attention, however, were the gold coins resting in seven of eight identical shaped recesses on the tray. They were all facing the same way with Hitler's head neatly aligned. She was glad they were positioned that way because otherwise she would have felt compelled to waste time lining them up neatly, alignment being another of her compulsive traits. Well, she would have tried to do so but for the solid glass casing covering it, just like the other one.

One of the slots in the tray was empty and, as she heard distant voices echoing down the corridor, she decided it was time to leave. Something niggled at the back of her mind and told her that she ought to know what all this meant. She had also noticed a weird and very subtle force or presence in the room, a sensation that was almost what she imagined seeing a ghost might feel like.

She stepped outside and closed the door, then ran down the corridor towards the Doughnut and away from the voices. She would have to think this through later, providing she wasn't caught, which was still her most obvious first priority.

Exiting the basement into the building on the ground floor was easy. Once inside GCHQ, the security of the building was relatively lax – getting into the Doughnut itself was the difficult bit – with the various top secret sections having their own zones and secure access. That meant the staff had free access to roam about without restrictions outside those areas.

With some clever timing to avoid both people and cameras, and keeping her head down, she made her way to one of the ladies' toilets and did her best to clean herself up. Mud, human blood and something unpleasant and yellowish that had leaked from one of the waste bags she'd hidden behind were duly dispatched down the sink from her sweatshirt after a very quick and very amateurish wash. Using the hand dryer, she tried unsuccessfully to dry the garment but it was still damp as she pulled it on over her head again. 'Ugh,' she said, but she knew she looked a whole lot better.

Many of the GCHQ staff dressed very causally and quite a lot seemed to occasionally forget to wash, presumably a by-product of being so dedicated and obsessively focussed on their work, so Natasha was confident her appearance and smell alone wouldn't alert the guards. No alarms had gone off, but she knew she was racing against the clock. Sooner or later one of the internal cameras would detect her or somebody would see her, and then the security people would probably send out a snatch team to quietly grab her so as to avoid making her capture a public incident.

Five minutes later and with impeccable timing she walked quickly through the foyer to the main exit as part of the morning crowd heading for the coffee van, the vehicle being parked outside the main entrance but within the secure perimeter fencing. The barriers were opened daily at eleven o'clock to allow staff to leave and queue for their refreshments, but their passes and PIN numbers would be needed for re-entry.

Natasha knew this, of course: nobody ever thought of people leaving a building as a security risk, just those trying to enter with their various bits of equipment. It was a bit like customs and immigration control at an airport.

Heading down past the van she made for the revolving gates on the perimeter that would allow her an unrestricted exit.

She was still about fifty metres away from the gates when the main security alarm went off. That required all staff to stay where they were until security approved their return.

Natasha started to run and almost immediately collided with a security guard who was heading the other way.

'I'm sorry,' he said. He bent down to help her up and then stopped when he obviously recognised her. 'Stay right where you are,' he ordered. 'Don't move.'

His only weapons seemed to be a walkie talkie on his belt and the finger he was pointing at her.

Natasha did the most obvious thing she could think of: she bit his finger, scrambled back on to her feet and ran as fast as she could.

She collided with the full height metal turnstile. A second later it opened away from her and she stumbled through, out of the perimeter fence and into freedom.

Looking back for the last time she saw that the guard was holding his finger in pain, his walkie talkie held awkwardly in his injured hand as he spoke into it.

'He should probably get a rabies shot for that,' she muttered to herself with a smile. 'He's got no idea where I've been.'

Then her smile disappeared as she noticed three armed soldiers behind the guard, all advancing towards her, their guns raised.

She knew that by now the alarms all around the site would have been activated. And that meant she needed to be somewhere else, and fast.

As quickly as she could manage, she ran across the road and into the cluster of council flats directly opposite GCHQ, her sole intention being to disappear.

Chapter Sixteen

1946: Bletchley Park, Buckinghamshire, England

Just over seventy years before Natasha Black had left Room 23 completely bewildered, Captain Fletcher had also exited it in much the same state of mind.

Sitting again in Major General Parker's office with the two guards having disappeared, taking with them the heavy coats the two officers had been wearing, Fletcher knew he was in for a grilling. Now there were no coffee cups and the twinkle had gone from Parker's eyes.

'So I won't mess around, Nick. You need to tell me the truth when I ask you some questions. Trust me when I say that I will know if you're lying and – I'm sorry to say this – I will consider it treason if you do. I can have you shot today, in the yard outside this building, if I'm not completely happy with what you say. No trial, no argument, no appeal. Do I make myself clear?'

'Perfectly,' Fletcher replied, figuring he had nothing whatsoever to hide but also knowing he would need to be careful. The old man had been in the military a long time, was clearly ruthless and would know every trick in the book. That included the senior officer now using his first name, a friendly gesture that was the verbal equivalent of a mailed fist inside a velvet glove.

'I saw the look on your face when I produced that gold coin so I know you must have been with Corporal Mitchell when he found them in Berlin. Is that true?'

'Yes, sir.' Fletcher thought some deference was called for here, as well as honesty, believing his life to be quite literally on the line.

'Good. Now think carefully before you answer this question. How many of these gold coins did Mitchell find after the German blew himself up in that cupboard space?'

Fletcher hesitated. Parker clearly knew all about the incident. That information must have come from Corporal Mitchell himself, the only other person involved, which meant the corporal had already been interrogated. But Fletcher also knew that neither Mitchell nor Parker could possibly know that he had also taken a coin because he'd been alone in the room when he found it.

He decided to gamble and confess half the truth.

'The explosion blew a hole in the wall, sir, and scattered the coins on the floor right in front of us and Mitchell picked them up. I even helped him do so. I knew he would keep them, and I know that I failed in my duty as an officer because I should have stopped him. I'm sorry for that, but the simple truth is that he'd saved my life on at least two occasions, and I almost felt that he somehow deserved them. I can't offer any other excuse. As to your question, I believe there were six or seven, but I'm not totally sure.'

Parker looked intently at him. 'I see,' he said. He placed the gold coin gently on the table in front of him. 'How would you describe this coin, Captain Fletcher?'

Fletcher picked it up and weighed it in his hand.

'It looks like a gold coin,' he replied, 'but it's bigger and thicker, more like a medal, I suppose. And it's quite heavy, but not as heavy as it would be if it were solid gold.'

'Go on.'

'I'm not sure what else there is I can say, sir. My only contact was picking up some of them and handing them to Corporal

Mitchell. At the time I believed them to be gold, or at least gold-plated because they're not as heavy as they look, but now I assume they're neither but some sort of magnetic material because of what you demonstrated downstairs when you made one of them float.'

'Was there anything else with the coins? Say a journal or book?'

Fletcher hesitated. The question suggested that Parker knew or at least had guessed that there had been a book, so he knew he had to come clean.

He nodded and was about to speak when Parker put up his hand, a single finger to his lips and shook his head.

'I see, no journal nor anything of that sort,' he said, his action surprising Fletcher. 'Are you absolutely sure about that?'

Fletcher caught on immediately. 'No, sir. There was nothing with the coins that I could see.'

'Very well.' Parker paused for a few seconds, looking down at the notes on the desk in front of him, then apparently came to a decision. 'I'm sorry about this, Captain Fletcher, but I'm going to have to ask you to undertake a small task on behalf of the government. These coins are valuable, but not because they're gold because of course they aren't. As you may already have worked out they're made from the same material as that floating ball downstairs. They also appear also to have multiple copies of the Z3 computer circuitry embedded within them. We only have this one coin but we know there must be as many as seven others currently in the possession of Corporal Mitchell. The problem we face is that the Corporal has now disappeared.'

Parker slid a slim envelope across the desk, took a deep breath and continued.

'That contains your new military identification card. Your commission has been reinstated with immediate effect and you are now in receipt of full pay, back-dated six months. You will report directly to me and to no one else. Your mission is simple.

Or at least, it's simple enough to say. Your task is to find Corporal Mitchell and retrieve those remaining coins.

'Now, I must remind you that you remain under the Official Secrets Act with all that that implies. This mission is classified Top Secret and is of crucial importance to the nation.' Parker handed him a small card. 'If you need any additional resources just call me on this telephone number at any time, day or night, and I will do my best to provide what you want, where and when you want it.'

Fletcher took the card and glanced at it, then looked back at the senior officer. 'This is all a bit sudden, sir, not to say unexpected. I assume I have no choice in the matter?'

'None whatsoever, Fletcher, because this is a direct order. But what I do have that might help you in your search is a little bit more information.'

Fletcher looked interested and waited for Parker to continue.

'First of all, we found out about these objects entirely by accident. We would have been none the wiser about any of this if Corporal Mitchell hadn't tried to sell this single coin in a remote auction house in Worcestershire, not far from where he lives, or where he was living at the time, anyway. His home was in a tiny village called Littleton, only a few miles from the auction house.

'Anyway, one of our people accidently stumbled across it in a box of other stuff – coins, medals, curios and the like – that Mitchell had put in the sale. He didn't know what it was, but realised it was something unusual and possibly valuable. He bought the whole box immediately for over twice the pre-sale estimate before the auction had even begun to avoid getting into a bidding war. He handed it over to some of our boffins who ran tests on it, and it ended up here at Bletchley.

'When we looked at it we started a full investigation. It's still early days but pieces of the jigsaw have started to fall into place, starting with the Worcestershire auction. The man who bought the coin was offered huge sums of money for it from two separate people as he left the auction. One was a well-dressed foreign-sounding gentleman and the second an elegant lady, possibly Italian. Both rather stood out in rural Worcestershire but no one we questioned who'd been at the auction seemed to be able to offer more precise descriptions of them other than a posh foreigner and a pretty lady.

'But the implication is clear enough. One or perhaps two overseas powers are aware of the existence of these coins and are trying to gain possession of them, and for that reason alone we want them. One of my people tracked Mitchell down soon after the auction and talked to him, which is how we found out about where the coin had come from, but before we could seize the others we assume were still in his possession, the man simply disappeared. We don't know why he vanished and nor do any members of his family, so we have had to assume that either he has been abducted by agents seeking the coins or has gone into hiding. But he would probably trust you, Captain Fletcher, because of your history together and that's why we need you to find him and recover the coins.'

Fletcher nodded. 'I understand, sir. So I presume you'll want me to head over to Worcestershire as soon as I can. But I will need to go back to Cheltenham to pick up a few things from home before I start the search.'

Parker nodded. 'That won't be a problem, but you will have to be quick about it. This search needs to start immediately. Now, one other thing. Before you leave here, you need to go to the armoury and collect a pistol and ammunition.'

'May I ask why, sir?' That was something else Fletcher hadn't anticipated and immediately added another, darker element to the task he had been set. He hadn't expected to handle a pistol again now he was a civilian. On the other hand, he realised, as of about twenty minutes ago he was effectively back in uniform.

'Yes,' Parker replied. 'The presence of two foreigners clearly looking for these coins worries me. I'm not going to send you into danger without providing you with the means to defend yourself. I've authorised the issue of a pistol, a box of ammunition and a shoulder holster because you obviously won't be wearing a uniform for this mission. The armoury is on the left just before the guardhouse when you leave here.'

Parker's slightly strange behaviour earlier in his briefing had puzzled Fletcher, but the fact that he wanted him to be armed during the mission really worried him. What the hell was he getting himself involved with?

'Finally, would you mind walking back to the station, please, as I need my driver for another job?'

Fletcher nodded. The Major General was still acting very oddly, and he had been hoping that in the car on the way back to the station – which was the way he had expected to leave Bletchley Park – would have provided an opportunity for Parker to explain what was actually going on, rather than just expect him to interpret the senior officer's gestures and raised eyebrows.

He shrugged mentally, stood up, saluted, shook Parker's hand and then left the room.

-o0o-

Once Fletcher had left the building, the tall elegantly-dressed man who had been listening to their conversation from the adjoining office entered the room.

'What do you think then, Hugh?' he asked.

'Fletcher described what happened in Berlin exactly the same way as Mitchell did so I think both men are telling the truth. Fletcher – remarkably – was a vicar before the war and lying wouldn't come easy to him. So on balance I'd say he really hasn't a clue what's going on.'

'So why is he helping us so readily?' Sir Roger Sinclair asked. He was the Chief of the Secret Intelligence Service or SIS, part of which had decamped from Bletchley Park and returned to London only the week before.

'He's still unemployed after four years of hard combat, he has very little money and he's lost his old religion. Basically, his life now lacks a purpose. This mission will restore some of that, so I'm not surprised he's on board. Its simplicity and the debt he feels he owes to Mitchell – he told me that the man had saved his life more than once in France and Germany – means we don't need to explain the dangers or what we think we know about the other players. And I've warned him and given him a pistol.'

The Chief nodded, a smug expression on his face, and left the room without another word.

Parker sat back in his chair and reflected. He had, he thought, been right in his guess that Fletcher most likely had the missing journal, and although an earlier covert search of his cottage hadn't yielded it or any more of the coins, he was pleased that Sinclair seemed convinced Fletcher was clean.

Parker knew Sinclair of old and didn't trust him. Despite his job and rank, the man had no natural manners or grace, though Parker could have overlooked that: nobody said you had to like the people you worked with. Much more importantly, given what was at stake, he wasn't convinced Sinclair wouldn't act in his own best interests rather than those of the country.

Parker and Sinclair knew that both a group of escaped Nazis as well as several agents of the Catholic Church were actively looking for the coins and the journal. It might only have started as wild speculation, but a legend had developed and quickly gained traction, a story they had heard from many different sources. The coins, the rumour stated, were somehow the key to a vast amount of stolen Nazi treasure held in a hidden vault, its location a closely-guarded secret.

It was already known that after the war escape routes for many Nazis continued to be enabled by the Vatican in Rome, using what were called Rat Lines to get the fugitives out of

Europe, with many of them ending up in South America. The Allies were already aware from statements by informants that at least three hundred very senior SS officers had fled by this route since the war had ended, using false documents and with safe passage supplied by the Church's global network. A very high priority in the past twelve months had been to prevent them from entering the United Kingdom. Hunting them down would be a task for another day, and in another country.

Despite the mounting evidence there had, of course, been no admission or acknowledgement of its involvement from the Catholic Church, which was actively attempting to disown its support of the Nazi regime, both its past and current involvement. But Parker knew loyalties within the Church were still split.

Several informants had also confirmed the existence of a document signed by a high-ranking Nazi that allegedly specified the origins, ownership and disposal of the vast wealth stored by the Church on behalf of the Third Reich. The two suggestions for the signatories were Heinrich Himmler or even Adolf Hitler himself on the Nazi side and Pope Pius XII. The document's location was unknown, but it would be interesting to see how the Church reacted when – or if – it ever came to light, Parker thought.

Swivelling his chair, Parker looked up at a black and white photograph of him in uniform standing beside Winston Churchill in the Western Desert. He wondered how Winnie was coping now he'd lost the election that should have been a solid certainty for him. He would be as mad as hell, he suspected.

What bothered Parker was not Nazi treasure or the like held by the Vatican, although he suspected Sinclair had personal plans for anything that might be recovered, but the mysterious and apparently purposeless golden ball. There was something about it that made him feel uneasy, something he knew he was missing.

But even if Fletcher did succeed in his mission and all the coins were found, then what? The Catholic Church would admit nothing because it never did, and even if the document allegedly signed by Himmler or Hitler and the Pope was produced, it would no doubt be proclaimed a forgery. Without an army to back them up, any possible architects of a Fourth Reich – because they would be the most obvious recipients of any hidden store of Nazi loot – would just hit a brick wall.

The answers had to be written in the missing journal, and it was that book, not the coins, that was important. And he believed he now knew where it was.

With that thought in mind, Parker made a quick phone call. Ten minutes later he was speeding in the black Jaguar towards Cheltenham.

Chapter Seventeen

Present day: GCHQ Cheltenham, Gloucestershire, England

Sir Charles Martin paced up and down his office, his face an angry mask though his moment of incandescent fury had passed. But he was concerned, even frightened, because Natasha Black had not only killed one of his bodyguards but for over a day she had evaded capture by a highly trained special forces unit equipped with all the latest technology. She'd even had the audacity to covertly come back into GCHQ. That was bad enough, but far worse was the fact that she'd obviously entered Room 23 – the database records showing her retina scan proved that – and then for a second time had managed to escape.

He opened her personnel file once again to see if he'd missed something. Had she had specialist training in escape and evasion or even assassination techniques? The SAS, for example. Or, much worse, the Russian Spetsnaz? Perhaps she wasn't simply an analyst but a highly trained foreign agent? That would be the most obvious nightmare scenario: a Russian agent working in GCHQ at the very heart of the British Intelligence community. But there was nothing at all in her file to suggest anything of that sort. Her life seemed to have been quite straightforward with all her time accounted for and she'd passed every GCHQ security check and screening without even a suggestion of a doubt.

What his men had seen when they'd examined the corpse of the ex-soldier she'd killed was alarming. The body had one destroyed eyeball, literally cut to pieces, and his throat had been slashed violently, his windpipe and carotid artery severed. And the pilot had described the back of his helicopter as a complete bloodbath, like a scene from the most gruesome and violent slasher horror movie.

The woman had obviously had a knife concealed about her person and had been quite prepared to use it. On the other hand, she'd been fighting for her life so it was difficult to decide if she'd just lashed out in a panic and simply got lucky, or if she had known exactly what she'd been doing and had first incapacitated the soldier – and stabbing him in the eye would certainly have done that – before using a killing blow to slash open his throat. On balance, Sir Charles guessed she must have known some martial arts techniques and perhaps she had carried a knife for self-defence purposes, although as far as he knew the metal detectors at GCHQ had never detected her owning such a weapon. And a knife wasn't the sort of item normally found in most women's handbags.

But either way – whether she was dangerous or just lucky – she needed to be found and dealt with. Fast.

As Sir Charles pondered his next move, he also reflected upon what he knew about Room 23, which was actually surprisingly little.

As Director-General of GCHQ he had, upon his appointment, become the official custodian of Room 23 and its contents. As part of his induction briefings, his Director of Research had explained to him that the room had been taken in its entirety from the sealed underground bunker at Bletchley Park in 1952 to Benhall in Cheltenham, where it had remained sealed until GCHQ's final move to the Doughnut in 2003. That had only been possible because the structure had originally been constructed as a reinforced concrete box, as a unit.

He had also explained that the broken gold fragments were an example of the earliest type of computer chip, invented by the

Germans during the Second World War, and that even today they couldn't identify its precise molecular structure but they knew it had been years ahead of it time. It appeared to be somewhat similar to graphene, a material only discovered as recently as 2004, which as a single layer of atoms can replicate the behaviour of neurone cells in the human body. The material also appeared to have qualities that allowed it somehow to have an inbuilt power source and also to exhibit binary logic using nano-magnets.

That had all washed over Sir Charles as being probably quite fascinating to his somewhat geeky Director of Research but of absolutely no interest to him. But the gold coins sitting next to the fragments had initially grabbed his attention, as had the intelligence report he had then accessed from the SIS archives, because they suggested the coins were the key to a vast hidden vault of looted Nazi treasure.

Untouched for over sixty years, that old red and faded file had been classified Top Secret, and then given a restricted-access caveat that ensured it remained hidden in the filing system. It had not been without difficulty to even discover its existence, let alone access it. His authority alone, even as GCHQ Director-General, hadn't been enough. Some coercion and the calling-in of substantial favours had finally released it. But when he had finally read it, the contents had confirmed that most of the rumours he'd heard had been true.

The first coin had been found and bought at an obscure auction house in England, purely a lucky find by a member of the intelligence community who had simply recognised the object as unusual and therefore potentially interesting. Later research had established that a Captain Fletcher and a Corporal Mitchell had found the cache of gold coins hidden in an abandoned building in Berlin. Another six of them had been retrieved from Mitchell by the SIS when they had caught him in Dublin trying to flee to America with them. He'd been aggressively questioned – a more acceptable term than 'tortured,' though that had been the reality of his fate – and then shot, his body thrown into the sea.

That meant seven of the original eight coins had been found and were then in the possession of GCHQ but the eighth had disappeared, its location lost in the distant fog and confusion of the last days of the war. One thing had puzzled Martin when the Director of Research had explained all this to him.

'So at no point have we ever had all eight coins in our possession?' he'd asked him.

'No. As I've just explained.'

'Then how do you know there are eight of them? How do you know the full set isn't just those seven coins?'

The Director of Research had just smiled at him. 'That's the easy bit,' he'd said. 'They're numbered one to eight, but we don't have number three.'

Martin also knew that the Catholic Church had apparently sent out its own agents looking for a share of the spoils, but all the indications were that it had given up the search long ago. What really intrigued Sir Charles was the translated transcript of the interrogation of a high-ranking Nazi general at the end of the war, which had also confirmed that the rumours were true.

A plan – fraught with risks but potentially offering unimaginable rewards – had then started to form in Paul Scott's mind, a scheme that would take him far beyond his current persona of Sir Charles Martin, which he was starting to find quite tiresome, and lead to the acquisition of untold wealth.

Chapter Eighteen

Cheltenham, Gloucestershire, England

The extent of the vast housing estate opposite GCHQ made it easy for Natasha to disappear and within ten minutes of running into the maze she knew she'd left any possible pursuit well behind her. It was a warren of back streets, abandoned cars, scattered groups of people standing and talking or just walking around, and broken fences galore. She knew the streets well and, she realised, her current tattered and dishevelled appearance after a day on the run and sleeping rough meant that she fitted right in.

There was, she reflected, something of a sense of irony in that one of the world's most secret establishments existed side by side with an area of transient social housing in the middle of a town. Despite being a literal island of secrecy, GCHQ wasn't in any way remote in terms of its physical location.

Natasha knew the area reasonably well because one of her guilty secrets or pleasures involved the fish and chip shop in its centre. Many a time, when she felt she needed a mental lift, she would sneak over there for a lunch of cod and chips with lashings of salt and vinegar. There simply was nowhere else in the area that did them better.

Her clear advantage was that, by hiding out in a housing estate with its fair share of illegal immigrants, suspected benefit fraudsters, petty criminals and other people usually considered to be socially undesirable, no-one there would ever admit to seeing anything or anyone if they were questioned by the authorities, and certainly there were no cameras or other surveillance mechanisms.

Natasha was greeted with the familiarity accorded a regular customer when she arrived at the takeaway, but nobody on the estate ever asked for names or anyone's business and there was certainly no prolonged eye contact. Police cars were a rare sight and nobody could ever recall seeing an officer – or even a group of officers – on foot. The locals effectively self-policed the area and that suited the authorities fine, as long as everything stayed calm.

Natasha's takeaway meal today was a necessity rather than a pleasure. She knew she needed calories to survive, and to simply help her think straight. Being slim and athletic, she knew she needed fuel for her body, and there was no better option than her favourite fast food. But she barely tasted what she was eating, her mind occupied elsewhere.

The answer to everything, she guessed, lay in Room 23. She had known of its existence, though not why it was important or what was inside it, for a couple of years. It was as her mind raced over everything that had happened when it suddenly came to her. She finished the last piece of cod and licked her fingers.

Leaving a couple of chips that had stuck to the paper and tossing it into a bin, she set off on a journey back to her home.

Chapter Nineteen

1946: Cheltenham, Gloucestershire, England

On the train journey back to Cheltenham Captain Nick Fletcher had the opportunity to think long and hard about what had happened and what he'd been told.

Parker had clearly been tasked to find out what he knew, and the book or journal or whatever it was seemed to be the key. Given his hand signals and facial expressions during the briefing it implied someone else had been listening. What he hadn't been told at first was that his mission was going to be dangerous, but the moment Parker had ordered him to draw a pistol, a weapon that was now tucked fully-loaded and heavy in the unfamiliar embrace of a leather shoulder holster under his jacket, his attitude had changed. He was a soldier once again, but the difference was that this time he had no idea who the enemy was. What he did know was that he had to consider himself in danger.

The first thing he needed to do was to retrieve the journal and the gold coin from their present hiding place and conceal them in a much more secure location. He decided he would then quickly pack a bag and set off for the village of Littleton by taxicab, as the fastest method of transport available, and find a place to stay. That probably wouldn't be easy at the time of night when he'd be likely to get there but he was sure he'd find a pub or something offering rooms. Then he'd start looking for Mitchell the next day.

It wasn't much of a plan, and it didn't even last until he reached his home.

He walked down the lane from the bus stop, where he'd stepped off the vehicle he'd caught at the railway station, and as soon as his house came into view he knew he had a problem. Or rather another problem.

His front door, which he'd shut, locked and checked before he'd left home, was standing open. Looking inside, even from a distance, he could see the place had been ransacked.

Fletcher took out the pistol. It was familiar to him, a Browning 9-millimetre semi-automatic, the same weapon that he had carried as his sidearm during the last few months of the Second World War instead of the cumbersome Enfield and Webley revolvers that were the standard weapons of British officers. He cocked it and made sure that the safety catch was on. Then he walked slowly down his garden path, watching the house for any sign of movement – perhaps the intruder or burglar was still in the building – and listening for any sounds.

But he was looking in the wrong direction.

He heard a sudden shuffle and exhalation of breath and before he could even turn or aim his pistol a heavy object hit the back of head. He crashed sideways into one of his flowerbeds and immediate darkness.

-o0o-

'Are you all right, old boy?'

Fletcher heard Parker's voice as if from a distance. As the light and consciousness and confusion returned, he suddenly vomited and rolled over to clear it away from his face. Turning back, he looked up into Parker's concerned face.

'I thought you might have been a goner there,' the senior officer said.

'I'm still alive,' Fletcher replied, 'though my head feels like it's about to split in two.'

He started to rise to his knees. Parker grabbed his left arm and helped him to stand up. Fletcher staggered, grabbed the back of his head and then groaned at the pain. To his surprise, his pistol was on the ground where he had been lying. He could only assume that whoever had attacked him hadn't realised he was armed, and that when he fell the weapon had been invisible under his body.

'What happened?' he asked, turning to look at his home.

'Someone broke into your house. I suspect it was the foreign friends I mentioned because there's a faint whiff of cologne in there if I'm not mistaken. But it looks as if they're long gone. It's the coins and journal they're after and I think I know why,' Parker replied. 'Let's have a cup of tea and a proper chat.'

They walked into the house and they both tidied up as best they could. It didn't take very long to bring some sense of order to Fletcher's few pieces of furniture and possessions.

Sitting on the opposite side of the kitchen table, Parker took a sip of the tea he'd made for them both and then began his long-overdue explanation.

'I've got a lot to tell you, and I'd appreciate it if you kept any questions you've got until I've finished.' Fletcher nodded but said nothing and Parker continued. 'A long time before the war finally ended the Germans had realised that they didn't have anything like the numbers of soldiers or more importantly the resources they needed to keep invading other countries, despite Hitler's dreams of global domination. In fact, we now think that Britain was planned to be the final occupied nation, and the Germans would then seek a peace treaty with Russia and the United States. We also know that Hitler's senior generals had started to put a plan in place that would include all this in the Third Reich. They even secretly factored in the demise of the Fuhrer and how the succession of a new leader would work.

'The problem they encountered was that Hitler was quite mad, totally deluded and almost daily becoming more obsessed with the occult and his own destiny. His disastrous invasion of Russia and the losses at the Battle of Britain were only the start of a series of bad decisions and ultimately the seeds of self-destruction for the Nazis. The generals could see what was happening and guessed what the future – the real future – held for them. Back in 1941 eight of them decided to put a secret contingency plan in place to be implemented if, or rather when, Germany lost the war.

'Over the course of the Second World War the generals had arranged with the Vatican Bank to store vast quantities of stolen treasure in a secure vault in a secret location, for a hefty fee, obviously. The Catholic Church has spread its wealth spread across the globe, not just in Italy, so this vault could literally be anywhere. The Church was of course quite happy with the arrangement, as it allowed them to increase their own wealth at the same time.

'We're unsure who in the Church knew of this arrangement, but it appears to have been a plan authorised at the very top, hence the rumours of a document signed by the Pope and by either Himmler or the Fuhrer.

'The other rumour, and I must assume this is now a fact rather than just speculation, is that all eight of these gold coins are needed to gain access to the vault and that all eight of the rebellious generals or their descendants would have had one each. How you and Mitchell came to find them all in one place in that building in Berlin I have no idea, but you did and that's to our benefit.'

Fletcher raised his hand to say something, then thought better of it and kept his silence.

Parker ploughed on. 'The other factor was technology. The generals knew that Germany's scientific and engineering knowledge were years, maybe decades, ahead of other nations and that this would not only be a bargaining chip but would allow the swift resurrection of the Nazi vision with a Fourth

Reich driven by its technological superiority over its enemies. A bit like this atom bomb that the Americans now have. That's an excellent example of the way new and advanced technology can dominate other nations until those countries manage to catch up.

'Anyway, I believe the book that was secreted away with the coins lays out this masterplan and gives the locations of both sites. One is a vault containing unimaginable wealth and the other is a laboratory full of world-changing scientific developments and achievements.'

Fletcher was not surprised by any of this, though he hadn't expected to find himself at the centre of it. But he had read the book properly, despite it being written in German and Latin, and had made one or two subtle changes to some of the information it contained.

'So why the hand actions and funny faces when we met earlier, sir?' he asked.

'Somebody else was listening. The Secret Intelligence Service and a few other groups of people are interested in all of this. I don't trust any of them and neither should you. In my opinion, any of them would be quite happy to torture you if they even suspected you had either the book or the missing coin.'

For the briefest of instants Fletcher caught sight of a fleeting shadow in his peripheral vision, a shape passing across his window. He grabbed his pistol and stood up but stopped as he heard Parker gasp.

The man had slumped forward onto the table and was gasping for air. For a moment Fletcher didn't understand what had happened. But then he saw the knife sticking out of Parker's back just to the left of his spine. The 'shadow' – whoever it had been – had obviously thrown the weapon from the doorway, the knife-point slamming with utter precision into his target and, from the angle, piercing the man's heart.

Fletcher flung himself against the wall, aiming the pistol towards the open door, in case the invisible assassin intended to use another weapon against him. Despite what had just happened he was icily calm.

He had been in this kind of situation so many times his reaction was second nature. He could see no movement outside the house through either the doorway or the window. But he had no doubt the man who'd just killed Parker was still out there, and the house could become a killing ground any second if the man had also got a rifle or pistol. He knew he needed to get out. And as soon as he could.

Fletcher made a final check all around him, then strode straight across the room to the back door, the only other way out, his pistol held ready to engage any target that he saw.

But what he wasn't going to do was just open the door and step outside, because that seemed to him like a really good way to get himself killed.

Instead, he positioned himself behind the solid stone wall of his cottage, then reached over to the door handle. He turned it slowly to open the wooden door, then took a half-step backwards.

His instinct had been right.

As the door swung open there was a thunderous noise as a massive force hit it, blasting off the paint and shredding the wood underneath. A huge bearded man clutching a black double-barrelled shotgun appeared in the doorway, his gaze and the muzzle of the weapon sweeping the room, perhaps assuming that Fletcher had been behind the opening door and was most likely now a bloody, mutilated corpse. Or, more likely, that his target was still alive but in shock and could be persuaded to answer questions about a golden coin and an old book while looking down the barrel of the shotgun.

But Fletcher was very much alive and was standing against the wall behind the intruder, his pistol loaded and cocked and pointing directly at the man's back. And he was in no mood to try to take a prisoner or ask any questions.

Without hesitation and as efficiently as a trained assassin he shot the man twice, once in the lower back and the second round about a foot higher. Either wound, from Fletcher's wartime experience, would probably be fatal, which was precisely the result he wanted and expected.

The man instantly collapsed to the floor of the cottage, the shotgun falling from his lifeless hands.

Fletcher stepped forward, checked outside the back door to ensure that no other putative assassins were waiting outside, then bent down beside the giant and quickly searched him. But apart from another four 12-bore shotgun cartridges, a set of car keys and a little cash he found nothing.

His appearance – the man's tanned complexion and black hair – suggested he might not be English, a conclusion supported by his jacket, which bore a label from a tailor in Milan. And Fletcher wasn't entirely sure why, but his shoes looked not only expensive but also in some way indefinably foreign. Neither suggested the man had been a hired thug, and Fletcher's mind inevitably returned to what Parker had told him about the potential foreign interest in the gold coins.

Fletcher picked up the shotgun, reloaded it and again checked the view from the back door of the property. He saw nothing suspicious and walked out into his garden, alert for any movement and primed to kill on sight.

But there was nothing and nobody.

He walked around to the other side of his property and wasn't surprised at what he saw. In fact, it was almost what he had expected, bearing in mind what had just happened. Parker's driver lay flat on the front lawn, a dark pool of blood forming an obscene halo around his head.

Fletcher walked to the end of his driveway, still checking all around him for any hostile movement. He looked over his five-bar gate and checked the quiet lane. About fifty yards away was a burgundy left-hand drive Volvo PV60 on Italian plates, which he assumed had been the giant's car and which, incidentally, confirmed his suspicion about the man's probable nationality.

He approached the vehicle cautiously and searched it thoroughly but apart from a small crucifix dangling from the inside mirror he found nothing. He used the keys he'd taken from the man with the shotgun and turned on the ignition. It had a full tank of petrol and he decided that as the giant assassin clearly no longer needed it, instead of taking a taxi he could use the Volvo to travel to Littleton to try to find Mitchell. As far as Fletcher was concerned, his mission was still in place, even if he would now have to find somebody else to report to.

Neither the blast from the shotgun nor the pistol shots had aroused any reaction from his neighbours. If they'd heard the sounds at all they'd probably have assumed it was a couple of farmers out shooting rabbits with a shotgun and a rifle. Deep in the countryside those kinds of sounds were normal. So that gave him some time to think.

What he definitely couldn't do was go to the police because he was the unwilling custodian of three dead men, one of whom he had himself killed, and two abandoned cars. Even the most friendly and accommodating of country police officers would correctly assume that as the only person still alive at the scene of multiple murders he would need to supply believable and convincing answers to a lot of very difficult questions, and those questions would be put to him in a locked interview room in a police station, or even in a cell.

There was a substantial risk that whatever he said wouldn't be believed and he would be locked up while a full investigation was carried out. He was also very wary of the warning from Parker about shadowy government figures in the background that were operating to their own agenda.

Fletcher knew that if he were to be arrested that would make it easy for the SIS or some other organisation to take him away for 'further questioning' and he had taken Parker's threat of probable torture to heart. He had to retain his freedom at all costs. That meant sanitising the scene of the shooting as best he could, and as quickly as possible.

Fletcher returned to his cottage, went up to his bedroom and stripped off his clothes and checked them all to make sure there was no blood on any of them. Then he dressed in a set of overalls he used for gardening and a pair of old shoes.

He left the house and walked over to the body of Parker's driver. He crossed himself, then grabbed the man by the wrists and dragged him across the grass to the driveway, where Parker's Jaguar was parked. He pulled open the rear door of the car and, with some difficulty, managed to pull him onto the floor inside the vehicle. And that was the easy bit.

Then he walked around the cottage and into the back garden to the compost heap where he'd left his wheelbarrow and pushed it over to the rear door of the cottage.

The dead Italian assassin was much heavier than Parker's driver, and it took Fletcher a lot longer to manoeuvre his corpse onto the wheelbarrow. But he finally managed it and, grunting with the effort, he pushed the barrow around the cottage and over to the Jaguar. And then he had to do it all again to get the bloody corpse into the boot of the car. He guessed the body was just too heavy and cumbersome to try to get it inside the vehicle, but the boot floor was about the same height as the wheelbarrow so he could roll it sideways.

Then he slammed the boot lid shut, covered the body of Parker's driver with some old sacking as a rudimentary disguise, closed and locked all the car doors and pocketed the keys.

Fletcher felt as if he'd done a route march, and before he did anything else he walked back into his kitchen and made himself a cup of tea. While he waited for it to cool, he washed the bloodstains off the flagstone floor and then looked at Parker's body. He had too much respect for the man to dispose of his body the way he intended to 'lose' the two men in the Jaguar, so he knew he'd need to use the wheelbarrow again.

Feeling somewhat refreshed, Fletcher returned to the front garden and deposited compost over the section of the lawn where the driver's blood had spread to conceal it, though he knew that the first decent shower of rain would permanently dispose of the evidence. Then he took a spade and began digging a deep hole in his vegetable plot in the shade of a plum tree that he hoped would be a suitable grave for the major general. It was a beautiful location, but he knew that his days of eating produce from the plot had now quite definitely ended.

An hour and a half later Fletcher stood at one end of a patch of freshly turned earth, his bible in his hand. But when it came to it he found he couldn't conduct a service – he'd comprehensively lost whatever remained of the tatters of his faith in the ghastly carnage that had marked the approach to Berlin – but he said a few quiet and respectful words and bowed his head. He had felt compelled to say farewell to the major general with some dignity but to do anything more would have been hypocritical and blasphemous, particularly with what he had planned for the other two bodies.

Later that night Fletcher drove the Jaguar with its two permanently silent passengers down to the River Severn. He picked a spot near a weir where he could see that the water was deep and where the bank sloped down towards the water at what he hoped was a steep enough angle. He stopped the car above the slope, opened all the windows a few inches, then switched off the engine and checked that the handbrake was fully released and the steering wheel was in the correct position.

Then he opened the door, stepped out of the car and walked around to the boot. He leaned his back against it and extended his legs. At first the vehicle didn't move, but then he felt it shift. He applied more pressure and suddenly he fell backwards as the car moved behind him.

He scrambled to his feet and watched as the Jaguar reached the edge of the bank and tipped forward into the dark water. Being heavy it sank quickly with little fuss, just a surge of bubbles on the surface as the air trapped inside the vehicle escaped, carrying its two occupants to the bottom of the river. With any luck, the vehicle would retain the two bodies until they had been reduced to skeletons, but even if one of the windows shattered or the boot lid opened and allowed one of the corpses to escape, there was no link he could see that would lead to the police to his door.

The walk back to his house took Fletcher over an hour, which provided more time than he wanted or needed for some personal reflection.

Without returning to the cottage Fletcher collected the booklet and gold coin from the hiding place he knew was still secure. He studied them both for a few minutes and then hid them again, this time choosing a much more obscure location. Back at the cottage he created a suitable clue for himself as a reminder, then packed a bag, checked again that he could see no signs of what had happened there, locked up and walked away. He climbed into the Volvo and started the car to begin his journey to try to find Mitchell and work out the truth about the other coins and the claims that Parker had made.

Exactly fifty minutes and thirty-three seconds later Captain N.C.A. Fletcher MC lost control of the unfamiliar left-hand drive car as he entered Littleton village.

The vehicle veered off the road and its almost immediate high-speed impact with a substantial tree propelled Fletcher through the windscreen. Razor-sharp shards of glass ripped and tore at his body as he was ejected from the car, causing devastating, but not fatal, injuries. But when his head smashed into the trunk of the tree that had stopped the car, the impact crushed his skull and broke his neck for good measure.

The wrecked car rolled twice after hitting the tree, ending up in a ditch, Fletcher's battered body trapped underneath it.

It was a further hour after that when Sir Roger Sinclair and a team of SIS agents arrived at Littleton. The first thing they saw as they drove into the village was the scene of the accident. They already had the number of the Italian's car, though they hadn't expected to find it upside down in a ditch. The stopped their vehicles on the road beside the tree and began their search.

Apart from Fletcher's mangled corpse and an unexpected 12-bore shotgun and a loaded Browning pistol, they found nothing.

Chapter Twenty

1945: Berlin, Germany

Hitler was SS – *Schutzstaffel* – member number one, its supreme leader and holding the unique rank of Oberster Führer der Schutzstaffel and, while he never wore the distinctive uniform, he headed one of the most feared organisations ever created. With over one and a quarter million members its reach was far, and few Germans could escape either its powerful influence or its retribution for perceived crimes.

But the man who sat at the desk in the smart office in the centre of Berlin with two full length windows that allowed him to see the world passing by in the square below exerted just as much power as Hitler within the SS. Member number one hundred and sixty-eight, but holding the commanding rank of Reichsführer-SS, was Heinrich Himmler. He had joined the SS in 1925 and had personally overseen the growth of the organisation from just a few hundred people to a million-strong paramilitary unit, his personal strength and power deriving from his control of the Waffen-SS, its hard-line military wing.

His view of the square below the building was a source of daily pleasure to Himmler: he was able to enjoy a glass of expensive claret as he swung his chair round to watch the daily hangings or the actions of his firing squads from the comfort of his office.

Many senior Nazis believed that Hitler feared Himmler because of his obvious organisational skills, utter callousness, and meticulous attention to detail. And he was right to do so. Having personally planned and directed the killing of over six million Jews inside the death camps, and because of his effective control of the SS, Himmler was a dormant but ever-present and immensely powerful threat to Hitler's long-term command.

Himmler was aware of this but had not the slightest interest in taking over the command of a fatally-holed and clearly sinking ship. As early as the end of 1941 he had already begun preparing for what he knew would be the inevitable defeat of the Nazi regime. Every senior officer in the Nazi high command – all of them except Hitler himself, in fact – had recognised that defeat was inevitable once the idiots running Japan had launched their unprovoked and suicidally-stupid air attack on Pearl Harbor on Sunday 7 December 1941. If that event had not occurred, public opinion in America would very probably have kept the United States out of the war, which would have remained an entirely European conflict, a war that Germany and Italy acting together might ultimately have won.

But the Japanese action had not merely prodded awake a sleeping, angry and immensely powerful bear. It had hurt and shocked and infuriated the most powerful nation in the world and that meant the ultimate defeat of Hitler was as inevitable as night following day.

Himmler was nothing if not a realist, and with the connivance of seven other trusted generals he had begun preparing for the building of the Fourth Reich.

Their simple plan involved the creation of a secret vault of tradeable treasure that would fund the further development of advanced Nazi technology and scientific research that would ultimately allow Germany to hold the entire world to ransom.

The idea of eight gold keys, keys shaped like innocuous coins, would ensure that no-one else, not even the Church which was deeply involved, could have access to the vault, and all the generals had an equal share, one key each. The fact that all eight keys needed to be present at the same time to access the contents of the vault meant that the loyalty and commitment of the conspirators was guaranteed: the possession of seven coins or less would have no value. That would ensure a bond between the men and on the use of the treasure when it was finally removed from the vault, and by default created a kind of self-regulation that would guarantee the continuation of the great cause, the Nazi dream of world domination.

Once any man gained so much wealth that he could buy anything, the motivations for his actions and his need for a legacy tended to change. To further guarantee their loyalty and commitment, each of the key holders would be allowed enough wealth to protect themselves and to provide for their future generations of offspring. The acquisition of power and implementing the Nazi legacy would become their sole motivations.

The technology built into the coins gave them both a source of power and a code that couldn't be broken. The scientists had demonstrated their use to Himmler on his tour of the vault and it had been amazing, almost magical, to see them working. They had decided to put Hitler's head on them as a form of disguise, to make them look like a kind of medal or token, and if any of the keyholders were to be challenged about the coins they held they would argue that this was a tribute to Hitler's greatness as the leader of the Third Reich. Nothing more than a simple acknowledgement and a reminder of Hitler's power and status. The appeal to the Führer's over-reaching vanity and planet-sized ego would probably be enough to assuage any suspicions he might harbour.

Even though Himmler was not known for his sense of humour, largely because he probably hadn't got one, he had seen the funny and ironic side of this.

Himmler vividly remembered the day in 1945 when Hitler had ordered him to be arrested for treason. Though it was, admittedly, true that he had technically – or even actually – committed treason when he'd opened up discussions with the Allies to see if a truce could be negotiated, that was hardly the point. He'd seen the allied forces continuing their steady and inexorable advance across Europe, an advance that he had known would inevitably end in the fall of Berlin and the end of the Nazi dream, and he'd known that negotiation and a truce offered the only possible way out.

Himmler also remembered how the other generals had not come to his rescue and had protected themselves by conspiring against him, and he had fled for his own safety.

He hadn't honestly expected Hitler to survive those last days, but as the final allied bombardment of the city had begun, the seemingly endless tons of British and American bombs falling from the skies and the repeated crump of Russian artillery shells exploding, it was obvious that it was every man for himself.

He had already decided he would now keep all of the eight coins and his journal, still locked in his personal safe in his office in Berlin, for himself as his own personal security. The generals who had abandoned him would no longer receive their coins for their treachery. He knew he had been very lucky with the timing because he had been about to distribute the coins to them.

The contents of the secret vault would give him obscene wealth, more than enough to allow him to live out his days in both an impenetrable disguise and complete safety, and the whereabouts of the laboratory that had fabricated the keys was still known only to him. That might, he hoped, provide something of a negotiating tool if he were to be captured by the Allies, though he doubted if it would do much more than delay his inevitable execution. He knew that his undeniable involvement in the creation and the running of the death camps to permanently solve the Jewish problem made his fate a virtual certainty.

But even as he had unlocked his safe that afternoon to remove the coins, he had heard footsteps, the sounds of a lot of booted feet coming up the stairs towards the room.

Time was against him. He quickly shut the panelling that covered the safe and ran towards the tapestry that hid his escape door. He would have to return later for the coins. More importantly, he couldn't allow himself to be captured.

What he didn't know was that another member of his staff had also been in the building but had not had time to escape. Himmler had heard the crashing explosion of the grenade behind him as he'd walked carefully down the narrow dusty passage.

And he knew at that moment that his own dreams of colossal riches were over. He knew what the explosion of a grenade sounded like and knew that the detonation would most likely have ripped the wooden panelling apart to reveal the safe, the safe that he had unlocked just a few minutes earlier. And that whoever had been coming up the stairs – almost certainly a group of enemy soldiers – would even then be picking up the coins and his journal. The only comfort he could take from what had happened was the knowledge that they would probably never find either the vault or the laboratory.

The only option Himmler had left was to get out of Germany as fast as he could.

At the end of the passage he undid the wooden hatch, climbed out and slipped away into the crowded street below, his civilian clothes allowing him to blend in with everybody else..

Just over two weeks later, on 21 May, Heinrich Himmler was captured by the Allies at a checkpoint in Bremervorde. Two days later he was taken to the British 31st Civilian Interrogation Camp not far from Lüneburg. He was carrying a forged paybook that identified him as Sergeant Heinrich Hitzinger, it being standard practice for people assuming another identity to retain their original first name whenever possible to allow them to respond immediately when addressed by it.

Unfortunately for Himmler, the paybook bore an official stamp that was known by British Intelligence to have been found on other forged documents being carried by officers identified as being former members of the SS. That was more than enough to spark an investigation.

Himmler was interviewed by Captain Thomas Selvester, the duty officer at the Interrogation Camp. Perhaps surprisingly, Himmler finally revealed his true identity and Selvester ordered him to be searched as a routine precaution. Then he was transferred to Lüneburg where the Second British Army headquarters had been established.

And that building was where Himmler's life reportedly ended. According to official sources, a doctor was called to examine him, but Himmler would not let him examine the inside of his mouth, turning his head away every time the doctor tried to do so. The reason for his reluctance became clear moments later, when Himmler bit into a poison pill containing potassium cyanide he had hidden in his mouth. He was dead in minutes, taking his knowledge of the gold coins, his journal, the vault, the laboratory and everything else with him.

His body was dumped in an unmarked grave, its location still unknown, in the vicinity of Luneburg.

That was what the official records showed.

But in fact, something entirely different had happened to Heinrich Himmler.

Chapter Twenty-One

Present day: Gloucestershire, England

While Natasha was fit, a five-mile cross country walk avoiding drones, soldiers and a certainly hostile and possibly lethal reception at her home was unappealing.

She had purchased the near derelict cottage at auction after being seduced by its faded charm and air of neglect. And the lack of any immediate neighbours suited Natasha just fine.

The reality was that nobody else seemed to want to buy it, possibly because of persistent rumours of the body of a murdered man being found buried in the vegetable plot just after the end of the war, but that didn't bother her. It was also all that she could afford and it was just about habitable, largely because the immediately previous owner had been a travelling salesman who hadn't spent much on its upkeep at all, because for most of his time he had been out on the road.

She'd done some rudimentary digging – in the records, not in the vegetable plot – and had found out that the owner of the place well before the salesman had bought it had been a military war hero. He had tragically died in a somewhat unusual motoring accident shortly after returning home from the war, and the cottage had remained unoccupied for several years afterwards before seeing a succession of owners and tenants.

The fish and chips she'd eaten had jogged a memory and some questions about that man that Natasha decided she needed to explore. With a bit of luck, the answers might be found somewhere in her cottage. She'd already discovered some hints which had started her innocent enquires about Room 23, enquiries that appeared to have upset several people at GCHQ, and certainly some members of the hierarchy.

Actually, the word 'upset' was a huge understatement in view of what had happened to her. And what other people had tried – so far unsuccessfully – to do to her. Somewhat bizarrely, she found she was enjoying the intellectual challenge she faced more than her fear of the physical danger she was in, which was of course, she concluded, utterly illogical. But then Natasha Black knew she had never really fitted into the 'normal' category. Whatever that was.

None of the local buses were fitted with CCTV as far as she knew. To leave Cheltenham would be easy if she could avoid any street cameras and pay cash for the bus ticket because she dare not use any of the credit cards in her purse: that would leave an indelible electronic trail. She could buy a ticket that would take her as far as the Coombe Hill Bird Sanctuary. There, she knew, was an old canal once used for coal transportation and which led down to the River Severn, and that was a route she knew she could use and remain unseen.

Her plan was simple enough. She could access the back of her cottage from the river where there were no roads. She would then be able to creep closer and see if her house was physically guarded. There was only one road in and out of the village and she suspected that any watchers would be covering that access. Her plan beyond that point, checking the situation at her home, was unclear in every sense of the word.

It was as she stepped down from the bus and made her way along the towpath to the canal and bird sanctuary that she finally realised she would need a boat for the last part of her plan because she needed to get to the opposite bank.

She hoped somebody might have left a rowing boat somewhere nearby that she could borrow, but she also knew this was a very unlikely possibility. Slightly disheartened, she walked the mile or so to the shore of the River Severn, which looked quite full and a little angry.

'Shit,' she muttered to herself. 'I'm not swimming across that.'

Natasha looked around and spotted something a few yards away. It looked like a discarded scaffold plank, but when she walked closer she saw it was actually four planks of wood that had been tied together into a sort of rudimentary raft or platform. Normally no one of sound mind would have even considered trying to cross the turbulent waters of the Severn on such a broken and insubstantial homemade vessel, but right then Natasha was completely out of options.

The banks on either side leading into the village were heavily overgrown and completely impassable without a machete so this would be the only way. She knew that local farmers had deliberately let the undergrowth flourish to avoid walkers crossing their land and to prevent fishing from the banks. On the other hand, she was also quite certain that nobody observing her house could have come this way either.

The homemade 'raft' was heavier than it looked and was entangled in overgrowth, and Natasha had to take a breather once she had cut it free. The combat knife she'd taken from her attacker was still serving her well and she spent the next thirty minutes hacking and sawing at a stout and fairly straight branch to make a pole. There was, she decided, something therapeutic about what she was doing and she could see why some people took up wood carving a hobby, though she had no intention of doing so herself.

She retied a few of the knots of the bailing twine that linked the planks and then faced the moment of truth. She manhandled her DIY punt to the edge of the river, clumsily crawled on board the unstable craft and knelt down, held the raft with one hand and used the pole to push the ramshackle vessel out into the river.

'HMS Natasha,' she said to herself, and then had to cling on tightly as she was taken downstream far too quickly for her liking.

Fortunately, the river quickly widened and the current reduced, which allowed her to take some sort of control with the pole. By then she was soaked through, the wooden planks floating barely above the surface of the river water, which sloshed freely over the insubstantial craft. The planks of the raft seem to move independently of each other but the bailing twine somehow managed to hold it together.

She had never seen or approached the village from this direction, and the view reminded her why she liked the location so much: it was very pretty, quiet and unspoilt. She almost didn't recognise the fields that lay about a quarter of a mile to the west of her cottage and sloped down to the river. Stabbing the pole firmly into the water and the river bottom she was able to slow the raft's progress downstream and tried to steer it towards the opposite bank.

That worked until the end of the pole caught in something underwater, and in trying to wrench it free she fell off.

Swimming fully clothed is never easy but Natasha managed to struggle to the bank, gasping for air and swearing in equal measure. Climbing up the muddy bank, her feet alternately slipping and sinking into the ooze as branches tore at her clothes and skin took most of the strength she had left. When she finally reached the safety of dry and level ground she was very wet, very dirty, very angry and shivering violently.

As she lay there trying to catch her breath she started to sob, the emotional upheaval and life-threatening events of the last two days finally catching up with her.

Chapter Twenty-Two

GCHQ Cheltenham, Gloucestershire, England

Sir Charles Martin had signed off all the paperwork regarding the death of Hargreaves, concealing the facts of the matter under the heavy and immovable blankets of national security and the Official Secrets Act. And he released another statement describing the disappearance of Natasha Black as a high-level security risk caused by a possible mental breakdown following the suicide of her superior.

His actions now meant that in addition to his own team seeking her, every police force and agency, including UK Border Control and even HMRC – Her Majesty's Revenue and Customs – were also on the lookout. As lucky as she'd been so far, he knew she hadn't been trained in any of this and he was certain she would eventually be caught. He had also issued a standing instruction that no one was to talk to her but him because of her security clearance and her intimate knowledge of GCHQ's highly classified operations and the possible impact on national security.

He temporarily pushed the Natasha Black problem to one side of his mind and turned his attention to the much more personally interesting subject of Nazi gold.

Hidden Nazi treasure had always been a something of a myth, despite the ranks of conspiracy theorists claiming the existence of a Nazi gold train tucked away in some forgotten tunnel and priceless works of art concealed in undiscovered caves or secret passages, all just waiting to be found. In fact, the Allies had done a very thorough job of appropriating any valuables or loot that they discovered at the end of the war. Many of the parties had been happy to overlook the actual ownership of most of it and move on, regarding what they'd found as useful contributions to set against the massive debts caused by the long war as they began to rebuild their own economies.

Sir Charles knew from the files he'd studied that Sir Hugh Sinclair, the former head of the SIS, had spent the last years of his life searching the globe for the missing gold coin or key. It was he who had authorised that Room 23 be removed intact from Bletchley Park and eventually secreted under the new GCHQ building, partly to remove it to a more secure location but more, Sir Charles assumed, for it to become Sinclair's own personal project, near his home in the Gloucestershire countryside and hidden away from prying eyes.

In those earlier days, GCHQ had been only a small specialist unit quite often overlooked or unacknowledged by Whitehall, not the world-beating, high-profile spying establishment it was today.

Once he'd discovered the significance of Room 23, Sir Charles had decided to continue Sinclair's quest, and he was armed with two bits of information that had only recently come to light.

First, he'd discovered that Natasha Black lived in the old cottage that had been owned just after the war by Captain Nick Fletcher, one of the two men who had discovered the coins in Berlin.

Second, it had dawned on him that her enquires about Room 23 did not appear to be simply random curiosity, and that implied that she had seen either the journal or the eighth coin or perhaps discovered something else that was linked to them.

Chapter Twenty-Three

The Pope's Private Study, Vatican City

Pope Benedict XVII sat at his desk and read the intelligence report again. As with any organisation with such international power and massive wealth, the Vatican needed to protect its reputation and financial situation to ensure its longevity and purpose.

The Church had survived many scandals over the centuries and whilst its past conduct had on many occasions been bloody and murderous and completely ungodly, he believed those actions had been essential at the time to ensure the survival of the Mother Church, a survival that was of paramount importance to him and his successors. Without the Church, he believed there would be no organisation able to provide stability and guidance and be a long-term force for good in an ever-changing world.

His predecessor during the Second World War had been faced with challenges he could barely comprehend. Indeed, he was unsure how he himself would have faced Hitler's demands as the invasion of Europe began in earnest. The Vatican's difficulties would have been compounded by the views of many priests who clearly had sympathy for Hitler's cause and a desire for a purer world at the expense of the Jews, the racially inferior *untermenschen* as the Germans called them, and that had globally split loyalties across the Church.

He knew that compromises had been made to appease Hitler and an agreement made with Mussolini and by default, with the Vatican, to prevent the Nazi invasion of Italy. Much of the threat of invasion was nothing to do with any kind of religious ideology but was simply the prospect of Hitler getting his hands on the Church's huge global income and the astonishing assets and wealth it held, both in the vaults of the Vatican and in bank accounts around the world.

As part of that agreement a compromise had been arranged. The Vatican Bank became the Nazi's bankers, handling their vast and increasing wealth while ignoring the suffering and numberless deaths inflicted by the regime and certainly never enquiring into the legality, origin or provenance of the funds the bank handled.

When the war had ended and with Hitler dead, the Church had reneged on this secret arrangement and had kept the Nazi wealth for itself, refusing to disclose or even discuss the matter. With other nations ransacking the battered ruins of Germany and plundering what remained, there was no nation left that was able to pass a moral or any other kind of judgement on the Church for its conduct.

The Pope had been aware from reading the many files and records that had been passed down to him that a vault had been built somewhere in Europe inside which a vast amount of stolen treasure had been stored as a contingency should the Nazis lose the war. Himmler had personally overseen its construction using his own slave labourers, and the Pope also knew that it had been passed into the Church's safe keeping by a signed deed shortly before the end of the war.

Unlike Hitler's arrangement with the Vatican, this had been conducted in secret and Himmler had ordered the execution of all those who had known of its existence and location. This had included, alarmingly, one Bishop and three priests.

Upon confirmation of Himmler's death, and in view of the veil of secrecy that had surrounded the vault – which more or less guaranteed that nobody still alive even knew of its existence, far less its location – the Church had decided to claim the treasure for themselves. Only two obstacles faced them: they didn't know the vault's location and they also didn't have any idea who possessed the eight golden keys shaped like coins that were apparently needed to unlock the vault door, if they ever managed to find it.

Agents from the Church had been dispatched to Berlin in 1946 to search for clues to the location of both the vault and the golden keys, but without any success, and the matter had eventually been consigned to history as just another unsolved mystery, and no signs of either the coins or any indication of the vault's location had ever been found.

That had now changed. An employee loyal to the Catholic Church who worked at GCHQ had managed to make copies of some of the pages of a file so old that its security classification had virtually lapsed, and had sent them, along with a note about the apparent intentions of the current Director General Sir Charles Martin, a man who had just announced that he would be retiring in six months' time.

The Pope had been astonished to discover that not only had GCHQ been holding onto seven of these keys – or coins, as they were described in the file – for over seventy years, but there was a strong possibility that the officer who had found them in the rubble of Berlin had also recovered a book or journal personally written by Himmler as well as the eighth and final coin. He had then been killed in a car accident in 1946.

What made this even more interesting, the GCHQ employee had added, was that another employee of the organisation, a woman who owned and lived in the soldier's old house, was now on the run from the authorities. And the reason for her flight was that she had apparently broken into the room in GCHQ that contained the coins, but she had not taken them.

The Pope reflected on this.

The employee who had provided this information was none other than Sir Charles Martin's personal assistant, so the Pope could be certain that what he'd said was accurate and reliable. The anticipated value of the treasure, according to the British file, was around ten billion pounds; the Pope wasn't necessarily convinced it was that much.

But none of that was as important as the other matter. The Laboratory of Nightmares, as it had been described in church records, had been the sinister sister project to Himmler's secret treasure vault and its discovery would threaten the Church directly even after all this time. At all costs this information couldn't be revealed because the records the Pope had seen proved there was irrefutable evidence in the laboratory that the Church had not only willingly funded the work but, far more devastating, had provided living subjects for the Nazis to use in their bizarre search for a God they could worship. Or emulate. And far, far worse.

The Pope shuddered. If what had happened in that laboratory were ever to be made public the Church would never – and could never – recover or be forgiven, even after all this time.

Summoning his Head of Security, he sanctioned with his signature and his seal the immediate theft from GCHQ of the seven keys, the location, capture and detention of Miss Natasha Black and the execution of Sir Charles Martin, who was clearly far too dangerous to be allowed to live.

Turning away to face the simple wooden crucifix on the wall, the Pope knelt and prayed.

Chapter Twenty-Four

Gloucestershire, England

Natasha pulled herself together and realised she had to act, and act quickly. She removed her outer garments and did her best to wring them dry, item by item. She waited until her skin and body warmed slightly in the sun and then put them back on. It wasn't pleasant but even the damp clothing helped to restore some warmth after a few minutes. Luckily it wasn't a cold day and the gentle sun on her face helped lift her spirits.

Being partially covered in mud she felt quite at one with her surroundings, and as she began to creep alongside the hedgerows towards her home she knew she was, at least to some extent, camouflaged. She had dismissed the thought of carrying a leafy branch to hold up in front of her as a disguise as probably being ridiculous, but she kept her eyes open for one just in case as she did need something like that as she moved closer.

Despite not easily finding any of the gates between the fields, she eventually and quite suddenly found herself almost at the edge of her garden and overlooking both her back lawn and the infamous vegetable plot.

She crouched down and waited, holding her breath until she could hear and feel her heart thumping. Everywhere was still. There only a gentle breeze and no sounds other than birdsong and the rumbling of the diesel engine of a distant tractor.

Natasha's gardening skills extended to using an electric lawn mower, doing a bit of gentle weeding and not much else. The dry-stone wall that surrounded her garden was covered in ivy and within it was a wild garden that she had left more or less to its own devices. She had always rationalised that she should encourage nature and not try to interfere with it too much. And that decision, or perhaps that non-decision, was now acting in her favour as she crept slowly along behind the wall.

She smelt the enemy before she saw them, the faint whiff of cigarette smoke blowing downwind towards her. Looking at the man smoking, she thought he appeared to be quite nondescript and non-threatening.

If it wasn't for the fact that he was behind a hedge and standing right outside her drive she probably wouldn't have seen him as a threat, just as possibly someone lost or slightly odd.

The man appeared bored and was now pacing up and down the lane outside her cottage, and it didn't look as if he was expecting her to appear there any time soon. She guessed he'd been sent out on a 'just in case' job – just in case she was stupid enough to openly walk down the lane to her house.

As Natasha looked on a woman joined the watcher. She was wearing a Barbour coat and green Wellington boots and was jabbing at the screen of her mobile phone, talking to the watcher in an irritated manner and punctuating her conversation with increasingly frustrated hand gestures. As Natasha knew only too well, the mobile phone coverage was poor to non-existent around the dip in which the village was located and the woman was clearly becoming exasperated trying to get a usable signal.

She watched the pair for about five minutes and concluded they were the only two people covering the cottage and, given their appearance, body language and actions, were most likely part of a security team from GCHQ and almost certainly there to raise the alarm if they spotted Natasha. And to try to grab her if possible. But she guessed that the more likely outcome if they saw her would be that they would follow her and try to corner her in or near the cottage. And then they'd summon a professional team who would rapidly appear and arrest her. Or worse.

Natasha had no illusions about the forces ranged against her.

Stepping quietly and carefully through a gap in the clumps of brambles that concealed her tank of heating oil, she put her hand in her pocket to retrieve her house key, but her probing fingers found nothing. It was gone, most probably washed away during her impromptu swimming session in the cold and murky waters of the River Severn.

Luckily that wasn't a problem because she had a spare key tucked away in a small metal box under the oil tank. That was a legacy of having locked herself out on more than one occasion, and of suffering the expensively unpleasant experience of calling out a glazier and paying him a seemingly extortionate amount of money to replace the single pane of glass she'd had to break to get back inside her own home.

Holding the combat knife in her left hand, a hand that now had a large purple bruise spreading across it, she slowly stretched out her hand to open her back door, ready to turn and run away very fast if she'd guessed wrong and somebody was inside waiting for her.Natasha entered her kitchen without fuss and stood for a few moments just listening for any unusual noise disturbing the normal sounds of her home. But she heard nothing. At least she wouldn't have to venture up the somewhat creaky wooden staircase because her bedroom was on the ground floor, a choice that right then she was really glad she'd made, though the reason had nothing to do with security or the staircase, but only with simple convenience.

In fact, she'd picked that bedroom to use because it had the kitchen on one side of it, and she enjoyed having easy access to both coffee and tea, and the downstairs bathroom was on the other side. And, as a bonus, the bedroom window was easily large enough for her to climb out of if, for instance, somebody with hostile or murderous intent was pounding on the solid wood of the bedroom door. And that scenario, she thought, was a very real possibility if she made too much noise inside the cottage.

She locked herself in the bedroom, sliding the large bolt home, and listened for any reaction from inside or outside the property. Again she heard nothing to alarm her.

Making as little noise as she could, she changed all her clothes, just keeping her Doc Martens on after a perfunctory wipe but added two pairs of thin socks to keep out the dampness. She combed her hair into some sort of order, found her bobble hat and pulled on her waterproof climbing jacket.

There was no cash in the house, but she kept the knife, found some sunglasses, took her passport from her bedside drawer and the small pocket-sized bible next to it. She obviously couldn't risk having a shower or cleaning her teeth as the sound of running water would certainly alert the watchers outside.

Creeping out she debated about leaving the back door unlocked to reduce any unnecessary noise, but then realised the watchers would almost certainly have tried both doors when they'd arrived, and if they checked again and found it unlocked they'd know that she – or at least that somebody – had been in the cottage. And if nothing else that would give them a confirmed locus from which to start a search. So she turned the key in the lock as quietly as she could, replaced it in its hiding place under the oil tank and headed back the way she'd come.

Warmer and drier but unfortunately no cleaner, and now with a renewed sense of purpose, she set off for the ruins of the old village church. The remains of the building, fortunately, lay well away from the only road into the village which she presumed was now guarded, or at least being watched.

Checking all around her, she walked cautiously down the dirt track that led to it and, as she always did, felt a sense of sadness for the building's demise and its present state as she approached.

Architecturally, St Mary's had been a fine building and could have served the village as a place of worship and a communal centre for many centuries. But the population of the village had shrunk in size as many families left, both men and women looking for work in London and the towns of the Midlands during the Industrial Revolution, and that once the church attendances shrank and its income dried up to almost nothing, the Church of England had no longer seen any point in maintaining the building. And any building that isn't properly maintained will eventually crumble as nature reclaims the site.

Natasha had never been particularly religious, but when she'd cleared out the house after she'd first moved in she'd found a small old military bible, a bible that she was now holding in her left hand. She'd taken to reading it occasionally, though it hadn't brought her any particular joy or comfort, and she'd put it in her bedside cabinet rather than throw it away because she'd somehow felt to do that would be wrong.

There was no name in it but she had always assumed it had belonged to the war hero named Captain Fletcher, a man who some old lady in the village told her had – perhaps surprisingly – been a vicar before going off to the war.

There was a very good reason why she was carrying the bible rather than, say, a stout walking stick she could use to beat anyone who attacked her to a pulp. What she remembered from the front pages of the bible was a hand-drawn map of the churchyard annotated with the names of those buried there. And she'd also noticed, next to one of the marked graves, a very small sketch of a coin with the legend R23 beside it. Most people would probably have assumed it was of no importance, but Natasha's brain had immediately picked up on it and stored it away as background information along with certain other clues she'd found in the cottage. Perhaps that had subconsciously triggered her later interest in Room 23 beneath GCHQ.

As she checked all around her before stepping into the churchyard, she looked again at the sketch and checked the name on the grave: Beckett.

Once in the churchyard it didn't her long to find the last resting place of Cyril Beckett, who had died aged 98 back in 1865. Why he'd picked this particular grave she had no idea, but she assumed that Captain Fletcher must have had some reason for his choice.

As she looked down at the grass-covered grave and the lichen-covered tombstone bearing very abbreviated details of the life of Cyril Beckett – basically the dates of his birth and death and the fact that he had been married to a woman named Edith – Natasha wondered what she should do next. Uppermost in her mind was the thought that the coin might be buried with the corpse, or rather the skeleton, that lay in the grave in front of her, and that searching dead bodies was becoming something of a habit of hers. Or perhaps an unusual hobby, she thought with a smile.

Where would I place a coin in an old grave? she wondered. She assumed that the captain hadn't exhumed the body to hide it, not with his background as a vicar. That, she had no doubt, he would have regarded as verging on blasphemy.

But she could see nothing apart from the grass covering the grave and the stone marker. She looked at the page in the bible again but there were no other clues. She now knew what R23 – which she deduced months ago had to stand for Room 23 – was but everything else was a blank.

Natasha stepped away from the grave and sat down on the grass against the back wall of the churchyard in the shade of a tree and for the first time thought properly about the enormity of the situation facing her.

She was on the run from the police and, most probably, all the security services of the United Kingdom. She'd killed a man, granted in self-defence, though she doubted she would ever get the chance to offer that as a defence in court, because she was quite certain that the people chasing her had not the slightest intention of letting her get anywhere near a court. And right then she was sitting in a churchyard looking for a golden coin missing from a set that was securely locked away in a hidden government vault along with a document bearing both Nazi and Papal inscriptions. Mad didn't even come close to describing it.

But even if she found the coin, what then? Could she somehow negotiate a truce? She guessed that was unlikely. On past form the people she was running from would simply take the coin and put her in jail without trial or possibly just kill her and dispose of her body. After all, she had no family or even friends or concerned colleagues who might start asking awkward questions if she suddenly disappeared.

The body bag episode she'd already managed to live through clearly showed her the likely outcome she would face if she was captured. She was fighting for her life here and the only thing she could do was find the damned coin and see if this gave her any answers.

At that moment it started to rain.

'Great,' she muttered as she stood up, walked across the graveyard and again knelt by the last resting place of Cyril Beckett, the combat knife in her right hand and ready to be used to prod around.

Chapter Twenty-Five

Italy

Mario Mazerino was twenty-nine years old and believed he had been destined to become a Catholic priest like his father, a man who had always denied his son's existence because the child was living proof that he had broken his vow of chastity. This denial had fuelled rage in Mario from a young age because his mother had been castigated and humiliated for giving birth to him out of wedlock. She had not been able to tell the truth about his parentage to anyone but her son.

They had travelled from village to village trying to settle, but eventually his mother found she couldn't take any more and had killed herself just after his fourteenth birthday because of the unbearable combination of never-ending shame and abuse, and her constant and abject poverty.

There had been no note, no words of kindness from her and the young Mario had decided in that split second, quite literally as he watched his mother's corpse being lowered into a pauper's grave on top of several other bodies, to become a priest. But not just that, and not just for the obvious reasons. He had also vowed to himself that he would find his birth father, something he wouldn't be able to do from outside the priesthood, and take his revenge on him.

Driven onwards by his unwavering rage he had almost completed the first part of his ambition, but on a single day everything had changed. On that afternoon he had found a thief robbing the coffers of the church where he had been training. Mario, then only eighteen, had exploded with rage and beaten the man to a pulp in a blind fury. When he'd finally stepped away, his hands bruised and bloody, the thief lay dead on the floor of the church. The man had been six foot three inches tall, weighed well over two hundred and forty pounds and had been a known debt enforcer.

Mario had stayed by the body, simply staring at it, until the Italian police had arrived. He was arrested and had then been handed over, as was the tradition in Italy at the time, to the Church authorities for trial, judgement, and sentence.

He had expected no mercy, and it was something of a shock when he was released after only one day and ordered to travel to Rome with a chaperone for a private meeting to discuss what he'd done and his future, if any, in the Church.

Mario had never been to Rome and was overawed by both its size and the large numbers of people moving everywhere at high speed. The car they had travelled in was given priority on the roads by the policemen directing the traffic, but absolute chaos was his immediate impression and the most obviously apt description of driving in Rome.

Eventually they had arrived at a set of gates set within an arched pillar on the very edge of the Vatican City. Mario had barely moved for the whole journey and his chaperone, an elderly priest, had clearly had no wish to engage in conversation with him and had hardly said anything at all.

Walking down a very bare and undecorated passageway, Mario had assumed that he had been brought in through the back door as he was still a prisoner and for a few brief moments he had even considered trying to make a dash for freedom. But the facts that he was able to walk of his own free will, wasn't wearing handcuffs, hadn't been put behind bars and was there in the Vatican City gave him some faint hope that he could talk his way out of what he had done, given that he had been defending Church property.

In fact he hadn't needed to even try to talk his way out. He had been escorted to a stone-walled room with a wooden floor, furnished only with a table and two chairs and told to wait. A few minutes later a man had entered, a man who appeared to have no warmth or, Mario thought, perhaps not even a soul. Completely unsmiling, the man had sat down opposite him, stared at Mario for what seemed a disconcerting length of time, and had then finally spoken to him.

'It does not matter who I am, but you will listen to me. If you interrupt me even once or do not answer my questions with honesty, I will leave the room and you will be killed. Do you understand?'

'Yes,' Mario had replied. He felt sweaty and although the room was cold, he wasn't.

'I know who your father was. I know your mother killed herself and why she did so. And I know that you seek revenge. None of that is important to me. I only need an answer to one question. What you need to tell me is why you killed the thief in the church with such violence.'

Mario paused and waited.

'You may speak,' the man had said.

Mario had known he couldn't lie to this man whose eyes seemed to bore pitilessly straight through him. He had nowhere to hide and, strangely, felt a huge surge of cathartic relief, almost like a confessional, as he poured out his anger, his shame and his sorrow at what he had done in his short and pathetic life.

The man had stared at him again for some moments and had then seemed to come to a decision. 'I am going to make you an offer,' he'd said. 'An offer not just to keep you out of prison as we are well beyond that stage now, but for your life, in return for your absolute devotion to the Mother Church. This will be your only opportunity. If you do not accept, you will be killed immediately. The choice is yours.

'What I demand from you is your complete and unwavering allegiance to the Church, not as a priest but as a servant. To faithfully undertake any action I command in the absolute belief that it is for the good of the Church. Sometimes it may not feel so, but your unquestioning and unswerving loyalty is required.'

Mario nodded but kept quiet.

'I will only ask you this once. Do you accept this offer?'

Mario nodded again. 'I do,' he said, no doubt or hesitation in his voice. Or in his mind.

'Good. You will be sent to a retreat far from here where you will be trained in many skills. If you are judged to have failed at any point, you will be executed, as others have been before you. What we offer you in return is the chance of freedom, of wealth and the security of the Church in embracing you for the rest of your life.'

With that the man had stood up and left the room leaving Mario to his confused thoughts. He had been too overawed to even ask any questions, though in truth he didn't know what he *could* have asked. What had he got himself into? What had he signed up for, and how bad could it be? And would it be worse than a long stint in prison? That might even have been an easier option, but he had known it was already too late to change his mind.

The man had scared him to his core.

About half an hour later two other men had entered the room, blindfolded Mario and led him away.

He'd been transported to an unknown destination that he suspected was not in Italy but more likely somewhere in the Balkans. Over the next two years he had been trained to be an assassin, learning many skills and techniques. His weaknesses had been exploited and turned into strengths. His instructors realised from the first that Mario had been well chosen for his role: he had a natural and unusual aptitude to hurt and to kill, and he was able to follow any instructions without remorse.

That day he was sitting outside a small cafe in Rome drinking an iced orange juice. He didn't drink alcohol or smoke and he had taken a vow of chastity almost as soon as he had been transported to the training camp. His role had required him to forswear all weaknesses and temptations.

A few minutes after he had taken his seat at the outside table his phone had buzzed, announcing the arrival of a text message. He read it with a sense of satisfaction and anticipation. His new orders were to travel to England where he was to perform one theft, carry out one abduction and commit one murder. The details of the last one gave him the usual thrill, even after all this time and all the men and women he had sent to meet their maker.

He stood up, slid a banknote under his glass and left to prepare for what he hoped would be a short but satisfying trip.

Chapter Twenty-Six

Gloucestershire, England

Sir Charles Martin had become successful not just courtesy of his huge inherited – or rather stolen – wealth and title, but over the years by being more cunning, sly and dishonest than others.

But his big problem was money, or rather the lack of it. He had gambled away much of the vast wealth he had inherited on the stock markets, taking a massive hit in the financial crash of 2007/2008 that had nearly ruined him. The trustees of the estate had all resigned and his other properties had been sold off in tranches. He wasn't poor but he certainly couldn't afford to be careless with money. He'd even started to look at the value of his civil service pension – which had surprised him as it was much more than he'd expected – but even that would go nowhere near financing his current or anticipated lavish future needs.

To safeguard his intended lifestyle he needed to get his hands on the Nazi treasure he believed to be hidden in the secret vault, and the key to him achieving that, he was now certain, was information locked away in Natasha Black's impressive brain. In fact, the physical treasure wasn't actually what he was after, because he had a different plan in mind, but he needed all eight of the golden coins to make his plan work.

He was feeling much more relaxed than he had been for the last few days because he now sensed that the end-game was near.

Once Natasha Black had made her escape, his team had continued to search for her and they had – finally – been successful. Or rather one of the other assets he had requested had done the trick.

Through GCHQ, Sir Charles had arranged for an armed MQ-9A Reaper drone, controlled from RAF Waddington in Lincolnshire, to be tasked with surveillance in the Gloucestershire area. He'd sent a handful of photographs of Natasha Black to the station by email to allow the three-man team of operators to try to locate her. There had been several false starts when women who bore a passing resemblance to the target had been detected and then rejected, but finally he knew exactly where Natasha Black was.

What had surprised him was *where* she had been located.

The drone had been primarily checking roads, streets and pavements and looking for any single woman who broadly matched Natasha Black's appearance, and it was only when the drone had been repositioning and flying cross-country in transit between two search areas that she'd finally been spotted. Several clear pictures of a woman attempting to cross the River Severn using what appeared to be half a dozen wooden planks lashed together had been sent to Sir Charles by encrypted email.

He had recognised Natasha Black immediately he'd seen the images from the Reaper's camera, and he'd given orders that she was to be followed by the drone so that he could arrange for a team on the ground to arrest her. Or that's what he told the RAF squadron leader over at Waddington.

In reality, he would almost have preferred to have ordered the team controlling the drone to take her out. Almost, because she had proved to be a major source of irritation to him, but he knew he needed her alive to be interrogated.

And using a supersonic AGM-114 Maverick air-to-ground missile with its twenty-pound anti-armour warhead – the weapon carried by that particular Reaper – against a lone and unarmed female wandering around in the fields of Gloucestershire in peacetime would have been considered overkill by everyone and in any circumstances. In fact, Sir Charles seriously doubted whether the RAF team would have been prepared to order the strike, irrespective of the authority he possessed.

He had been surprised to learn that the drone was armed at all, but the senior officer he had spoken to at Waddington had explained that the crews were expected to operate the Reapers in a war environment, which meant carrying the usual missile fit even on training exercises. A bare drone flew and handled differently than one armed with almost four thousand pounds of lethal ordnance.

More importantly, he knew he needed to spend what he thought of as some quality time with Ms Black. Quality time for him, a rather less pleasant experience for her, but she would, he knew, eventually be persuaded to tell him what he wanted to know. Sooner or later everyone talked, and the men he employed were experts in the dark art of enhanced interrogation. Torture, in short. So all he really needed to know was where the woman was heading so that he could ensure she was picked up.

The drone would track her invisibly from a few thousand feet in the air and, as he sat looking at the big computer screen in his office on which a live streaming video of his target was now being displayed, he smiled for the first time in ages.

He had opened a link on his landline telephone to the team operating the drone at Waddington so he could talk to them directly rather than relay orders through a senior officer. It wasn't quite the same as actually being in the RAF control room but it was the next best thing. Once again he was grateful for the professionalism of the UK's armed forces and their command and control structure.

Sir Charles's full attention was locked on the screen on his desk as he watched Natasha Black's actions through the high-resolution cameras of the circling drone.

She had returned to her cottage and disappeared inside. That presented an ideal opportunity for the two watchers in the lane outside to bottle her up, a chance that he couldn't afford to miss. He muted the speakerphone link to Waddington, picked up his mobile and issued very specific orders to the operatives on the ground. Or rather he tried to, but the mobile phone network and the lack of coverage made it impossible. Ringing either of the numbers he had been given just produced a chirpily irritating message telling him that the mobile he had called was switched off – which he knew was not the case – or out of the area, which was also wrong.

Clearly exasperated, Sir Charles blurted out to the empty office: 'I'm sitting in the world's leading telecommunications centre and I can't even talk to somebody five bloody miles away!'

But there were other people he *could* talk to: the leader of the security team he had waiting on standby at GCHQ. He called him and issued the most specific orders. It was time he took control.

He knew the security team couldn't reach the cottage before Natasha Black could leave the building because there simply wasn't time, so he needed to wait just a little while longer to see where she went so that he could issue further orders.

Sir Charles watched impotently as Natasha Black emerged from the back door of her cottage a few minutes later, leaving both the watchers in the road entirely oblivious to her presence, and started to make her way across the fields.

Reluctantly, Sir Charles was starting to develop a niggling admiration for her ability to remain below the radar. And she certainly had the luck of the devil.

He stared at the screen as she made her way cautiously towards her objective, presumably some other part of the village. Maybe she had a car parked there or another means of transport that she intended to use to try to escape the net. If that was her plan, he knew it would be doomed to failure: the drone's cameras would easily be able to read a vehicle's number plate and the network of ANPR – automatic number plate recognition – cameras would do the rest.

But that wasn't her plan, he realised a few minutes later as he watched her enter the old abandoned churchyard. She was clearly moving with purpose and he suspected immediately that the last golden coin might be buried there. It would make sense as a hiding place.

It was time to move. He issued his final orders to the drone controllers at RAF Waddington, telling them that the 'GCHQ exercise' – the paper-thin excuse he'd used when he'd first contacted the base – was over and that they could resume their briefed mission. The last thing he wanted was an eye in the sky recording what was actually going to happen when his team finally caught up with Natasha Black.

Twenty minutes later, Sir Charles Martin stared though the windscreen of the Range Rover as the driver navigated the narrow lane that ran through the village, driving past the two watchers. As they approached the track which led to the ruined church, he felt a sense of excitement and satisfaction. His game plan was simple and carried minimal risk. Once the operation was over, he would approach the Catholic Church, offer them the eight coins and demand a massive sum of money in exchange. Searching for the hidden Nazi vault was, he thought, probably a waste of his time. Even the Catholic Church, with all its global resources, might take years to find it, and he needed funds right now. For him, it was far better to do a clean deal for a shedload of cash and just walk away.

His Cayman Island bank account was untraceable to him and there was no reason why the Church would want to double cross him. The Catholic hierarchy was well used to undertaking untraceable and deniable deals and even the large amount he would demand wouldn't cause them any anxiety given the huge wealth the Church and the Vatican possessed. The trick with deals of this sort was to always make the payment the easiest of all the possible options.

The driver stopped the Range Rover some distance from the churchyard and far enough away that the sound of its engine would have been inaudible to their target. The three men – Sir Charles and two of his security team – walked down the deserted track and then stopped. The two ex-soldiers split up, moving to positions that would prevent Black escaping, and to protect Sir Charles if she turned nasty. He still hadn't forgotten the images of the dead man in the helicopter.

Wishing he'd worn some boots and a raincoat, Sir Charles glanced up at the sky as it again started to rain.

Chapter Twenty-Seven

Gloucestershire, England

It didn't take Natasha long to find the old rusty tin. The knife hit metal at the base of the grave stone and she realised it had only been buried about three or four inches deep. She had nearly missed it as it had been buried on its side. As she pulled it out she saw that it was an old biscuit tin, quite narrow and about eight inches long.

As she refilled the hole with wet soil Natasha concluded that grave robbing could now be added to her list of recent indiscretions. Or qualifications.

She picked up the old tin and walked through the doorway of the ruined church and hunched down in a corner where she was slightly sheltered from the wind and rain.

The tin was rusted but intact, though the lid split open as she tried to pull it off. Inside was a small parcel of what looked like crumpled baking paper that she carefully unwrapped. Inside that was a small book with a burgundy leather cover embossed with a swastika, and on top of that, just as she had hoped, a single golden coin just like the others she'd seen in Room 23.

She studied the object and examined the Latin wording round its rim.

'I am the third key to the gloriousness of the Third Reich,' she whispered to herself, translating the script. 'A bit like *The Lord of the Rings* then.'

Natasha had a natural aptitude for some languages and had learnt Latin, French, German and Russian to help her in her work at GCHQ, but Chinese and Arabic had defeated her because of their structure and syntax.

As a child her photographic or eidetic memory had meant she could be lesson lazy and in exams she had always managed to excel, pouring out the relevant text onto the paper as easily as if she'd been copying it from a textbook. This ability had saved her from reprimand and expulsion from school on many occasions.

She hadn't completed A levels or gone to university to earn a degree but twelve straight A*s in her GCSE examinations and a sky-high IQ had signposted her potential. Rather than try to earn a living, Natasha had started professional gambling as a 'job' but had really only managed to scrape by. It was only when she'd realised how the odds were heavily stacked in the bookmaker's favour or the bias in the code of the online software that she decided to really use her intellect to try to beat the systems.

She'd started to make a lot of money and soon found herself banned from most of the online gambling sites which had been constructed, obviously, to fleece the punters, rather than to pay out large sums of money to them. Her watchwords then became little and often and she did her best to stay under the radar, using aliases to avoid being recognised, but she soon found gambling mundane and without real excitement, given that there was almost no chance or luck involved.

Natasha's break, if she could call it that, had come when she had been drinking heavily and then arrested for fighting after trying to protect a young girl from some bullies. With no parents and no one she could call to help her, she had spent a night in the cells at Cheltenham Police Station in Princess Elizabeth Way, where she had charmed the desk sergeant with her photographic memory tricks and winning smile.

Cheltenham is a sleepy, rather up-market town with the highest number of spies or spooks in the United Kingdom living there. Paul Whiteman, a Senior Intelligence Officer at GCHQ, had been in the station the following morning on another matter and had watched as Natasha had bedazzled the sergeant with her tricks. She had been released without charge and he had done a discreet background check on her, concluding she would make ideal spy material.

She had been recruited six days later.

Natasha shook her head, banishing the memories that had crowded her brain, and opened the book. It was clearly extremely fragile, the pages cracking and crumbling as she examined them, and had been hand-written in both German and Latin. She very slowly turned the half-dozen or so pages – according to one footnote they'd been written by Heinrich Himmler himself – and read them. The document was really little more than a booklet, and the leather cover only held about twenty pages, and roughly half of them were blank. But everything Natasha read made sense, and as she finished the final piece of text everything – the coins, the cottage, Captain Fletcher and even Room 23 – suddenly clicked into place.

'Blimey,' she said. Her mind was almost numb from the information she'd read in the journal, the pages of which were already starting to crumble because of the age of the book and, probably, because it had been buried in an unsealed container just a few inches underground for so long. And its condition certainly wouldn't be helped by the raindrops. She closed it gently to try and preserve the fragile pages.

Natasha stood up and walked back towards the ruined entrance of the church, trying to work out who she could go to, or what she could possibly do, with the book and the single golden coin.

She stepped through the archway and only just stopped herself from literally bumping into Sir Charles Martin who was staring at her with a smug smile, his hand outstretched, but not so she could shake it. Two men dressed in black stood silently behind and on either side of him, their pistols pointed straight at her.

There was nothing she could do and she knew it.

She sullenly handed him the book and the coin, looking him directly in the eyes as she did so. He looked away and started to examine the book. As he turned the pages they crumbled at his touch. Natasha knew that the only way they could be examined safely was in a museum or laboratory, where the fragile pages could be treated and preserved.

Sir Charles tossed the book away in disgust.

'Useless ramblings of some old German lunatic,' he said. 'Anyway, this is what I really wanted.' He stared down at the golden coin he held in his hand.

Natasha stayed quiet, because what she had read in the book was so much more valuable than the coin or a mystical treasure hunt.

At a gesture from Sir Charles, the team leader, whose face she had not seen before but whose name-tape on his combat jacket read 'Blake,' walked over and briskly turned her round, used set of steel handcuffs to secure her wrists together behind her back, roughly searched her and removed everything she was carrying, which wasn't much, just the combat knife and multitool, the old bible, her purse and passport. Leaning close to her he whispered in her ear.

'Don't expect an easy death, Miss Black. Me and the lads have plenty of things we want to do to you before you die. Whatever you can imagine, just trust me when I tell you it will be far, far worse.' He laughed harshly as he turned away.

Natasha was beyond scared. She was simply terrified. But she had, she hoped, one last card still to play.

Chapter Twenty-Eight

Oxford, England

Mario had landed at Heathrow and on the strength of his Vatican-issued passport he was waved through Immigration without fuss. He cleared customs, having no weapons or the like in his carry on bag, which was all the luggage he had with him. The Church had stationed a quartermaster able to act as a source of weapons and other specialised equipment in nearly every country of the world, so carrying a pistol or anything else was a pointless and unnecessary risk and, with modern airport scanning equipment, doomed to failure.

He took a public bus without CCTV from Heathrow to Oxford, where he was booked into The Randolph with reservations for breakfast and dinner for two nights. On the hotel check-in form he stated his reasons for staying were sightseeing and a short holiday. Stating the true purpose of his visit – theft, abduction and assassination – somehow didn't seem appropriate. Or sensible.

In fact, Oxford was also where the Church's English quartermaster was based and that evening Mario visited a secret location under one of the old university colleges and collected a silenced pistol and ammunition, a garotte and three small syringes pre-filled with a fast-acting tranquiliser.

Returning to his hotel room he packed the tools of his trade into his leather briefcase, had a shower and then knelt for an hour in prayer, a part of his daily ritual. He never prayed for his contacts and victims, past, present or future, because they were just a part of his work, non-people to be used, discarded or eliminated as he followed his orders. He prayed only for himself and his masters and, especially, he prayed that the operation he was undertaking would be successful.

He would drive to Cheltenham the following morning after breakfast, he decided, and then formulate a plan once he had viewed the area. With that decision made, he drifted off into a restful night's sleep.

Chapter Twenty-Nine

Gloucestershire, England

Natasha had been virtually thrown into the boot of the black Range Rover, her ankles also now lashed together with tape and a hood over her head and tied around her neck so tightly she was having to make a conscious effort to breathe very shallowly to avoid choking. Her imagination was still running wild as she mentally re-played over and over again the threat that the armed soldier had made to her back in the village churchyard. She just hoped – and she was trying desperately to convince herself that she was right – that Sir Charles Martin was only trying to soften her up so that when the vehicle reached its destination she would agree to whatever he wanted and answer all his questions.

If she'd known that her destination was actually the 'Farm,' the covert interrogation and execution centre that was intended to be where she would draw her final breath, her thoughts would have been very different.

The two soldiers – Blake and Timms – were a part of the GCHQ security force and officially worked for Her Majesty's Government, but Sir Charles topped up their incomes with regular cash payments for various unspecified 'jobs.' As they drove towards Oxford, he handed each of them an envelope containing ten thousand pounds. Both men tucked the envelopes away in their jackets without checking the contents or commenting. They each had a good idea how much additional pay they had been given, and what they would be expected to do to earn it.

When the Range Rover stopped just over an hour later, Natasha was manhandled from the vehicle and shoved into a dirty brick-walled cell where the hood was finally removed. The tiny room stank of human waste, had no natural light and had an enormous drain in the middle of the floor.

The two soldiers unlocked the handcuffs, only to attach them again when they'd moved her arms to the front of her body. Then they grabbed her hands and lifted her up and hooked the handcuffs onto a butcher's hook that was mounted directly above the drain. The strain on her arms as she took her full weight on her wrists was appalling, and the pain in both wrists virtually unbearable.

'Can I have some water please?' she asked meekly.

'There'll be plenty of water when we hose you down to shift all the blood,' Blake said with a laugh as they left the cell, slamming the door shut and leaving her in utterly impenetrable darkness. Natasha's shoulders ached abominably and the bruising she had suffered the day before simply magnified her agony.

After some minutes the pain began to be replaced by numbness as the blood supply to her hands became even more restricted, though the ache in her shoulders seemed only to intensify. Despite the sheer agony of her position and her barely-controlled terror, her lack of sleep and the exertions of the previous two days began to numb her brain.

She slowly started to lose consciousness, her mind wandering and her head filling with spurious and random thoughts. She found herself thinking about the parents she had never known, about the bible she'd found in the cottage which led her to ponder the obviously illogical but for some people still compelling belief in the existence of some kind of supreme being and even, at a more mundane level, whether she would ever see her cottage again.

The pain she was suffering and the confusion of images and thoughts tumbling around in her brain combined with the hopelessness of her situation, and she suddenly began crying softly into the silence of her prison. And then the exhaustion of two days largely without sleep finally overtook her and, despite hanging by her wrists from the ceiling of the cell, a few minutes later she fell into a troubled sleep.

-o0o-

Sir Charles Martin had decided on his way back to Cheltenham that now Ms Black was finally and safely secure and that he had all eight gold coins in his possession he could now open negotiations. After the last fiasco he had decided to travel with the soldiers to the Farm to make sure she was securely imprisoned. The slam of the door shutting her in the cell had been a particularly pleasing sound.

About twenty minutes later he realised that matters weren't going according to plan. Or at least not according to his plan. His contact in the church had answered immediately when he'd called. But the man had insisted the deal had to include both the book and all the coins for thirty million dollars, with no room or scope for negotiation. It was a one-shot offer. Without the entire package there would be no deal. And Sir Charles had obviously agreed because he'd had no other option.

As soon as he'd ended that call, he'd issued new orders, and within minutes he was back in the Range Rover and speeding from the Farm to the church, now in driving rain. The team leader was a skilled driver and had covered the ground as fast as anyone could have done, gaining time but to no avail. They had found the book lying on the ground exactly where Sir Charles had flung it. Or at least they'd found the cover, but many of the pages had been reduced to little more than fragments. And, irritatingly, all the pages that remained intact were blank, completely devoid of any text or markings.

Sir Charles took a deep breath, placed the cover and all the page fragments he and the soldier could find into an evidence bag, and thought hard.

Natasha Black had read the journal, he was sure. And according to her file she possessed an eidetic memory. He knew he was clutching at straws, but if she had read the destroyed pages, she should have remembered them. He was aware that there were a lot of assumptions in that train of thought, but right then assumptions were all he had.

And to finish his tally of assumptions, if Natasha Black had read and memorised what had been written in that slim book, if she were to be given sufficient 'encouragement,' she would be able to replicate what she had read. And, he hoped, that would probably be enough to satisfy the Church. The Vatican, after all, wasn't interested in the original pages, only in the information written on them. It was the message, not the medium or the messenger, that was important.

The moment he reached that conclusion, he immediately dialled the mobile number of the soldier who had remained at the Farm.

'Have you started on her yet?' he asked.

'Just leaving her to stew for a while,' Timms replied. 'But I can begin softening her up right now if you want.'

'NO!' Martin shouted into his mobile. 'Don't touch her. We're on our way back to the Farm right now.'

After a few moments he called Timms again and gave him some very specific further orders.

-oOo-

Natasha woke with a start when the cell door slammed open. But what happened next was not what she had been expecting, and dreading. Instead of a man with a whip or some other instrument of torture – because the position of the hook directly above the drain made the purpose of the cell clear enough – the person who entered was not the soldier who'd made the threats against her but the second man, Timms.

He was carrying a plastic bag which he placed on the floor beside the door, then walked over to Natasha. He wrapped his arms around her body and with a grunt of effort lifted her up and off the butcher's hook and lowered her quite gently to the floor, manoeuvring her so that she was in a sitting position with her back against the wall.

She sat there, her cuffed hands resting on her lap, her body numb and unable to function, and her mind virtually shocked into a catatonic state. She just stared at the floor and the disgusting drain in front of her, wondering what was coming next.

But the soldier clearly wasn't there to hurt or injure her. Quite the reverse.

He picked up the plastic bag, opened it and took out a sealed bottle of water and a packaged sandwich, both of which he opened and then placed beside her within easy reach.

He said nothing and neither did she, but she knew that his behaviour was encouraging. Maybe she'd been granted a reprieve for some reason.

She had.

And she had a good idea why.

-o0o-

With something of a sense of déjà vu, Sir Charles Martin headed back to the Farm via GCHQ. That stop was essential to recover the seven gold coins or keys from Room 23, now that he was so close to concluding the deal he'd been planning for more than the last two decades. He descended to the underground passageway and unlocked the door. Inside he unlocked the reinforced glass sheets protecting the golden coins, grabbed them and the wooden tray and left the room.

He climbed back into the Range Rover and told Blake to drive straight to the Farm. When they arrived, the industrial site was almost deserted and they were waved straight through the main gate.

At least he was in the right place, but at that moment he had no clear idea how he was going to get Natasha Black to reproduce the missing pages. That would be another challenge, and he would try being nice first, but he guessed that torture and drugs would probably eventually have to be used to get her to see things his way.

The first thing Sir Charles did was to use the CCTV system to check that his prisoner was still alive. It looked as if she had drunk about half of the bottle of water and one of the two sandwiches and was still sitting exactly where the soldier had positioned her. He stared at her image on the monitor for a few seconds, considering the best approach.

Then he nodded. First, he'd try gentle persuasion, and if that didn't work he'd let Blake do what he did best. The man was something of an artist with knives and pliers and especially with a blowtorch. The process wasn't pretty to watch, but the results spoke for themselves.

He instructed Timms to prepare a different cell a few doors down from where Natasha Black was being held.

This was a very different kind of room, with a small horizontal window mounted high on one wall and a level concrete floor that was devoid of furnishings. There was even a screened-off area at the back of the room which contained a lavatory, sink and shower, with a toothbrush and toothpaste, soap and towels. It was more like a really cheap hotel room than a cell, at least until you looked at the solid wooden door, which was clearly designed to ensure that the occupant remained inside.

The two soldiers brought in a camp bed with pillows, sheets and blankets and then went to the original cell and picked up Natasha from the floor where she was still lying. They removed the handcuffs and cut off the tape binding her ankles together and carried her to the new cell. The lifted her almost gently onto the camp bed and placed the bottle of water and the remaining sandwich on a small table beside it. A few minutes later Timms re-entered the room carrying a mug of hot sweet tea.

Throughout it all, Natasha Black neither spoke nor reacted in any way, letting her body remain completely limp and non-responsive, her eyes closed.

'How is she?' Sir Charles asked, watching the CCTV feed from the new cell after Blake had closed and locked the door.

'She looks in a bad way, far worse than I would have expected. She was only hanging there for a couple of hours, but she doesn't look good.'

Because of the nature of its business, which was mainly detention and 'enhanced interrogation,' the Farm had a regular team of medical staff on standby.

'Call the duty medic to take a look at her,' Sir Charles ordered. 'When he gets here, go into the cell with him and make sure she doesn't talk to him. Or at least doesn't say anything we wouldn't want the doc to hear.'

The doctor arrived about forty minutes later and spent twenty minutes examining the prisoner, with Blake looking on from the side of the room.

Natasha was fully awake and kept her eyes open, but just lay still and unresponsive as the examination proceeded.

'She's in no danger,' the doctor said to Blake.

He was a middle-aged man with the hardest and most impassive face Natasha thought she'd ever seen, and the kind of bedside manner that she guessed had been the norm among the Nazi death camp doctors who specialised in medical experimentation and vivisection on their helpless prisoners.

'What she needs right now is sleep and fluids, preferably water, so give her another couple of bottles. I'll monitor her through the CCTV system and I'll come back if I think she needs a medical intervention.'

Natasha hadn't realised that the cell was monitored by CCTV, though she knew she ought to have assumed that it was. And at least she now knew that she hadn't suffered any serious effects from her actions over the last days or from her recent abuse.

As soon as Blake and the doctor had left the cell, she swung her legs off the camp bed and onto the floor so that she was sitting rather than lying. Moving her arms and hands was still difficult, but she was able to finish the second sandwich and drink the last of the tea and finish the water. Then she stood up and walked slowly and with difficulty around the cell until she found the lens of the CCTV camera.

When she located it, she gave a brief wave to whoever was monitoring it and silently mouthed a single sentence, emphasising each word.

Then she lay down again on the camp bed and in a few minutes had slipped into an uneasy sleep.

Chapter Thirty

Oxford, England

Mario was woken by his mobile phone at five thirty that morning and was instantly out of the bed and wide awake. An encrypted message had arrived and he quickly read the contents.

His orders had changed. The Church's informant within GCHQ had provided details of Sir Charles's movements, which had been confirmed when the man himself had made a call the previous day. Matters had moved on.

Of more immediate interest was the fact that the Head of Security within the Vatican had been able to have his cyber experts hack into the mobile phone and tablet carried by Blake, the GCHQ security team leader. The Vatican team had recorded a video obviously being taken in real time by a drone and had forwarded it to Mario. The footage showed a young woman crossing a river on a raft made of planks, several minutes where the focus of the drone's camera had been a small house surrounded by fields and woods, and then the same girl leaving the house and walking into a churchyard. Then the feed had been cut.

Mario confirmed his understanding of his revised orders and decided he would skip breakfast and just get on with the job, which now looked like being considerably easier than he had expected. His credit card would be debited for the full two days he'd booked at the hotel but that didn't matter.

He checked his list of unregistered mobiles carried by covert helpers and enablers who had been recruited by the Church and made a call to one of them. That secured the very rapid delivery to the hotel of an anonymous hire car that would check out if he were to be stopped by the police. He made a coffee in his room while he waited, packed his bag and then went down to the lobby to wait for the car.

About half an hour after he had made the call a black 8-series BMW pulled up outside, driven by a single man and followed by another BMW saloon, again with a single male driver. Mario stepped outside.

'You're Mario?' the first driver asked.

'Yes.'

'Go with God,' the man responded, handed him the key to the car and shook his hand. Then he climbed into the front passenger seat of the second vehicle, which drove away.

Mario familiarised himself with the controls of the BMW, then started the engine and programmed the satnav with his destination and set off down the A34 towards Woodstock.

Even so early in the morning, the traffic leaving Oxford was slow-moving, caused by the sheer volume of vehicles and not helped by numerous sets of roadworks and cyclists veering in and out of side streets without warning.

It was a relief when the BMW cleared the city limits. Still on the A34 Mario began to gather speed as he headed out into the Cotswold countryside.

Chapter Thirty-One

Gloucestershire, England

Natasha had slept for what she guessed – and hoped – had been a few hours and woke in something of a panic, for several seconds not knowing where she was because of the unfamiliar surroundings. Then reality returned and metaphorically smacked her in the face, producing a single sob of despair.

She strengthened her resolve, sat up and took stock of her physical condition. Her wrists and shoulders hurt badly, and she couldn't lift her arms without the pain getting a lot worse, but she could now move her hands almost normally. Not for the first time, she wondered at the amazing ability of the human body to repair itself almost overnight.

She could also walk, which is what she then did. She already knew the interior of her cell from her exploration of the previous evening, or what she assumed might have been the previous evening. Certainly the light coming in through the single window was bright enough for her to assume it was then morning. Or daytime, at any rate.

Natasha had always read voraciously and one of the books she remembered very clearly had been written by a man who'd been kidnapped and imprisoned for several months. In that book, the author had stressed the importance of trying to establish a degree of dominance, or at least some semblance of control, over his captors rather than just dumbly accepting his fate.

She couldn't think of any good reason why she couldn't try the same technique herself. After all, she had nothing to lose.

She walked around the cell a couple of times, then stopped directly in front of the CCTV camera. She snapped her fingers at the lens in the manner of somebody trying to attract a waiter's attention.

'Breakfast,' she said crisply. 'Coffee – and that means a latte or a cappuccino and none of that instant crap – fresh orange juice, wholemeal toast, butter and English marmalade.'

Then she went back to the camp bed, because there was nowhere else to sit in the cell, and lay down, appearing entirely relaxed. Inside, her mind was in turmoil, wondering if what she'd just done would have made her situation better or worse. But she knew she still had one card left to play, and the fact that she'd been taken out of the other cell and was now being treated fairly humanely suggested that Sir Charles Martin knew all about it. It all depended on what happened next.

And no doubt he would have understood exactly what she had meant by her silent six-word message from the night before.

And, she reasoned, if it all went badly wrong, somewhat surprisingly she still had her set of razor-sharp titanium finger nails to use as a weapon of last resort. Obviously neither of the soldiers had realised what they were. They had already proved lethal and she was determined to fight rather than be tied up again. Blake's words had done their job; she would far rather die fighting for her life than dumbly submit to what they had originally planned to do to her.

About twenty minutes later – without a watch or clock she was finding it difficult to estimate the passage of time – the cell door opened and Timms walked in carrying a tray which he placed on the small table beside the camp bed.

Natasha looked at him, then at the tray. It wasn't exactly what she had ordered, but it was close. There were two slices of brown toast, a couple of foil-wrapped pats of butter, an unopened jar of marmalade, a glass of orange juice, a cafetiere, mug and small milk jug.

'We did the best we could,' Timms said, speaking to her for the first time. 'When you've finished this, Sir Charles would like a word with you.'

'I'm sure he would,' Natasha responded crisply. 'Tell him I can see him in about half an hour. You can go now.'

Somewhat to her surprise, Timms just nodded and left the cell, locking the door on his way out.

Natasha drank the orange juice – which probably came out of a packet – buttered the toast and ate it with the marmalade. She felt better after that, and took her time drinking the coffee, which was better than she'd been expecting. Then she used the bathroom alcove and washed and dried her face, and mentally prepared herself to meet Sir Charles Martin again, but as a prisoner rather than as a senior employee of GCHQ.

Again it was Timms who opened the cell door, this time to escort Natasha elsewhere in the building.

'Follow me, please,' he said, and walked out of the cell.

Natasha had no option but to follow him because she had no idea of the layout of the building or where the exits were located, and she was still weak and hurting and knew she would have zero chance of out-running Timms. Or an arthritic pensioner. Or anybody else, for that matter.

Timms led her down a wide corridor to the room at the end, the door to which was standing open.

'In there,' Timms ordered.

Natasha stepped inside the room, a large office, and saw Sir Charles Martin sitting behind a desk directly opposite her.

She stepped forward trying to exude an aura of confidence that she frankly didn't feel. 'Sir Charles,' she said brightly, extending her hand towards him.

The seated man smiled briefly and insincerely at her. And then, in that instant, everything changed.

'Not so fast, bitch,' a harsh voice snarled from directly behind her, and she felt her left arm wrenched painfully up behind her back in an arm lock that sent spears of sheer agony lancing through her shoulder.

Natasha didn't need to turn her head, assuming she had been able to do so. She had instantly recognised Blake's voice and knew that her plan hadn't worked as she'd hoped.

'You've had your fun, Black,' Sir Charles snapped, 'ordering breakfast as if you were a paying guest in some hotel. It's time you learned who's really in charge around here. Sit down.'

Timms appeared beside her and slid an upright chair in front of her, as Blake roughly manhandled her into it, before finally releasing his grip on her arm.

Natasha didn't feel brave but some of the old anger was starting to build up and she knew she would most likely explode in rage at some point.

Sir Charles stared coldly at her from his seat and Natasha stared straight back at him.

She thought he looked a bit ragged and had obvious bags under his eyes but she knew even being physically exhausted would have no effect on what he did. He'd acquired a reputation at GCHQ of being utterly ruthless and everything that she knew he'd orchestrated over the past few days had only reinforced her view of him.

'I got your message,' Sir Charles said. 'I suppose you thought you were being clever, standing there in front of the camera and just mouthing the words. But I already knew about your linguistic ability, you stupid woman.'

Natasha's message, the six-word sentence that she had hoped would give her an edge because of what had happened, had been simple enough: 'I can speak and read German.' But it was beginning to look as if the card she'd been hiding up her sleeve wasn't going to be high enough to save her.

She didn't reply, just sat there staring at her former boss.

'Thank you for finding the last gold coin for me. I'm indebted to you,' he said with patent insincerity.

'You could thank me by letting me go and stop trying to kill me for a start,' Natasha retorted, her anger bubbling to the surface.

'I'm not that indebted, as I'm sure you can guess. And, anyway, I need you for one last thing before we even consider what to do with you. But you should know that if you don't agree to do what I ask I will tell Blake to kill you. It may not be a quick death. For some reason he's very annoyed that you're still alive and making you suffer seems to be his highest priority at the moment. Now, as I said, I already knew that you read that German's journal, and that you have a photographic memory.'

'Eidetic,' Natasha interrupted.

'What?'

'I have an eidetic memory. Only stupid and ill-educated people call it a photographic memory.'

Sir Charles Martin stared at her in silence for a few seconds, then he shook his head.

'In your situation, trying to annoy me really doesn't make sense. I thought you were bright enough to realise that, but perhaps I was wrong. So what I want you to do is use your *eidetic* memory – is that right? – to write down every word that you read in that book.'

'In German?'

'Of course in German, unless Heinrich Himmler scribbled anything down in another language. And you can translate it, though I'll get a professional to do it as well so I don't have to rely on your probably amateurish effort.'

'What about the Latin?'

'There's Latin text as well?'

'If you hadn't thrown the book away you'd know that,' Natasha responded.

'Yes,' Martin ground out the word through gritted teeth, 'obviously you will write out the Latin text as well. And translate it.'

'And then what happens to me?'

'And then you'll stay here as my guest for a few days until I've been able to check that your memory is as accurate as you seem to think it is, and just in case I have any other questions. And after all that, if you've done a good job, I'll let you walk away, with one condition. To save you asking, that condition is very simple. Yes, I'll let you leave here and live your life as long as you never tell anyone what has happened to you or anything about the contents of that book. If you do, I will have you tracked down and killed. Is that clear?'

'Crystal,' Natasha replied.

'Good. Now it's time for you to get started.'

Timms placed a small table in front of her, on which were two pens and a blank exercise book similar to the ones that Natasha remembered using in her primary school.

She didn't, of course, believe that Sir Charles had the slightest intention of honouring the agreement he himself had proposed, but she knew she could play for time and hope that by some miracle an opportunity for an escape would present itself. And, inevitably, any extension of life was always going to be better than an immediate death, the only other choice she'd been offered.

'I agree,' she said. 'I will need some peace so don't rush me. I'll also need to review it to make sure it's accurate.'

'Don't try to play games with me, Black. I'll give you thirty minutes to reproduce each page and as far as I remember there were only about ten or eleven in total.'

'Thirteen,' Natasha corrected him.

'Fine, thirteen. So the whole thing should take you about six and a half hours to finish, so let's say seven hours. That's less than a day's work, so you should be finished by this afternoon.

Just as an incentive for you to work quickly, for every ten minutes that you take over seven hours, I will tell Blake to remove either one of your toes or one of your fingers, so I suggest that you crack on with it. He will apply the same punishment for every error you've made when we check the document.' He paused for a moment, then added: 'I have a client for the coins and the text of the book. I don't understand why the text is important but trust me when I say my client will know if either your memory or the transcription is wrong.'

Natasha couldn't help herself and mocked him.

'So you have a client for the coins but you've thrown away the book and you've only just found out why that was a stupid thing to do. Heavens, I wouldn't want to be in your shoes, Sir Charles. You're in real trouble whether you kill me or not. You do know that, don't you?'

Sir Charles stepped forward, his face red with fury. He slapped her violently across the cheek, almost knocking her off the chair.

Natasha nearly snapped but didn't; she just laughed.

He was about to lose control completely and kick her when Timms stepped forward and placed a hand on his arm.

'Sir,' he said quietly but firmly. 'We need her to replicate the book.'

Sir Charles stopped and composed himself as best he could. 'You're right. Just get on with it, Black, or you'll be sorry. Really sorry.'

Chapter Thirty-Two

Gloucestershire, England

Mario regretted the choice of the BMW the moment he hit the single-track country roads. With its bulk, rear wheel drive and low suspension it was far from the ideal car to handle the narrow lanes and numerous potholes.

He eventually made it to the village of Ditchley where he was forced to park outside the village hall as that was the only available space he could find. From there he'd have to walk, but he'd come prepared for a hike. He was dressed in walking gear with boots not only to act as a disguise – he'd discovered that the area was popular with recreational walkers – but also because the best and most covert and secure approach to his destination was on foot. Before he got out of the car he switched the contents of the briefcase into a small rucksack.

Putting on a black beanie hat he set off, using the Google Maps app on his tablet as the most convenient and accurate way for him to navigate because it showed the public footpaths and other routes he could use. His destination was the industrial unit inside which the Church's informant believed Sir Charles Martin's men had taken the woman Natasha Black.

The footpaths were well signposted and looked well used. It surprised him that members of the public would be allowed to walk freely so near to a government site. He couldn't imagine that situation ever occurring in Italy.

Mario found an ideal position, a small thicket of trees and undergrowth at the edge of a small hill, that enabled him to look down at the target site. It looked, strangely enough, more like a farm than anything else, but he had been told that the single steel barn with its corrugated roof would be both reinforced and guarded.

He settled down to watch the site. He was hampered by not having been able to look at plans of the interior of the structure and had no idea what he would find when he went inside. He also didn't know how many of his targets would be present because the information he'd been passed was now several hours old. He really needed to know that at least some of them would be there.

After almost forty-five minutes, he finally saw movement. A pedestrian door on the left-hand side of the building opened and a man wearing dark combat clothing emerged. He walked across to a black 4x4 utility vehicle that Mario thought might be a Range Rover, opened the driver's side door, took something out and then returned to the building.

Mario hadn't taken his eyes off the man the entire time he was in view, committing every detail of his appearance to memory. As soon as the vehicle had driven off he opened up his smart phone and checked the image gallery he had been sent. His search didn't take long: as soon as he looked again at the slightly blurred photograph of John Blake, one of Sir Charles Martin's bodyguards and mercenary muscle, he was able to confirm the identification.

That was enough of a clue for Mario to act. At least he knew the place was in use, which gave him somewhere to start. The best scenario for him was that Sir Charles Martin would be somewhere inside the building, so that was where he needed to go. If he wasn't, he'd just have to hunt him down individually.

He put the rucksack back over his shoulder, pocketed the syringes and garotte and tucked the pistol into the waistband of his jeans, where it would be concealed by his waterproof jacket but still immediately accessible.

Slowly and cautiously he began to descend the hillside towards the building, aiming for a section of the boundary fence where a substantial branch of a tree had fallen and largely flattened it. That was an unanticipated bonus and maybe, he thought, a good omen for the mission.

Chapter Thirty-Three

Gloucestershire, England

Natasha reproduced each page of the German and Latin text of the book accurately. When she'd finished, she smiled slightly as she again appreciated the size of the operation the Germans had tried to put in place and the sheer madness of it all

Sir Charles returned to the office when Blake told him she'd finished. He picked up the copies of the sheets of paper she'd written – Timms had run each of them through the photocopier as she'd finished – and looked at her.

'I told you to do it in English as well,' he hissed. 'Get that done before I come back. I'll be about twenty minutes,' he added to Blake. 'I have to send the information to my contact.'

Then he strode out of the room.

Natasha picked up a sheet of paper and began to write the translation – the easiest bit of the operation – under the silent threat of the gun held by Blake, sitting in the chair Martin had occupied. The moment she'd finished, Blake walked over to her and taped her wrists to the arms of the chair she was sitting in and secured her ankles to the chair legs.

She didn't resist but couldn't avoid another smile appearing on her face as she was bound. She'd done exactly what Sir Charles Martin had told her to do, completely accurately, but there was one thing that she'd kept to herself. One thing that she knew that nobody else in the world was aware of at that moment:

the coordinates, the two lines of six numerals, written in Himmler's book giving the location of the vault were incorrect. And she knew they were incorrect because when Nick Fletcher had read the German text well over half a century earlier, he had realised the full scope of the Nazi plan and had altered them. And Natasha knew that because of a cryptic note on one of the first pages in Fletcher's old bible.

She assumed that he'd been so appalled by what he'd read that he'd decided to prevent anybody who only recovered the coins and the journal from locating the vault. To be successful any searcher would need both the stated coordinates and an entirely separate six-digit numerical sequence to deduce the location.

That was her final ace in the hole. If she got the chance to play it. What she couldn't do was tell her former boss about it immediately, because she now knew he'd simply order Blake or Timms to torture her until she revealed what she knew. She just had to hope she'd get an opportunity later. But, she reflected, if it all turned to worms, at least she'd go to her grave knowing that Sir Charles Martin would never get his hands on the Nazi loot.

A few minutes later, Sir Charles returned with a sinister smile on his face.

'Ms Black, it appears my client is happy, which is surprising. I've just sent him scans of the pages you produced and he believes your memory has served you well. Apparently the German and Latin text are exactly what he was hoping for. So now all I have to do is deliver the coins to him and then I'll be able to enjoy a very comfortable retirement, thanks to you.'

He stared at Natasha for a few moments, then shook his head.

'Frankly, you've been a bit of a disappointment to me. I expected you to need a lot more persuasion and lose a few fingers. I suppose you thought I might treat you better if you did what I asked. If you did, you were sadly mistaken. Now, I'll take that translation, just so I can see what's so important about that bloody book.'

He snatched it from the table. 'What does it say?' he asked.

'That's easy,' Natasha replied. 'It says you're an arsehole.'

He glared and punched her in the face.

'Goodbye, Ms Black. Enjoy the rest of your short stay here with my friends. I'm going back to GCHQ. Blake, she's all yours.'

'What about our deal?'

'We never had a deal. You should have realised this was only ever going to end one way.' Then he left the office, snapping out orders to Blake and Timms.

Her nose had started bleeding and her eye was already swelling, but Natasha realised it hadn't been a very heavy punch and she concluded that – if she ever had the chance – she could most likely beat Sir Charles Martin in unarmed combat.

She ran her tongue around her teeth to check that they were all still there,

The gun Blake was pressing against the back of her head moved away after Sir Charles left the room.

'We aren't going to shoot you, bitch,' Blake said. 'That would be far too quick and easy.'

'I wouldn't do that if I were you,' Natasha replied, trying to make her voice sound strong and confident. 'I think you'll find Sir Charles will need my help later on.'

Blake laughed and shook his head. 'No bloody chance,' he snapped. 'You heard him. He's already left the building so we can make a start on you right now. I'm going to make sure you take days to die. Long, painful days. At the end, you'll be begging me to kill you. But that'll just mean we'll slow down a bit. Take our time, you know. Really make sure we can enjoy the moment.'

Natasha closed her eyes and, almost picking a religion at random, prayed. There was no escape and she knew the best she could hope for was a quick death, and the only way she could get that would be by provoking the men and using her nails to go down fighting.

Now locked into a world of her own, she braced herself for what was to come.

Chapter Thirty-Four

Gloucestershire, England

Mario had reached the rear of the building without incident, seeing nobody. He assumed that as the structure was on government property it was protected by preventing access to the site as a whole rather than by mounting sentries or guards on the building itself. Whatever the reason, it made his task slightly easier.

He heard shouting from inside the building as he approached, keeping low and taking advantage of every scrap of cover, and stopped beside one of the few windows on that side of the structure. The horizontal blinds inside were partially open, and he was able to supplement what he was hearing with a clear but slightly obstructed view of the room.

As he peered through the window, Mario saw a man he knew to be Sir Charles Martin ranting at a woman he recognised as Natasha Black sitting at a small table on which were a few sheets of paper. Then he watched Martin punch her in the face, grab the papers from in front of her and walk out.

Mario was tempted to act immediately. He had few standards and had eliminated numerous women during his long career, but a man punching a helpless woman in the face, a woman tied to a chair and who was clearly being held prisoner by another man holding a pistol to her head, was beyond the pale in his opinion. For that alone, Sir Charles Martin deserved to die, but not at that moment. Timing was the key here, he decided, and first he had to get inside the building.

He worked his way around towards the door of the building he had seen Martin use, but as he approached it the door swung open and his principal target stepped outside, a broad smile on his face. That smile faded abruptly as Sir Charles Martin registered the presence of a tall and slim man, apparently a hiker, standing right in front of him.

'What the hell do you think you're doing here?' he snapped. 'This is government property and you're trespassing. Consider yourself under arrest.'

Sir Charles pulled out his mobile phone, but as he did so the stranger replied.

'I don't think so,' he said politely and pulled a pistol from beneath his jacket.

'What the –?'

'You made an expensive mistake, Sir Charles,' Mario said. 'Nobody tries to rip off the Vatican and gets to live. Roberto Calvi found that out, the hard way.'

Sir Charles scrabbled in his jacket pocket for his own pistol, but he was a lifetime too late.

Almost casually, Mario aimed the Glock 17 with its bulbous suppressor and squeezed the trigger once. He was an expert marksman, and at that range one bullet was all he was ever going to need. The shot sounded like a wet slap, inaudible from more than a few yards away, but the effect on the other man was terminally dramatic.

The bullet ploughed into the centre of Sir Charles Martin's forehead and exited from the back of his head in a cloud of blood, brain matter and bone fragments. He was already quite literally dead on his feet but his body remained upright for a second or two before collapsing almost elegantly backwards onto the stained concrete.

Mario had started moving even before Sir Charles's body hit the ground, walking across to the pedestrian door that was just starting to swing closed, and stepped inside the building.

From his observation through the window, he knew exactly which room the woman Natasha Black had been held in, and he walked briskly down the corridor and turned right. He stepped inside the office and instantly appraised the scene in front of him, which had barely changed since he'd first looked through the window.

The two black-clad men were still in the room, one bending over the prisoner and doing something with the ropes or tape that secured her to the chair. The other man was leaning against the wall, a black automatic pistol held loosely in his right hand.

Too loosely, as it turned out.

Barely seeming to aim, Mario took aim and fired twice.

Blake, taken completely by surprise, was hit by both bullets before he'd even begun to lift his own weapon, and collapsed backwards, his pistol dropping from his dead hand.

Mario effortlessly shifted his aim and fired directly towards Natasha.

She'd been shocked into immobility by what had just happened, and her bound limbs prevented any movement. But as the pistol swung to point at her she screamed and instinctively turned her head away.

Another two suppressed shots sounded in the room and Timms collapsed backwards. Neither man had been on Mario's kill list, but that fact they had been in the office where a woman had been imprisoned and beaten meant that in his opinion they had forfeited their right to live. Or they were just collateral damage. He didn't care either way.

Mario turned around and walked out of the office. About five minutes later, having cleared the building room by room to avoid any surprises, he walked outside to the Range Rover, pausing only to use his smart phone to take a photograph of Sir Charles's dead body to confirm he'd completed that part of his contract, and to remove the vehicle's keys from his jacket pocket. He unlocked it and removed the eight gold coins and the wooden holder from the back seat, all of which he transferred to his rucksack.

Then he strode back to the building and walked all around it, checking for cameras. As a black ops site, he found no sign of any surveillance devices, which was precisely what he had expected, but it never hurt to make certain.

He entered the room where the woman had been tied up and where he'd left the bodies of the two soldiers. The glow he felt after a kill still left him exhilarated and he looked at the two corpses, savouring the moment as he photographed each one. A pistol or other firearm was undeniably an efficient killing device, but Mario really preferred getting both very close and very personal and using something like a knife or garotte or just his bare hands. He liked to see the light going out in his victim's eyes at the moment of death.

The only killings that didn't give him quite so much pleasure were the children he was very rarely tasked with eliminating, but his training at the retreat had efficiently brainwashed him into believing he was merely fulfilling God's work and that their souls would be blessed as special for all eternity.

The woman in the chair looked as if she had fainted. Mario walked over to her and nudged her arm with the end of the suppressor.

Chapter Thirty-Five

Gloucestershire, England

After the totally unexpected arrival of the unidentified man, and his extraordinarily efficient assassination of Blake and Timms, Natasha had closed her eyes tightly and waited for the bullet that would end her life, but there had been no fifth shot. Or any other sound. Finally, after what had felt like a lifetime but was probably less than a minute, she slowly opened one eye and looked around the room. There was no one there. Or nobody alive, anyway.

Wriggling on the chair she tried to find a way to use her titanium nails on the duct tape wrapped around her wrists but the way she'd been secured made it impossible. She simply couldn't bend her fingers back far enough to reach even the edge of the tape. And the pain from her wrists and shoulders, and now from her face as well, meant that there was a limit to how much effort she could physically make.

She tried again, but still couldn't reach the tape. She closed her eyes in despair, and simply gave up.

Something touched her arm and she jerked in surprise and opened her eyes. Standing in front of her was the intruder, but she hadn't heard him come back into the room, or in fact heard any other sound. Now that she wasn't looking down the barrel of his gun she saw that he was dressed as a hiker with a rucksack on his back. And he was, she couldn't help noticing, a remarkably good-looking man with olive skin and deep brown eyes.

'Hello,' he said. His voice was quiet with no accent that she could detect. 'Please do as I say, and you'll be fine.'

'Who the hell are you?' Natasha asked.

'I'm a friend, Natasha, I suppose you could say. But you must come with me quickly so we can get out of this place.'

Natasha stared at him as he pulled out a pocket multi-tool, selected the knife blade and opened it. Then he bent down and cut the duct tape around her wrists and offered her his hand to help her stand up. She stood slowly, rubbing her wrists and touching her nose that was throbbing courtesy of Sir Charles, but even her gentle touch sent shafts of pain lancing through her head.

'Ow,' she said. 'That bastard. I'll kill him for this.'

Mario smiled slightly. 'That may be a little difficult,' he said. 'Now we must leave.'

Natasha looked at the silent corpses of Blake and Timms lying where they'd fallen when Mario's bullets had ended their lives.

'Who are you?' she asked again, 'and how the hell do you know my name?' Then she went on before he had time to reply. 'Not that I'm not glad you walked in when you did. That one over there –' she pointed at Blake's body '– had promised me I'd take a very long time to die. His schedule was several days.'

She took a couple of rapid steps over to where Blake lay and launched a couple of powerful kicks to his face. Her Doc Martens weren't football boots, but the effect was much the same, and she was rewarded by the sound of bone cracking under her assault. As quickly as she had started her attack she ended it and turned back to the hiker.

'God, that felt good,' she said. 'Sorry about that,' she added, 'sometimes I do tend to lose it.'

The man grinned at her and shook his head slightly. 'Now we need to go.'

'Hang on a minute,' Natasha said. 'These bastards took my passport and purse. I need to find them.'

'Sorry, we don't have time. Whatever they took can be replaced. We need to get out of here right now.'

He took her by the arm and led the way out of the building.

The first thing Natasha saw was Sir Charles Martin's dead body lying a few feet from the door. Her dormant anger surfaced again and she started to move with malicious intent towards his body.

'He's already dead,' Mario told her, grabbing her arm, 'and we need to move quickly, so perhaps you could restrain yourself.'

'I suppose so,' Natasha responded, sounding reluctant. 'I hate that man. I mean I *really* hate him. Did you kill him as well as the other two?'

The hiker shrugged. 'Somebody had to. I was just in the right place at the right time. And you did say you were pleased I turned up when I did.'

'Oh, yes. You are now my newest, bestest friend,' Natasha said, smiling as best she could with a bloody nose and an emerging black eye.

The assassin seemed nonplussed by this. Natasha guessed he was probably more used to people dying around him than anyone actually being glad to see him.

Chapter Thirty-Six

Gloucestershire, England

On the walk back through the woods to his car Mario found himself talking rather more than he normally would. Natasha learned that he was Italian, was named Mario, was employed by a client he did not and would not identify, and had been sent to Britain specifically to locate and, if necessary, rescue her. But he did confirm that the gold coins and the transcriptions and translations she had done were to be handed over to the client and that they were going to meet him. And he would, Mario assured her, be very grateful for what she had done.

Given what had happened in the last three days, Natasha knew she had no one left to turn to or to rely on other than this mysterious, very polite and gentlemanly, ruthless Italian assassin. And she knew that when it was discovered that the Director General of GCHQ had been killed on a secret government site as well as the two soldiers she already knew about and, she assumed, perhaps some other people in the building, the hunt for her would undoubtedly rapidly intensify.

Whilst Mario was quite demonstrably a cold-blooded killer and a man Natasha had first met literally minutes earlier, she found she liked and even, to her surprise, actually trusted the Italian. She acknowledged that he was a handsome man but that was merely the surface layer. She sensed there a kind of innate good in him, a feeling she had that he would act in the right way in any given situation. Of course, because he had rescued her from a certain and painful death that might have substantially clouded her judgement but walking beside him through the woods she felt surprisingly content, as well as indebted to him.

They arrived at the BMW and Mario opened the back door for her to climb in. She sank back in the seat grateful for finally being able to stop walking and just sit. She hadn't realised how weak she felt after her ordeal and the maltreatment she'd suffered, and the pains in her joints had got worse, seemingly with every step she'd taken.

It was probably because of the constant ache that she didn't feel the tiny pinprick of the injection Mario skilfully ministered to her as he helped her sit down. Though she was unaware of what had happened, the effect was virtually instant. Her eyes closed and she fell sideways across the back seat, unconscious.

Mario strapped her in with the seat belt, then climbed into the driver's seat, reprogrammed the satnav for Kidlington Airport and started the engine. Once he was on the road, he called an Italian mobile phone number to confirm that his mission had been a success. He also provided a rough estimate for his arrival time at his destination in the private jet that had been booked for him. And he would, he added, be returning with all the merchandise.

Chapter Thirty-Seven

Cessna Citation, en route to Rome, Italy

Natasha stirred and awoke quite slowly. She opened her eyes and immediately knew one thing: she had no idea where she was. Or rather, she knew she was in an aircraft but that was all.

She was sitting in a comfortable wide leather seat with a belt strapped across her lap. The engine noise was clearly audible but muted. Looking around, it was quite obvious that she wasn't in the first-class compartment of a regular passenger jet, and definitely not in the cattle class accommodation endured by most people who needed to take to the air to reach their business or holiday destination. She was obviously in a small and seriously upmarket aircraft, and she appeared to be the only passenger.

'At least it's not a body bag this time,' she muttered. She tried to move but found, to her immediate alarm, that her limbs weren't responding to her thoughts. After initially panicking at the thought that she could be paralysed, she noticed her fingers and toes had pins and needles, so it she guessed it was just the effect of the drug – because she was certain that was what had happened to her – wearing off.

Having established where she had to be, and with feeling returning to her extremities, Natasha examined herself by touch. Her nose had a thin plaster on it, her right eye had almost closed and someone had removed her Doc Marten boots and put soft slippers on her feet.

'Someone cares then,' she said to herself.

A few minutes later she realised that she wasn't the only passenger when the Italian stood up from one of the seats at the front. The seats were so big he'd been invisible to her.

'You're awake,' he said, stating the obvious. 'I'm sorry about the sedative but –'

'Sedative?' Natasha interrupted him. 'Knock-out drug more like. What you gave me could have sedated a bloody elephant.'

'I know, but it was the most efficient option. My client wanted to meet you and time was against us.'

'You could have just asked me. If I'd known I was going to get a ride in an airborne knocking-shop like this I'd definitely have agreed to come along.'

Mario shrugged.

'I apologise again. Please follow me and I'll show you the onboard bathroom where you can freshen up, and then we have a meal prepared for you.'

Natasha tried to get angry – she had, after all, just been kidnapped – but found that she couldn't. Wherever she was going would probably be a far better option than running around Gloucestershire like a fox with the hounds in hot pursuit as the forces of law and order attempted to find her. Or worse.

'Thanks,' she found herself saying.

What's the matter with me, she thought? I've been drugged and kidnapped by an Italian assassin. I should be fighting and screaming to get away, but actually I'm feeling quite happy about the situation.

Mario led her to the rear of the luxurious private jet and showed her a small cubicle that contained a shower and toilet. A somewhat limited selection of clothes had been laid out on the closest seat, something she was grateful for when she looked down at what she was wearing. She felt like she'd been living in the same outfit for about a month, and virtually everything she had on was destined for a bin rather than a washing machine.

There were rips and tears from her trek through the woods with Mario and a selection of mysterious and unpleasant-looking stains she'd probably picked up in the first cell where she'd been imprisoned.

She picked out a bright yellow sweatshirt, sports bottoms and trainers, and put her new outfit on the lavatory seat. Then she stripped off and examined herself critically in the full-length mirror attached to the back of the cubicle door. The bruising to her body and face was now quite extensive and the swollen eye hadn't opened yet either. She grimaced at her reflection but knew there wasn't much she could do to improve the way she looked, not without the services of a competent make-up artist. Or, perhaps better, one of those people who worked their cosmetic magic on corpses. Whoever she was going to see would just have to take her as she was.

'Ugh,' she muttered, and stepped into the shower. The water was hot and it felt luxuriously decadent to just stand there and enjoy it, ten miles high or whatever altitude the aircraft was maintaining.

About twenty minutes later she emerged, trying to look as dignified as possible.

She walked towards the front of the aircraft where a table had been laid with cold meats, pasta and fruit, and sat down in the leather swivel chair opposite Mario. He poured her a glass of chilled water and a cup of fresh black coffee.

'Please eat and drink as much as you like,' he said. 'Your clothes will be washed when we land and returned to you later.'

'I think they're a bit far gone for that,' she replied. 'I'll need to hit the shops as soon as possible. There are shops where we're going?' she asked after a moment.

'Of course. Italy has some of the best shops in the world.'

At least she knew where they were heading, Natasha thought, though it hadn't been a particularly difficult conclusion to reach.

'And some of the most expensive shops,' she pointed out, 'and I have no euros. And all my credit cards are somewhere back in Gloucestershire but even if I had them with me there's a good chance they've all been blocked.'

'I'm sure we can come to an arrangement,' Mario said, which could have meant almost anything, and Natasha flushed slightly as her mind considered what some of those 'arrangements' might involve.

She ate and drank her fill, finding that she was famished, a combination of simply not consuming anything like her normal food intake and from the stress of the whole situation.

'Not quite the date I'd envisaged,' she said finally, leaning back from the table and holding back a burp.

'Just relax and enjoy the flight,' Mario said. 'If you need anything, just press one of the call buttons.

He reached over and did exactly that, and almost immediately the door at the front of the cabin opened and a steward appeared to clear the table.

For the rest of the flight she sat in the leather seat with the seat belt loosely done up, looking out at the clouds with her good eye. She had decided not to bother asking questions on where they were heading or risk changing the quite enjoyable status quo.

No doubt she'd find answers when they reached their destination. Or maybe there'd just be a load more questions.

Chapter Thirty-Eight

Rome, Italy and Vatican City

As the jet began its descent Natasha looked out at the towns and the landscape below. She already knew they were landing in Italy, though nothing about the terrain told her that. Mario hadn't told her who they were going to see or why, but from her knowledge of the contents of the book Himmler had written she had a pretty good idea that they would be heading to the Vatican. The Catholic Church had real and devastating reasons to know what the book had contained, and to find both the Nazi treasure vault and the secret laboratory.

When she had transcribed the text word for word from her memory, as instructed by the late Sir Charles Martin, she had realised from an annotation written in Captain Fletcher's old army bible that a passcode needed to be applied to the location co-ordinates.

She had worked on cybers and codes for years at GCHQ so she was familiar with the techniques. Fletcher had clearly realised the nature of the document and had changed the co-ordinates to provide a degree of added protection before he'd buried the book. The Vatican now had a slight problem, whether anyone there was aware of it or not, because the coordinates she had written down in her transcription would not work without the passcode. She alone could solve that problem and that, she knew, was why they would have to keep her alive.

As soon as they landed and the aircraft had parked, Mario led her down the steps and into the back seat of a waiting air-conditioned limousine but didn't join her.

'I've enjoyed our brief time together,' he said, holding the door open and looking down at her, 'and I hope to see you again.'

'I'd like that,' Natasha replied, somewhat to her own surprise.

He closed the door and the driver, sitting in front of the closed glass partition, quickly drove her away.

She looked out of the window as they left the airfield, which looked like a private establishment. Security was obviously a high priority and she saw armed guards on its borders. Maybe, she thought, it belonged to the Church and was where the Pope's flights arrived and departed.

Surprising quickly, given the volume of traffic, the car arrived at the entrance to the Vatican City, drove into an inner courtyard and then stopped. As she looked around her, the car door beside her opened.

'Welcome, my child,' a voice said. 'Please come and walk with me.'

The old priest in front of her looked strangely familiar and exuded an air of gentleness and kindness. Natasha climbed out of the limousine and slowly they walked together into a walled garden, an oasis of silence and tranquillity that felt like a world apart from the noise and hustle and bustle of the streets of Rome that she'd just been driven through. She breathed in the scents of the flowers and plants and realised the garden felt utterly peaceful – almost enchanted in some way.

'God works in strange and sometimes complicated ways,' the old priest said gently, 'and I am sure that is why we are both here today. But I must confess I am unsure how to resolve the dilemma of the secrets that I believe you hold.'

'I too am confused,' Natasha replied. 'The last few days have been the most terrifying time of my life. I've been chased, kidnapped and beaten, and now I find myself walking through a lovely garden in the Vatican talking to a priest who seems to know a lot more than I do.'

The old man laughed gently. 'That you are here is God's will, so that part is easy. Being frightened is one of the many challenges He gives all of us, and this lovely garden is simply down to the skills of our gardeners. It's one of the places I come when I feel the need to meditate and get closer to nature and the mind of our creator.'

Natasha smiled at him and then, like a bolt from the blue, she suddenly realised exactly why the priest looked so familiar. She froze in her tracks and just stared at him.

'Yes, my child. As I think you say in England, the penny has dropped for you.'

Natasha nodded, simply unable to speak.

'As Pope, I remain just a priest with no belongings, but I do carry a weight of immense responsibility, responsibility sometimes so great that the pain is almost unbearable. The fact we are talking together shows you just how serious this situation has become. It also should tell you that the Church, Natasha Black, needs your help to survive.'

Natasha finally found her tongue. 'I already know what you need from me,' she said, quickly adding, 'your holiness.'

He nodded.

'I suspected you would. The words you have read, and the implications of our actions, will impact billions of people. Let us retire to a quiet room where we will not be disturbed to discuss this more fully.

'We simply must, with the help of almighty God, find a solution to this appalling dilemma.'

PART TWO – THE JOURNEY

Chapter Thirty-Nine

The Pope's Private Study, Vatican City

A small fire flickered, sending shadows that fluttered across the exquisitely decorated room where Natasha Black, His Holiness Pope Benedict XVII, and the Vatican's Head of Security Pierre de Ronson were sitting. Officially designated as the Pope's study, it had been chosen for its warmth with old beams and wooden floors rather than the standard cold stone slabs that lay elsewhere in the building.

Natasha's chair was well upholstered and comfortable but she scarcely even noticed as she stared across the room at the two men. The thought that had lodged itself immovably in her mind almost as soon as she'd walked in was of Dr Jekyll and Mr Hyde, albeit in two different people.

The Pope appeared serene and conveyed a sense of goodness, even godliness, an aura that was the very antithesis of that of his Head of Security. De Ronson looked like a well-dressed thug and his eyes, eyes that seemed able to look right into her soul, had not stopped staring at Natasha since she'd walked into the study.

After her short walk through the garden with the Pope, Natasha had been taken to the quarters she had been allocated, which were quite sparse and basic. But she was pleased to find that all her old clothes had been left on the simple bed, repaired where necessary, and washed and ironed. She could only assume that there was an incredibly rapid and efficient laundry service available in the Vatican.

She took almost an hour to bathe and do what she could to her somewhat battered face in the adjacent bathroom and then rested on the bed before dinner was delivered to her by a young priest. He had blessed her and the meal, then looked at and tended the wounds on her face before leaving.

The meal had been chosen for her, and when she lifted the lid she saw that it was roast beef, Yorkshire pudding and garden vegetables, which seemed something of a cliché, but she ate it with relish along with a glass of fresh orange juice at the small wooden table in the room.

She also saw that Captain Fletcher's bible had been placed in the room with her and spent a few minutes looking again at what he had written decades ago.

'Thanks a lot, Captain Fletcher,' she said to herself, closing the old book.

After she'd eaten she was escorted back to the room she'd been told was the Pope's study, and where the two men had been waiting for her.

'So what can you tell us, Natasha?' the Pope asked, looking at her expectantly.

Natasha nodded and then summarised what she had learned from the German and Latin text.

'I've read the book and I know exactly what Himmler wrote. I'm also aware that the coordinates of the vault were changed by Captain Fletcher and that a six-digit code needs to be applied to the numbers to reveal the true location. The gold coins or keys somehow unlock the vault to reveal whatever the Nazis stored inside it, and this may include a laboratory charged with developing special technology. On each coin is an inscription and a number from one to eight. I assume this may be important, perhaps meaning that the coins have to be used in a particular sequence to unlock the vault. The wording in the book suggests that the laboratory is separate from the vault and I assume knowledge of its location will only be discovered once the vault has been opened.'

Natasha paused for a few moments and chose her next words carefully.

'It's logical to assume that there may be items and evidence in the vault that the Church would rather not become public knowledge. I also assume that anything of value needs to be removed in a covert manner.'

'You're an intelligent and if I might say quite a forthright young lady,' the Pope said, nodding at her.

Natasha gave him her best winning smile which the Pope duly reciprocated, but de Ronson's face remained entirely unchanged and expressionless. He almost glared at Natasha when he spoke.

'This whole episode needs to be handled with the utmost discretion. Outside this room no one else knows what we have. With Sir Charles Martin now permanently silenced we have two challenges. One is to find the six-digit code that Captain Fletcher used to amend the coordinates, and the second is to locate and then open the vault.

'Let me be perfectly frank with you, Miss Black. You have not suffered the same fate as Sir Charles only because we know you are an outstanding code-breaker. You've also proved yourself quite adept at breaking into and escaping from secure areas, in the process killing a highly trained soldier to evade capture.'

Natasha felt her cheeks go red at this accurate but somewhat clinical description of her actions, and felt slightly ashamed at what he'd said in the presence of the Pope. This quickly turned to anger at what he said next.

'Please believe me when I tell you that if we decide you have outlived your usefulness your execution will be both certain and immediate.'

'You would have me killed?' She directed her question at where the Pope had been sitting.

But as de Ronson had been speaking, the Pope had silently risen from his chair and was now studying a painting on the far side of the room, clearly not wishing to be a party to this part of the conversation.

'Oh, I see,' she said.

De Ronson attempted a smile that made him look as if he had severe toothache.

'As long as you do what we ask you will be perfectly safe. What the Church would like you to do is break the code and locate the vault. You will travel only with Mario, who you have met, and report only to me. Once you have found the vault, I will join you and take whatever decisions are needed at that time.'

'And then you'll kill me, I suppose,' she muttered.

'If you do what we ask, no one is going to kill you, Ms Black. You will only become a liability to us if you fail. And if you do succeed the church will be grateful and reward you. Money is not a problem, so what price will buy your loyalty?'

Natasha thought hard. And quickly. It was tempting to seize the chance to become a millionairess but she decided she had to be honest.

'It's nothing to do with money. I don't want your money. The chance to be involved in an adventure to find a hidden Nazi treasure vault is so cool I can't tell you. I also want to do this because whatever is in that hidden vault and the laboratory definitely needs to stay hidden. What the Nazis were planning and what the Church may have felt needed to be done to protect itself in the confusion of a war that involved virtually every European nation should never see the light of day, for the future good of mankind.'

She thought she'd phrased that lengthy last sentence quite well.

The Pope turned back to look at her. 'On that we both agree, Natasha,' he said. 'There are many things the Church has done of which I am ashamed but which cannot be undone. I'm so pleased you think that way and I hope and expect that you will be successful. God will be with you, my child.'

Opening a small side door, the Pope left.

She looked almost nervously at de Ronson, but he attempted another smile at her, which she found just as unnerving as his first attempt.

'Your room now has a laptop computer and stationery in it. Please let me know when you have worked out the coordinates. A priest will be sitting outside your room for your convenience in case you need anything.'

Obviously more like a guard than for her convenience, Natasha thought, but she said nothing and just nodded.

As she walked down the corridor, accompanied by yet another priest, she hoped she had already cracked the code. Certainly she knew of one six-digit number that seemed significant. She would have to check that she was right, and then play for time and do some research using the laptop to keep them happy.

While she was doing that she would try to formulate a plan to ensure that she stayed alive because she didn't trust de Ronson at all.

Chapter Forty

Vatican City

Back in her cell – she assumed that was the proper name for such basic accommodation in the Vatican – Natasha lay down on the bed and tried to work out her best course of action, her brain racing with possibilities and probable outcomes, most of them fatal. It certainly wasn't going to be easy, she knew that.

What was happening in England now that the bodies of Sir Charles Martin and his men had presumably been discovered and with her missing in action she could only guess. She knew she was safe in Italy for the time being at least, as long as she was doing what de Ronson wanted, so she had to focus her thoughts and look forward. Working out the location of the vault should be easy enough if she had correctly guessed the six-digit passcode – that was what she'd been mentally calling the number Fletcher had come up with, though it was really a misuse of the word. So her main problem would be trying to devise a viable escape plan if, or more likely when, things turned nasty.

She wasn't stupid and she knew her demise would conveniently and without much risk close off a loose end for the Church. And, having already seen Mario in action she assumed this would be the most probable outcome. Although he'd treated her well, no doubt because he'd been ordered to do so, she'd also seen him murder two men as casually as most people would kill a fly. She needed a backup but at that moment was at a loss to know who or what it could be.

Unable to sleep, she sat down at the desk and fired up the laptop. A top of the range Apple MacBook Pro, it was very fast and she had no doubt it would be stuffed full of trackers and keyloggers and other surveillance devices to follow her activities on the Internet. She suspected the room also had a camera hidden in it somewhere so she would need to make all her actions credible to any third party.

She had already deduced that the six digits had to correlate to something associated with her cottage, the bible and when Captain Fletcher had altered the coordinates in the book. And the one thing that linked all of these was the grave of a man named Cyril Beckett who had died aged 98 in 1865.

If 9-8-1-8-6-5 wasn't the answer in some way she knew she was in real trouble.

She spent the next hour producing the same document she had done before from her memory of the book, first in the two original languages – German and Latin – and then carefully translated the text to English, trying to ensure that any nuances wouldn't be lost in the translation.

Using a pencil and paper rather than the laptop, for obvious reasons, she devised her own code on top of Captain Fletcher's, which simply involved adding the 9-8-1-8-6-5 sequence to the two sets of numbers – the latitude and longitude coordinates – written in the book, presumably by Heinrich Himmler himself, for degrees, minutes and seconds.

Natasha knew that degrees of latitude, the parallel theoretical lines on the surface of the planet that run east-west, ran from -90 to +90 while longitude, the lines running north-south and which converged at both poles, had values running from -180 to +180, and the two sets of coordinates in the Himmler book had only six digits and neither a plus nor a minus sign in front of either. But that didn't bother her, because if she'd guessed the correct passcode, the number of possible combinations – with or without a plus or minus or a leading digit of 1 – and hence the number of locations was actually quite small.

She knew it was also quite possible that the code was 1-8-6-5-9-8 or some other combination of those six numbers, or that the passcode had to be subtracted from each of the coordinates rather than added to them. Google could produce maps of the revised coordinates in seconds, but Natasha obviously wasn't going to just type them in, not just yet.

She needed to confuse the situation and started to enter dozens of different possibilities based on the amended coordinates and with different passcodes added or subtracted, the handful that she thought were the most likely hidden within the list. One of her abilities was to focus analytically and produce vast quantities of data at speed. Hopefully by doing this anyone else would have to spend hours analysing each possibility and trying to make sense of them.

Three hours later she had input over a thousand sets of coordinates all loosely connected to Captain Fletcher's and asked the priest outside if they could all be printed. The young man looked remarkably alert, smiled and nodded. He handed her a memory stick onto which she downloaded the list of coordinates and, speaking into a walkie talkie, arranged for the USB drive to be collected and confirmed the printouts would be sent up.

What he didn't do was leave his post right outside her door.

Forty-five minutes later there was a knock on the door. Outside was a stack of A4 paper, each sheet with a colour printout of a map on it.

They must have the fastest printer in the world, Natasha thought.

Carrying the printed maps into the room, she spread them like tiles over the bed and much of the floor of her room. That, she thought, would confuse any watcher and also make it look as if she was earning her keep.

Much later that evening, when the daylight had completely vanished from the single narrow vertical window of her cell, a late supper was delivered, consisting of lemon cake and English tea.

Natasha ate and drank and then, exhausted by the events of the day, decided to go to bed. She cleared away the printed maps, carefully placed the back of the chair under the handle of the door to provide some security – the door had no lock she could work from the inside – and then took a quick shower. She hoped the hot water would relieve the pain of some of her bruising. She checked herself in the mirror and noticed her eye was still bruised but she could now open it. And the scab on her nose was nearly ready to pick off. She was, she thought, starting to look almost presentable.

As she slept, another young priest took over the guard duties outside her door. What Natasha didn't know was that under their simple robes each of them carried a Glock 19 pistol and both were members of the Vatican's Pontifical Swiss Guard.

Chapter Forty-One

1945: Bern, Switzerland

The federal city of Bern lies more or less in the centre of Switzerland and was the location of a series of secret negotiations towards the end of the Second World War between Nazi Germany and the Western Allies to arrange for the surrender of German troops in Europe. It went under the code name of Operation Sunrise.

The lead Nazi negotiator was Waffen-SS General Karl Wolff, but the surrender of the German forces was a cover for his real purpose. Despite Himmler's grandiose plans for a Fourth Reich, Wolff and the other generals knew their only real chance of personal survival was to negotiate a form of immunity for themselves with the Allies.

This immunity was granted by the Americans to the seven generals without either Russia's or the United Kingdom's approval in Bern in 1945. This immunity was given in return for the specific disclosure of the whereabouts of all other high-ranking SS officers and details of the provable death of Adolf Hitler.

As part of this agreement Himmler was to have been arrested, but he'd managed to slip the net and got out of Berlin. He was captured shortly afterwards but the records showed he had committed suicide whilst in captivity. The Americans had then reneged on their agreement in order to appease both Russia and Churchill who had reportedly been furious at their action.

In fact it was Heinrich Himmler alone who had the last laugh, or maybe not.

His 'suicide' had been a sham. He'd been positively identified by his British captors and had then been subjected to prolonged 'enhanced interrogation,' or torture. He had answered every question put to him, and had also revealed the exact whereabouts of Hitler, which had led to the orchestrated 'suicide' of the Nazi leader in the infamous bunker and thereby secured Himmler's own freedom.

He had lived out his days as a free man in Bern, under the noses of the authorities and using a false identity supplied by the Allies. This freedom had come at a high cost: Himmler had suffered a severe stroke brought on by the torture only a week after his release and had then required twenty-four-hour medical care.

Age and various illnesses had added to the effects of the stroke. His appearance had changed over the following years until there were no obvious physical links evident to anyone that they were looking at the monster who had orchestrated the Holocaust.

A secret trust had paid for both the house where he lay in bed and the substantial monthly medical bills, and none of the Swiss medical team, or anyone else, was inclined to ask questions as long as the supply of money didn't stop.

Himmler still had his voice, but he was only rarely lucid and, whenever he started talking about the hidden Nazi vault or the secret laboratory, what he said was treated by his carers and the doctors as the ramblings of a sick and mentally ill old man.

He had however received three visitors at different times to his bedside before he died.

One was Sir Roger Sinclair, the then head of the British Secret Intelligence Service, the second the former Waffen-SS General

Karl Wolff, and the third was Heinrich Himmler's illegitimate son Hans.

All of them had the same two things in common. They all wanted to know the location of the treasure vault, and none of them ever did get the information from Himmler.

Both Sir Roger Sinclair and Karl Wolff went to their graves never having found it. What was not common knowledge was that for both of them it became an obsession and as old men they had even agreed a truce to work together.

Himmler's son Hans was a lot younger and this played to his advantage as the memories of the Second World War began to fade and people involved in the conflict simply died of old age. Now in his eighties himself, Hans had remained convinced that he and his family were entitled to the wealth that his father had acquired and then hidden.

He had only met his father twice as a boy. The first time Himmler had been dressed in casual clothes and smoking a pipe. He knew from his mother that he had younger half-sisters but he was Himmler's only son. At that first meeting his father had spent just ten minutes telling him how he would have to carry the family's legacy into the future.

The second meeting, about three years later, had made a rather different impact.

Dressed in his black SS uniform, Himmler had looked and acted like a monster towards the boy. He had forced Hans to listen as he told him about the treasure vault and the laboratory and the reasons that he, Hans, would carry forward the Nazi dream and lead the Fourth Reich. Repeatedly slapping the boy across the face, his father had made him promise to remain loyal and swear allegiance to the Nazi cause. As he departed, he said that once the war was finished, he would arrange for Hans to be collected to join him.

Aged just eight, Hans had been terrified and had nightmares for many years. However, the story stuck in his memory and as a young man the idea of untold riches had been one he had wanted to pursue.

Now an old man, he had spent a lifetime looking for the vault and failing to find it. But he had passed the story and the legacy on to his twin sons as they grew up. Their names were Leon and Jonas and both had taken the Himmler surname which their father had refused to use. He had called himself Potthast, the maiden name of his biological mother.

Genetically they had both inherited a ruthless and callous nature from their grandfather and had both been drawn into crime, becoming debt collectors for loan sharks. They both enjoyed their work and were proud of their infamous grandfather. They carried his name and legacy as a badge of honour as they meted out violence to their victims.

Leon had been broken-hearted when Jonas died.

His brother had taken a short holiday in England and had naturally gravitated to the crime-ridden East End of London. Drinking in a pub, he'd had decided to pick a fight with one of the men in the bar. Unfortunately, his victim was a member of a powerful local gang. They had turned on him as a mob high on drink and drugs and beaten him to death. As was usual at that time and in that area, nobody in the pub had seen anything when the police finally turned up to investigate.

Why Jonas had done something like that when he was a relatively rich man made sense only to Leon. As his twin as he might well have done the same; for both of them the temptation to enjoy a fight ran too deep to resist.

With vengeance in his heart he had tried to track down members of this mob, but they had simply disappeared and the police had no leads, no evidence and no witnesses. Or at least, none that were prepared to testify under any circumstances. It had been a really cold case, and the murder of the German was quickly forgotten, though not by Leon.

He had then joined the Italian army where he had been able to vent his pent-up anger and aggression legally while wearing a uniform, and he even got paid for it. His physical strength and callous attitude meant he had been a natural recruit for the Italian Special Forces. He ended up in the 'Col Moschin', the 9th Paratroopers Assault Regiment where his ability to kill without compassion was noted and, in some circumstances, overlooked and even encouraged.

Eventually he had gone freelance as a mercenary after having been given an honourable discharge that was really nothing of the sort and he had ended up working in England for the British Government, despite his parentage.

His grandfather's identity had been acknowledged by the British Security Vetting team without comment and he had eventually been assigned to Sir Charles Martin, the Director General of GCHQ, as a kind of fixer and useful muscle.

What Leon didn't know at the time was that Sir Charles had signed off his vetting based purely on his relationship to Himmler, in the hope he might know where the last gold coin – or even where the vault – were located.

In fact, what had transpired was that Leon had become better informed about his father's claims and quests thanks to Sir Charles, rather than the other way round. He had served him well as a bodyguard but had confessed he knew nothing about either the missing gold coin or the vault, which had annoyed Sir Charles immensely.

Leon had been retained and had simply bided his time, handling the kind of dirty jobs that nobody else wanted to touch. He had been at GCHQ arranging for a body bag to be taken away for covert disposal when news of Sir Charles and his two colleagues being executed was radioed through.

He already knew about the capture of Natasha Black and had intended to join the team later for some fun with her. And with Sir Charles Martin now permanently out of the way, Leon saw no reason why he couldn't help himself to the rack of gold coins secured down in the basement in Room 23.

Now was his moment to act.

Chapter Forty-Two

Vatican City

Natasha awoke, her body aching all over as had become the norm over the last days. She felt she could barely move, but somehow made it into the shower, kicking maps to the floor as she went. After what seemed like ages she emerged from the bathroom and got dressed. Right on time her breakfast arrived, heralded by a quiet knock on the door.

Hoping for a full English, instead she got muesli, croissants, fresh black coffee, and iced water.

'I'll need to introduce them to the concept of a bacon sandwich on cheap white bread with brown sauce,' she said to herself, but loudly enough for whoever else was most certainly listening to hear, just to drop the hint.

She spent the next hour shuffling through the maps and looking at some of the locations she had chosen, including those that she thought were at least possible, and found two that made some kind of sense.

The first was in modern day Poland in the Owl mountains in Lower Silesia where she knew the Nazis had built a huge network of underground tunnels near Ksiaz Castle, as usual using prisoners and slave labour. The complex had been rumoured to be both an arms factory and an alternative strategic command centre for the Third Reich. It had been intended to end up as a small underground city with a full infrastructure including fresh water supplies and even a complex rail network and hospitals.

The area had been searched rigorously by the Allies after the end of hostilities, so any secret vault there would almost certainly have been found.

And that was probably too obvious anyway, Natasha thought, and when she checked the map more carefully, the precise location of the coordinates was about a mile away and under a lake. So that made it a bit of a non-starter. Or did it? She stared at the printed map and began wondering if she could use that location to play for time, time she could use to try to save her own life.

The second possible location was more interesting and the coordinates precisely matched one particular spot on a small island. Natasha couldn't quite believe it, but it did make some sort of sense. She tossed that map aside in apparent irritation for the benefit of the hidden camera and began studying other sheets. She now thought she knew where the vault was most probably located.

Some time later she 'found' the map showing the area surrounding Ksiaz Castle and began to show visible signs of excitement, again playing to the camera she assumed was watching her. She hoped that de Ronson would fall for her selection, her application of the code and the modified coordinates. And she knew she could argue that the resulting co-location with the known underground base was compelling.

The obvious danger was that if he or some member of his security team decided to apply her suggested passcode to some of the other possibilities and to generate revised coordinates, and particularly to the island that she thought was the most probable location. If that happened, her obvious defence would be to suggest that the island seemed improbable because of where it was located. She'd have to think up a few other convincing reasons for not having chosen it.

She thought long and hard about this and was afraid she would end up being trapped because she knew de Ronson would see straight through any obvious lies. So maybe her best option would be to hedge her bets, to not tell a lie but to simply shade the truth slightly. The more she thought about it, the more that seemed to make sense.

She made up her mind. She would supply de Ronson with both locations but suggest to him that the castle seemed to be the most likely site, and that the first place they should look was in the underground tunnel system beneath it. And then, if that search drew a blank, they could then move on to the island. And hopefully she would be able to work out a way for her to escape from the clutches of the Church and get out of this mess.

She sighed and opened the door to her room. She asked the guard – a different man, she noted – if she could speak with Mr de Ronson.

Chapter Forty-Three

Gloucestershire, England

Leon Himmler had received a full report from the GCHQ security team on the incident in Oxfordshire, which told him little more than that both Natasha Black and the gold coins were now missing. And that an unknown but clearly very efficient assassin had been involved in the deaths of Sir Charles and the other two men. Forensic analysis of the bullets that had caused their deaths had revealed very little except to confirm that the weapon had almost certainly been a Glock. The Austrian company wasn't the only arms manufacturer that used a polygonal barrel in its pistols but Glocks were far more common than handguns made by Heckler & Koch, Kahr and Walther.

He had to track down the woman as he suspected she would lead him to the treasure vault that he absolutely knew was real. The fact she had escaped again meant she was highly dangerous. Or probably more likely, bearing in mind that she was some kind of an academic, a code-breaker, that she had been kidnapped by an unknown third party, maybe by the unknown assassin.

What he had to do was quite easy, but whether it would work only time would tell.

As the most senior remaining member of Sir Charles's team, Leon had been interviewed or more accurately interrogated by some faceless government people who had picked his story and background to pieces. They also knew about the coins but seemed uninterested in them. Their clear and obvious focus was on finding Natasha Black and whoever had killed Sir Charles Martin and the other men.

They'd finished the interview shortly after he'd proved he'd been in Cheltenham at the time of the killings. Somewhat surprisingly, they had agreed to his request to let him track down Natasha Black, on the grounds that he had access to her GCHQ personnel file and other information they didn't possess that would help him to find her. He was to remain on the GCHQ payroll and report daily by text to a mobile phone number he was given.

With this authority he immediately returned to the command centre they had set up at the airfield. There, he'd issued an update to the team on site and confirmed the target's last known whereabouts as Ditchley, Oxfordshire. As search commander, all information would come to him first.

The other asset he possessed, which again the British police did not, was access to the super computers at GCHQ, which meant he could use all the United Kingdom's spying capabilities and additionally tap into certain international police and border control infrastructures that he could order to be tasked with hunting down Natasha Black.

Once she'd been located, he would either continue to track her or have her captured and interrogated to find out where the vault was.

One way or the other he would make his grandfather proud.

Chapter Forty-Four

Ksiaz Castle, Poland

Mr de Ronson, as Natasha now addressed him, not out of any respect but to try and convey the impression that she was being totally compliant, had listened to what she'd said, looked at the coordinates she'd produced and the maps, nodded and immediately leapt into action without questioning her further.

Within five hours she and Mario had flown into Krakow Airport on the same private jet they had used to get to Italy and had then been driven away in a large four-wheel-drive military vehicle. The journey had been much longer than she had expected, taking almost three hours before the vehicle finally stopped. She climbed out with a real sense of relief and looked at their destination, the vast and castle-like Hotel Ksiaz where, she quickly learned, a small command centre had already been set up.

Everyone but Natasha seemed to be dressed in black and, looking out of the window of her very comfortable room, she noticed that the huge vehicle they had travelled in was also black with dark tinted windows.

'Everything's black, even me,' she said, chuckling quietly at her own pun.

Mario hadn't said anything to her on the flight to Poland. He had taken a seat near the front of the plane before she boarded and appeared to have slept all the way. He'd also occupied a front seat in the vehicle that had driven them to the hotel, seemingly engrossed in a laptop.

Natasha had done her part of the job and was apparently expected to wait in her hotel room and amuse herself while the team from the Church began their investigation of the underground chambers. When she'd asked Mario if all the other people had driven to the hotel, he'd told her they'd travelled in a much larger chartered jet and had arrived in Krakow only an hour or so after them.

The area around the castle was honeycombed with tunnels, both natural and man-made, and the team downstairs began by examining old plans, blueprints and numerous geographical surveys. Natasha knew they wouldn't find the vault marked on any document because not only had it had been one of the most secret projects attempted by the Nazis but she was also certain it was nowhere near Ksiaz. In fact, if she was right the vault wasn't even located in mainland Europe. But she speculated that given the huge amount of Nazi engineering in the area and that Hitler had intended to make this place his long-term base, they might stumble on some anomalies that they would decide merited investigation.

None of which helped her, of course, and whilst she wasn't technically a prisoner, she also knew she wouldn't get very far if she tried to escape.

She remembered Mario's nonchalance after he'd killed Sir Charles and the other men. She knew he would certainly kill her without hesitation if the situation demanded it, and quite possibly he had already been ordered to do so once the vault was found. When this thought crossed her mind and then lodged firmly in her brain, the deep-fried chicken wings and chunky homemade chips she'd just ordered from room service suddenly lost some of their appeal.

On a positive note, her weapon of last resort, her titanium nails, had lasted well, and she kept them carefully polished and sharpened them as best she could. She was prepared to take the risk of scratching herself either awake or asleep as a trade-off for keeping them sharp enough for another stab and slash if that was what it came to.

Her luck had lasted well over the last few days, perhaps helped by the mixture of bravado and timing that she'd cultivated, but she knew matters would soon come to a head when her luck would run out and there would be no avenue of escape she could take.

The next day she didn't bother going downstairs to watch the team operating, wishing that they would simply forget about her.

But any possibility that this would happen was shattered at about mid-day when there was a rapid knocking on her hotel room door.

She opened it about six inches and peered out.

'Hello, handsome,' Natasha said.

Mario stared at her, opening his mouth to say something but then shut it again.

'Natasha, please come with me,' he finally said, his arm outstretched to guide her down the corridor. 'We have found something.'

That was absolutely not what Natasha had expected, but she left the room, locking the door behind her and taking her key, which was old fashioned and quite heavy. She had thought it might be used as a possible weapon but doubted if it would offer her much of a chance of overpowering Mario or anybody else.

As they entered the temporary control room on the ground floor it suddenly occurred to Natasha that they were the only guests in the hotel. Clearly the Church had paid for total privacy and this was impressive.

She had no idea what the room was normally used for, but it now resembled a cross between the control room at Cape Canaveral and the villain's lair in a typical James Bond film. Several large screens had been mounted on the walls and the numerous desks were dotted with computers, all tended by operators again dressed in black. There was a buzz of anticipation in the air and even a few smiles. Images from sonar, from drones and static and mobile cameras were displayed on the screens, some of them split to provide additional data. Natasha had to admit she was again impressed at how quickly all this had been set up and the system made operational.

Mario turned to her. 'We have found an underground structure at the end of a disused tunnel that may be the vault,' he explained. 'It is not far from the lake that the coordinates indicate, and we believe there may be an underwater entrance, possibly for a type of small submarine. We are working on the hypothesis that the Nazis might have transported the treasure here by air or rail – there's an airport and a railway station at Wroclaw they could have used – and then transferred it into the vault through the underwater entrance.'

That struck Natasha as being extremely unlikely for at least two reasons, but she didn't dispute Mario's statement. Sometimes, she thought to herself, two plus two really can make five. But what he'd said did prompt a question she'd been meaning to ask.

'I didn't know there was an airport at Wroclaw,' she said. 'But if there is, why didn't we fly in there rather than go to Krakow? Wroclaw must be a couple of hundred kilometres closer to Ksiaz.'

'It is,' Mario agreed, 'but because of the nature of this operation we needed to use an airport where the Church had significant influence, and that meant Krakow. We also needed sympathetic contacts in the Polish military, hence the vehicle we used to get here, and that too was easier to organise at Krakow. And being under the protection of the military ensures that we will not be disturbed by the police or anybody else, and also means we have access to aqualungs, diving gear and other equipment that we might need.'

Natasha looked with interest at the various screens as Mario explained what their sensors had detected.

'I'm not sure,' she said. 'That void looks bigger than I was expecting. Can we tell if any metals such as gold are within the structure?'

'Our experts think it's lined with concrete so our sonar and detectors can't see what's inside it. We have equipment on the way to drill though into the chamber to inspect it, and a small underwater team is preparing to approach from the lake to see what is there.' He paused and smiled at her. 'If you know how to scuba dive, would you like to join the underwater team?'

'I do and I would, please,' she said, then hesitated. 'As long as someone isn't going to try and kill me while I'm underwater.'

'Signorina Black, I promise you they will not. The Pope himself has blessed your involvement and you will come to no harm if you do as you have been asked and help the Church. Please just enjoy the moment.'

Natasha was unsure about this. Mario being kind was not, she thought, a characteristic of his core nature but on the other hand he'd been unfailingly polite to her – as well as saving her life – and what he'd said did make some sense. And discovering a lost Nazi secret chamber was a bizarre sort of dream come true and very, very exciting, the more so because she had no idea what they would actually find in this void. All she was reasonably certain about was that it was not the vault that Himmler had ordered to be constructed.

She decided against giving Mario her best winning smile and instead sat down on a chair at the back of the room and settled down to wait.

Chapter Forty-Five

Gloucestershire, England

At about the same time that Natasha had walked into the command centre in Ksiaz, Leon Himmler was also looking at a lot of screens in a temporary command centre. But unlike the one in Poland, where the mood was buoyant and optimistic, the room in Cheltenham was full of serious faces because Natasha Black appeared to have simply vanished into thin air.

And it wasn't just the woman who had disappeared.

A suspiciously large number of CCTV cameras covering various bits of Oxfordshire had experienced different 'technical issues' which meant no footage had been recorded in large swathes of the area. Obviously any piece of equipment could malfunction but the cameras were usually very reliable and for so many to go down at the same time in such a small area was more than suspicious. Leon suspected that bigger forces were at play, forces with tendrils that could reach into almost any organisation. And right at the top of that particular short list was the Catholic Church.

It had crossed his mind that people like himself, descendants of Nazi generals, could also have been in the game but he knew that most of these just wanted to forget their genetic legacies. Urban myths of the Fourth Reich actively rebuilding its forces in South America were just that, myths.

No, it had to be the Catholic Church and the speed and capability shown in the CCTV cover-up confirmed this. No other organisation outside of the British Intelligence community, of which he was a part, could have done it this in the United Kingdom.

He studied the enormous map of Oxfordshire projected onto the wall and thought about how he would have escaped had he been in Natasha Black's position. It had to have been by air because there really were no other options. River transport was too slow, and in any case there weren't any waterways she could have used. Railway stations had cameras, and as far as he knew none of those had been affected by the blackout, so if she'd taken a train he would probably already know about it. And any cars leaving the county would have been recorded on the traffic cameras outside the immediate area and those images, coupled with facial recognition software, would have alerted him.

The only other option was an aircraft, and in that case there were several possible escape routes. The killing site at Ditchley had helicopter pads and there were two local airfields at Enstone and Kidlington.

Ditchley was under the control of GCHQ and nothing had gone in or out apart from the clean-up teams and investigators, but the other two private airports were a possibility. Leon needed flight manifestos and air traffic control reports for the day Natasha Black had vanished, and he needed them quickly. He made the call and, as he did for a few minutes every day, thought about his brother. Doing that always strengthened his resolve, fuelled his anger and increased his long-denied desire for revenge. It also shortened his already notoriously short temper.

'Find this bloody woman right now,' he yelled at the team of people working in the room. Everyone kept their heads down and kept tapping away at their keyboards.

Thirty minutes later he was looking at the flight records from both the private airports. It appeared that the number of take-offs recorded by Air Traffic Control at Kidlington Airport had exceeded the number of flight-planned departures by one.

Try as he might, and even with the authorisations he possessed by virtue of his position, nobody could tell him what the extra flight was. He ordered copies of the recordings of all the CCTV cameras from the airfield, but that would take hours to go through because he had no idea what he was looking for apart from an aircraft. And, just as the best place to hide a tree is in a forest, the airfield tapes would be full of aircraft and at that stage he had no idea which one he – or rather his staff – were looking for.

To narrow down the search, Leon ordered copies of the ATC records to be compared to details of the parking and landing fees charged – as is often reported as a joke, all aircraft take-offs are free, and airfields only charge for each landing – to try to identify the elusive missing aircraft.

Somebody at Kidlington, he was certain, was either in the pay of whoever operated the missing aircraft or had accepted a one-time payment to 'lose' its details. But Leon knew that he needed to find the Black woman as soon as possible and he couldn't waste any more time, which meant he had to reluctantly play his last card and admit his lack of progress.

He prepared a text to his new masters on the number he used for the updates he sent every day. In it, he explained the situation and asked them if they could help track the aircraft.

The mobile vibrated in his hand thirty seconds later and, without any introduction, an arrogant voice – it sounded like the product of a lengthy public-school education and contained more than a hint of exasperation – informed him that the aeroplane in question belonged to an Italian aviation company but had been hired by the Catholic Church. And that in the last hour it had flown into Krakow Airport.

Then the line went dead.

Chapter Forty-Six

Poland

The orange neoprene wetsuit fitted her but had been designed for a man, which meant it was baggy in some places and tight in others. The fins and goggles were a good, tight fit and once she'd tested the air supply Natasha gave the 'OK' sign, ringing her right thumb and forefinger, then tumbled backwards from the stern of the small boat that was moored about forty feet from the shore of the lake.

The water was muddy with very poor visibility, and she swam a few feet away from the boat to allow the next divers to follow her in. As she suspended herself in the lake, she realised how deep it actually was. She couldn't see the bottom because of the murk but she could see the shapes of the other divers through the swirling brown mist. And that, it suddenly dawned on her, was probably why they were all wearing the bright orange wetsuits.

She swam alongside the three other men, all of whom had powerful torches and were carrying weapons that looked like harpoon guns but with thicker barrels. All the suits had a small flashing white light on the right arm to assist visibility. She had no doubt they would be keeping a close eye on her throughout the dive, though realistically escaping while wearing an orange wetsuit and an aqualung was never going to be a viable option.

Methodically the divers swam along the bank and came to a stop at a certain point. Natasha could see nothing and assumed the control room had radio contact and were tracking their positions.

Suddenly a hand appeared from out of the gloom and grabbed her foot. She kicked out but the grip held firm and then another hand grabbed her shoulder to restrain her movements. She cried out into her mask as the pain shot up into her neck from the old bruising where she had been punched in the helicopter what felt like a month ago.

Had Mario lied and this was the spot where she was to be killed and her body dumped?

One of the other divers swam over to her shaking his hand from side to side for her to calm down. Then she saw her 'attacker' was another diver who then released his grip and pointed downwards.

She looked and saw layer upon layer of old and rusty barbed wire just below her feet. Had she swum into this or even caught her foot in it, it would have created a nasty and painful wound. More importantly, extracting her from it would have been an awkward rescue exercise for the team.

Natasha gave him a quick OK signal with her forefinger and thumb and slowly moved away feeling a little bit silly and very paranoid.

The quantity of the barbed wire and how it was laid across the lake floor and along the steep bank they were approaching was no accident. It was clearly protecting something of value.

The divers all seemed to suddenly congregate in front of her. Natasha floated on the periphery of the group trying to see what they had found. Snagged in the barbed wire were many pieces of rag that looked like old clothing and resting, almost staring at them from near the centre of the tangled mesh of wire, was a complete human skull. It was positioned almost as if on display in a gallery.

Natasha shivered and not from the cold.

As she turned, she could now see the light from two of the divers' lamps cutting through the darkness and illuminating the bank itself.

There before them she could see a huge round metal object – Natasha thought for an instant that it looked something like the hobbit doors she'd seen in the film *The Lord of the Rings* – but far, far bigger. She guessed it was about twenty feet in diameter. In the centre of it and clearly visible even after all this time was a huge embossed swastika.

They had found the underwater entrance to the chamber.

Chapter Forty-Seven

Gloucestershire, England

Once Leon knew where the aircraft had landed he also knew where to start looking. It was comparatively easy to hack into several of the Polish information systems and members of his team quickly traced the arrival time of the plane and then began checking CCTV images of road traffic out of the airport at around that time.

Despite the blacked-out windows of the military style 4x4 truck, windows that completely concealed the identities of the occupants, Leon had deduced from the timing and the footage that it was the most likely form of transport for the Black woman to use. The Church, he reasoned, would not have wanted her face to appear on any traffic or other cameras, hence the choice of vehicle.

As a precaution, he also ordered surveillance of about a dozen other possible target vehicles, but his gut told him Natasha Black had been in the truck. And as the ongoing footage from surveillance cameras was covertly collected, collated and analysed, his belief was strengthened. His team traced it all the way to a part of Poland that was now a tourist area dominated by a large castle. He also knew from what his father had told him that this was the castle from which Hitler had intended to rule his global empire.

A final set of images from a traffic camera outside a hotel in Ksiaz picked up Natasha Black climbing out of the vehicle and entering the building, which confirmed his deduction.

Now he knew where Black was, he had to get to Poland to complete his assignment. And, having lost three of the original team he had worked with, he decided he would do the job alone. This would allow him to travel quickly, and speed was vital as he was at least a day behind the woman. More importantly, working by himself would allow him to act independently and quickly, depending on what was found.

He was sure that he was being played by the powers that be in London, but he guessed that Poland was near the limit of their reach, so he could make his own decisions once on site. He had already decided to keep any treasure for himself and deliver Black's dead body to them as his parting gift.

To do that he would need to disappear very fast with a new identity. He studied a map of Poland on his phone, trying to get his bearings. He knew he would need to be careful and for his plan to work whatever treasure was found had to be both portable and of sufficient value to afford him a new identity and wealth.

But even if this didn't transpire, if he couldn't carry enough of whatever the vault held to begin a new life, he could abandon that part of his plan and just kill the woman. That would appease his controllers and might even earn him a bonus or a promotion.

Just under two hours later he walked briskly across the tarmac at RAF St Athan on the Welsh coast just west of Cardiff towards an Embraer Phenom 100 multi-engine aircrew trainer, marked with RAF roundels. He had no idea what strings his masters had pulled to requisition the aircraft, but he was to be the only passenger on a flight-planned but otherwise undocumented training flight to Krakow.

He could have driven but the roughly 1200-mile overland journey would have taken him at least two days to complete and probably more like three, and in three days his quarry could be almost anywhere in the world. But the Phenom T1 would get him there in under four hours, even with a refuelling stop in Germany.

He climbed the integral steps just behind the cockpit on the port side of the plane with a sense of purpose and nodded to the crew member who was waiting for him to board. Leon was carrying a small rucksack that held the bare necessities – clothes, washing kit, a tablet computer and chargers for that and his mobile phone, a couple of continental adaptor plugs and full box of nine-millimetre ammunition for the Glock pistol in his shoulder holster. In his jacket pocket was a new diplomatic passport in his name that would allow him to bypass immigration and customs at Krakow and avoid the Glock sending the metal detectors at the airport into meltdown.

'Any change in the flight details?' one of the two pilots asked. 'For the flight plan, I mean.'

'None,' Leon replied shortly. 'Krakow, and as quickly as you can.'

The officer nodded, showed him where he could find refreshments and the toilet.

Ten minutes later, the plane climbed into the greyish skies over the Bristol Channel before turning east to join the airways system over Gloucestershire.

In the passenger cabin, Leon Himmler ate a couple of sandwiches and drank a cup of coffee, and then fell into an uneasy sleep.

Chapter Forty-Eight

Poland

The dive team had immediately returned to the surface and been taken back to the hotel. Whilst Natasha was excited, none of the other men seemed to be particularly elated, apparently treating it as some sort of standard exercise. Or perhaps they were intimidated by the sheer size of the structure and the door they were going to have to try to open. When she had seen the swastika, her heart had missed a beat. The size of it on the door had been deliberately imposing, almost defying anyone to challenge it.

The other issue that had been niggling away at her was that this could in fact be what they were looking for. If it was, it meant she had almost been too clever for her own good. The other location had seemed more probable to her but this alternative set of coordinates had led them to what was clearly a Nazi-built large hidden underground chamber with a big and obviously very heavy underwater door, several feet below the surface of a lake.

Could there be more than one vault? Was one of them the laboratory? Was the Himmler journal cleverer than she had initially thought? Mathematical probabilities always made random events look organised, but sometimes events genuinely were organised. She would have to be patient, see what was in this chamber and then decide.

That evening at dinner she was sitting some distance from Mario at the long table, she suspected at his request. She would have preferred to use room service, but he had insisted she join them as the brains behind the discovery, and the mood was buoyant because of what they had found.

In all Natasha counted twenty personnel, all youngish men, at the table. One obvious change was that they were no longer all dressed in black. Each was wearing the same style of shirt and a jumper draped stylishly over their shoulders in the way only Italians can properly carry off. She had visions of a Church supply shop where they all queued up to collect one black sweater, one wool jumper in random colour, one computer and one pistol holster. She chuckled to herself.

Interestingly no one seemed inclined to talk to her and she was left alone to eat and observe.

When coffee was served, Mario came over and sat in the now vacant seat next to her.

'An interesting day, don't you think?' he asked.

'Absolutely. So what do you think is in that chamber, Mario?'

'I do not know, but I am sure God will protect us from its evil.'

That gave Natasha a moment to pause. The Italian was clearly religious, which was a bit of a surprise. In fact, if she hadn't seen his lethal handiwork first-hand, she could have assumed he was a priest. How his religious beliefs could be reconciled with killing people in cold blood she had no idea. Or, she then thought, perhaps she had. After all, she'd killed the man who had attacked her on the helicopter without even thinking about it because she had been fighting for her life. That was the only real justification for what she had done. Whether or not she was on the side of good hadn't even crossed her mind.

But if the Catholic Church was fighting for its very survival – and if the kind of Nazi relics she guessed might be hidden in the vault could be linked to the Vatican, its survival might well be in serious jeopardy – it could certainly be argued that Mario, as an instrument of the Church, was morally justified in taking the lives of the people who threatened it.

Breaking the short and uneasy silence, Mario rose and wished her a good night's sleep. She noticed when he had gone that she was now sitting at the long table all on her own, and the room was deserted apart from two hotel staff clearing away the remains of the meal.

'A room full of Italian men and not one of them wants to stay and talk with me,' she muttered.

She reached up and touched the large scab on her nose and then felt the swollen bruising on her eye and decided she really couldn't blame them.

Suddenly feeling very tired she climbed the stairs slowly back up to her room and went straight to sleep.

Chapter Forty-Nine

Poland

The next day there was a palpable sense of purpose down by the lake as the divers, including Natasha, pulled on their wet suits. She noted a lot of cutting equipment and what looked like boxes of explosives stacked up on the bank. The weather was calm, and as the sunlight broke through and hit her face Natasha felt the warmth and started to relax very slightly.

Sometime during the night, a temporary metal framed jetty had been built that stretched out over the lake, presumably above the location of the door they had discovered.

Sitting on the jetty, Natasha pulled the air tank onto her back. It was heavy and cumbersome and her movements didn't help her aches and bruising, but she wasn't going to show any weakness. She turned a grimace into a smile to anyone who might be looking.

Stepping into the water after the other divers, she swam out about fifty feet and waited there just below the surface, regulating her buoyancy and trying to see what the divers were doing. Their intention was that the door would be opened physically using whatever levers and bars they had to force it. If that didn't work, the contingency plan was to blow it off with explosives.

After about thirty minutes and without any obvious signs of success, Natasha and the other three divers were recalled to the jetty and climbed out of the water.

It was time for Plan B, which involved two of the divers who were presumably qualified in the use of explosives underwater. They disappeared below the surface taking the boxes with them and reappeared almost an hour later.

Now back on dry land, dressed and standing a safe distance away, Natasha looked on with the other members of the team, waiting for the detonation.

She was disappointed with the explosion.

She'd been expecting a bang and a spout of water, but in fact heard only a dull muffled thud followed by a swirl of largish bubbles on the surface of the lake.

'Is that it?' she asked, but no one answered her.

-o0o-

While all this was happening, Leon Himmler had made himself comfortable on the opposite side of the lake, sitting on the bank with a fishing rod and a large rucksack.

He had arrived late the previous evening and while still in the air he'd realised he would need both a means of transport and a base. So he'd decided to combine both requirements and used his mobile phone to hire a campervan that came equipped with provisions for a week as well as a fishing rod, hiking sticks and the like. He had also hired a wetsuit and air tank along with a harpoon gun and had collected everything that morning. No one seemed inclined to ask questions if it was all paid for in cash with a hefty deposit.

At that stage he didn't need to hide because he was far away enough not to be of concern to anyone, but he was also close enough to see what was going on. All the roads down to other side of the lake had been closed and were guarded, but from his vantage point he could simply wait and see what transpired. Once he knew what was happening he could decide on his own course of action, and when to make his move.

Night-time was always the best cover for any infiltration, and with the closed roads his obvious – and in fact his only – avenue of approach was directly across the lake. This was what he had anticipated, which was why he had hired the diving equipment. If the people he was facing were guarding the roads, which they were, he had no doubt they would also be guarding the approach across the lake. But guarding the approach *under* the lake would have been far more difficult for them to monitor, which was why that was probably going to be his best option.

To his surprise he had also caught two fish, which he hoped might be a lucky omen for the tricky mission he faced.

Chapter Fifty

Poland

As Natasha and the team looked on, the surface of the lake suddenly started to erupt with debris.

For a few minutes nobody could work out what was happening, but then the man operating the ground-penetrating radar shouted out that he'd seen something. Mario and some of the other men gathered round him and stared at the screen of the device as he explained what the image showed.

Then the Italian walked over to Natasha. She'd heard the rapid chatter in Italian but that language was not a part of her repertoire and she'd understood almost none of it.

'What's happened?' she asked.

'The explosives breached the door of the chamber,' Mario replied, 'but there was a second door further inside the cavern and that has opened as well. We don't know if it was blown open by the explosion or if it had been left open when the site was abandoned. Either way, it doesn't matter because we now have a way to get inside.'

Behind him, a shout went up as several of the team stopped what they were doing and just stared at the lake. The kind of debris being pushed out as the chamber under them had started to fill up, which had mainly been bits of wood and fragments of cloth, had been replaced by what looked like hundreds of white footballs. White footballs that floated up to the surface and then sank.

The human eye is a highly-evolved organ but the most important part of the entire process of seeing is the brain, which interprets what the eyes are looking at. If the scene is something the brain can't recognise, it will be difficult for this interpretation to work. The brain really does have to know what it's looking at in order to see it properly. The short version is that knowledge and recognition is requisite to seeing.

Natasha stared at the lake, simply not recognising what she was looking at. And then it suddenly dawned on her, and she shuddered, leaned forward and retched.

What she was seeing were hundreds of human skulls, presumably buoyed up by the air inside the cranium, rising to the surface of the lake and then sinking as the air leaked out.

Mario stood beside her and looked on impassively.

'What the hell happened in there?' Natasha asked. 'Who were those poor people?'

'Slave workers, probably,' Mario suggested. 'Left to die in the chamber when the Nazis left. That would have been cheaper than shooting them. And easier. All the Nazis had to do was lock the door and walk away.'

Five minutes later and without another word she and Mario returned to the truck and were driven back to the hotel in silence.

Natasha was simply trying to process the horror of how all those human skulls, those countless anonymous lost lives, came to be there.

Beside her, Mario seemed deep in thought, and Natasha guessed he was wondering how de Ronson would react when he was told that the hidden chamber was now flooded and, possibly, that at least some of the contents had been scattered across the bottom of the lake.

Mario's demeanour worsened as they entered the hotel lobby where de Ronson, dressed in black military style clothing, was standing, his arms folded and staring out of the panoramic window that looked over the valley below.

'I had hoped we could have got inside without destroying what we were looking for,' he said, his voice cold and laced with menace.

Natasha thought he was about to explode, but he turned round, glared at her and Mario, and then stalked away.

'We will talk later,' he snapped.

He turned and left the room.

'Mr Happy comes to town,' Natasha said to Mario. She'd recovered her composure after the scene at the lake.

He didn't smile but nodded slightly, and then promptly also left the room.

Natasha decided her best course of action, as she was feeling hungry and had no idea if or when lunch was going to be available, was to order a club sandwich and some strong coffee as she sat alone in the hotel lounge.

About thirty minutes later, just as her club sandwich arrived and she had ordered a second coffee for herself, Mario reappeared, de Ronson a few paces behind him.

Mario looked weary and, unlike Natasha who had adapted quickly to her constantly changing world because of her ability to rationalise things without too much emotion, seemed neither as efficient nor as cold-hearted as he'd been when she had first met him.

'Signore de Ronson and I have spoken,' Mario said. 'He is not happy but not as angry as I had expected. I have explained that the breach of the second door was probably inevitable in the circumstances. We have now used diggers to gain access to the site from above, and he wishes us to continue our search of the chamber this afternoon.' He hesitated for a moment. 'This will not include you, I'm afraid.'

Natasha clenched her hands and stared angrily at Mario.

'I thought –' she began, but he interrupted her immediately.

'What we have already found in that chamber is abhorrent, the work of the devil. Thousands of dead souls were locked in there and they will never find any peace.'

Across the room de Ronson spoke. 'What Mario is trying to tell you, Ms Black, is that we've found a Nazi death pit. There were hundreds, maybe thousands, of prisoners and slave labourers working on this site and when they were of no use for whatever reason they were simply left in this concrete pit to rot.'

Unlike Mario, de Ronson didn't seem particularly perturbed as he described this. His tone contained no more emotion than if he'd been talking about the design of a new building or something equally innocuous.

'What is concerning me more,' de Ronson went on, 'is that as far as I can tell this isn't the vault we are looking for. Our search will continue, but all we have found so far are simply dead bodies or rather skeleton after skeleton in there.'

Natasha wasn't going to ask who had the job of checking that out and just nodded.

'So, Ms Black, tomorrow we will travel to the second destination you suggested. You will be picked up in the morning so please be ready. Any clothing or anything else you need please tell Mario and he will arrange it. Let's hope for your sake this one works out better,' he finished ominously.

That night Natasha had repeated nightmares about skeletons, dark pits and de Ronson himself. She awoke early the next day feeling almost more tired than she had the night before.

The only positive thing was that the bruising on her eye had turned from purple to yellow and now it almost matched the other one in size.

Chapter Fifty-One

Poland

Leon had watched all the activity across the lake with interest. Like Natasha and Mario, he hadn't known what the white roundish objects were that had suddenly appeared, but unlike them he wasn't close enough to eventually identify them.

Watching the equipment being packed up later that afternoon and the apparent loss of interest in the site, he decided he would check it himself that night, but he concluded that the treasure wasn't there. Having seen the Church's efforts and the reality that at least some of the stories his father had told him were true – he had known about several Nazi underground structures located in Europe – he started to daydream about how he would spend the huge sums of money that would accrue when he'd recovered the treasure. A super yacht, perhaps, and drink, women and general debauchery were right at the top of his current list, as they always were, in fact. He'd briefly forgotten about both his brother's memory and the much bigger issue of continuing Nazi world domination.

That night he pulled on his hired wetsuit and aqualung and finned slowly across the lake about ten feet below the surface. This was something he had trained for and undertaken many times before and for much longer distances during his army career and he was barely out of breath when he hit the first line of barbed wire.

Whilst this hadn't done any real damage, other than a tear in the neoprene wetsuit and a scratch on his leg, he cursed inwardly for his stupidity for not being more careful. He swam back out and made his way towards the shoreline further along.

He could only see one guard indiscreetly silhouetted against the skyline and knew there would be at least one other. Their sloppiness suggested they weren't really expecting any trouble. Either that or they had nothing of real value to protect. Or possibly both.

Leon assumed that the team from the Church had gained access to the chamber from below the surface of the water, but he could also see that an opening had been constructed above ground.

He slipped ashore well away from the sentry he could see, took off his fins and aqualung and concealed them in some undergrowth, then made his way towards the opening. He knew where to head as a kind of corridor of tape had been erected around a large hole in the ground. Two large mechanical diggers or backhoes were still on site and had presumably been used to excavate the area he was approaching.

He crouched down and worked his way slowly towards the tape. He knew from his military training that sudden movement would catch the guard's eye, so he concentrated on making all his moves fluid and gentle. Strong nerves were needed, and he knew for sure that he had those.

The hole was huge and had a low square brick wall constructed around it like a wide chimney. The backhoes had only had to remove the topsoil and the grass covering it to expose the structure. It appeared that a large iron grid or gate that had covered the entrance had been swung open, probably by one of the diggers, but had broken away from its corroded hinges.

Removing the waterproof infrared torch and a night vision headset from his pouch, Leon looked into the black abyss and at the heavily rusted steel staircase that led down into the depths.

The pit was filled with murky water from the lake, but he could quite easily see the bones and skulls within. He knew in that moment that it was a mass grave not a treasure vault, and he also realised the significance of the white floating spheres he had seen that morning. He swore silently.

Turning to go he suddenly felt a gun barrel pressing on the back of his head.

'Do not move,' a voice instructed him in Polish with, he noted, a definite Italian accent.

He raised his hands and responded in a mixture of Polish – he did speak a little of the language – and German: 'I am a poor farmer. I only wanted to see what was going on.'

The guard clearly didn't understand him either way. He tapped Leon with the pistol and motioned for him to turn around.

That was all the time Leon needed. He instantly twisted, grabbed the gun barrel, rammed his other elbow into the man's face with the sound of breaking bone and pushed him face down into the mud. The guard never stood a chance. Leon began increasing the pressure and slowly broke his neck in a way that he had done so many times before to so many others. He slid the guard's dead body quietly into the water to join the others in the pit.

He swam silently back over the lake to the campervan and spent the next hour sterilising the site, removing every trace of his presence, conscious that the guard's body would eventually be found.

But when he drove off into the night there were no signs yet of that having happened.

Chapter Fifty-Two

Poland and the Bailiwick of Guernsey, Channel Islands

Leon knew that the Vatican, along with the governments of other micro-states like Andorra, didn't own any aircraft, so that when the Pope flew anywhere the Vatican chartered an aircraft, usually from Alitalia, Italy's national carrier. The aircraft was allocated a special flight number, A74000, and might also use what has become known as the Pope's personal callsign, Shepherd One.

But clearly members of the darker forces within the Vatican had other options. The Cessna Citation with Italian registration – the letter 'I' followed by four other digits on the side of the fuselage was clearly visible – was the aircraft he now knew had carried Natasha Black from the UK to Poland. And it would no doubt also carry her to wherever the next part of the search took them. The jet was parked at the John Paul II Krakow-Balice International Airport – the name of the airport was itself almost a slap in his face with its reference to the Pope – and he knew his team back at GCHQ would be able to track it as soon as it took off and follow it electronically to its new destination.

Parked on a different hardstanding at the same airport was the Phenom T1, fully fuelled and with the crew in an airport hotel at ninety minutes' notice for departure.

-oOo-

Natasha and Mario were unaware of the intrusion on the site or the death of the guard because they were driven back to the airport at Krakow early that morning. She noticed that Mario had a serious looking metal briefcase cuffed to his wrist and, as they sat down opposite each other in the cabin of the private jet about three hours later, Natasha couldn't bear it any longer.

'What's in the case Mario?' she asked, her winning smile on display.

'Guess,' he said, looking serious.

Natasha was about to make an inappropriate suggestion but remembering Mario seemed to take offence quite easily she played it straight.

'Cash?' she suggested.

'Close.'

She tried again. 'The gold coins?'

He smiled, then stood up and moved to another seat near the front of the jet on his own and made a call on his mobile phone.

Natasha had guessed he would distance himself from her as he'd done that twice before rather than sit near her on a flight, presumably so he could make or receive phone calls with some degree of privacy. She consoled herself by going into the small kitchen area and selecting a couple of packs of sandwiches and a carton of orange juice for the flight.

The wide leather seat was comfortable and she put on her seat belt ready for take-off. Once the aircraft reached its cruising altitude she ate her scratch lunch and then, still tired from her recent lack of sleep, she dropped off for a couple of hours, only waking up as the Citation hit some mild turbulence.

Rubbing her eyes, she sat there and again thought about what Himmler had written. Something was niggling at her, but she was still almost certain that where they were now going was the final destination, the actual location of the hidden vault.

She'd discussed their next stop with Mario in the hotel the previous evening and had suggested, to try to throw off any possible pursuit, that the aircraft should land somewhere other than its actual final destination.

'Maybe we could we land at Alderney?' she'd asked. 'And then we could take the inter-island ferry to Guernsey. Keep a low profile, that kind of thing?'

'I'll give the pilot a call,' Mario had replied, 'because that sounds like a good idea.'

He'd returned about an hour later and had shaken his head.

'It's impossible,' he'd said. 'The runway at Alderney is less than nine hundred metres in length and isn't fully tarmacked. The Citation – our jet – needs an absolute minimum of one thousand and seventy metres and a solid surface. And even that would be tight. The pilot told me it's all to do with the approach path and pavement strength and the fact that an aircraft never lands right on the end of the runway and something about undershoot and overshoot and other stuff that I didn't understand. But the short version is that we have to land at Guernsey. That has an international airport and the runway can handle most jets: it's almost sixteen hundred metres – about a mile – long.'

A short while after the turbulence had jolted her awake Natasha felt the Cessna begin its descent and tightened her seat belt slightly. As the small jet came into land her nervousness about returning to British soil increased, not least because she didn't have her passport and she was almost certainly still on various wanted lists. On the other hand, the Catholic Church didn't seem to need any documents or authority to fly or land anywhere.

Stepping off the private jet, Natasha put on the thick overcoat and a new bobble hat she'd requested from Mario and climbed into a waiting black Range Rover. She knew the Channel Islands could be cold and windy and Mario had also wrapped up but had topped off his outfit with some very cool looking sunglasses.

It didn't take long for them to reach their destination of St Peter Port, which was only about three miles from the airport.

The island that Natasha had identified as the most likely location from the decoded coordinates was Guernsey, which had been occupied without a fight by the Germans in the Second World War. And that was where Himmler's vault of treasures, hidden for decades, would now, according to the words written by the long-dead Nazi general, be found.

Chapter Fifty-Three

Bailiwick of Guernsey, Channel Islands

Natasha read from a tourist information board beside which she and Mario were now standing.

'"The German occupation of Guernsey lasted from June 1940 through to the end of the war in May 1945. The Channel Islands were invaded without any resistance being offered by the British armed forces as Churchill and his government had deemed them not to be of any strategic military value." Ouch!

'"The Germans very quickly established a civil administration with the islanders who had largely remained compliant to avoid severe retribution and threatened mass civilian executions. Hitler felt the invasion of the Channel Islands was a huge moral victory and ordered the fortification of the islands, particularly Guernsey, using prisoners from Russia and France as forced labour.

'"Even today there are many tunnels and bunkers that have been left unexplored beneath the island. The German Underground Hospital with over seventy-five thousand feet of tunnels remains the biggest Nazi structure on the Channel Islands."'

'So that means as well as being open to the public as a tourist attraction the tunnels have been maintained over the years and are well documented. That is both good and bad,' Mario pointed out.

If ever there was a place where a Nazi treasure vault would be hidden, the German tunnels probably looked just right, Natasha thought, even better than a film set in an *Indiana Jones* movie. She imagined wet concrete tunnel floors, curved brick walls and string lighting with fading painted swastikas.

'I need to make a call,' the Italian said and walked out into the town square to get a better signal.

Natasha looked around and spotted a small cafe with Parisian style tables outside. It was early afternoon and whilst she had slept on the jet her sleep pattern was all mixed up and she felt somewhat dozy.

A double expresso and two almond croissants later, Mario re-joined her.

'Mr Grumpy's coming, isn't he?' she asked, a direct reference to de Ronson.

'Yes, but we have some time before he arrives. Our computer experts are now examining all of the documentation available for this site and accessing whatever systems they need to. We should go and get some rest. The hotel has been booked.'

The opulent Les Rocquettes Hotel was only a short walk away and Natasha thought it looked quite splendid.

Mario didn't seem particularly interested in guarding her, but she knew she had to keep in line and behave. She suspected they had tagged her somehow, maybe with a tracker, so if – or rather when – she made her break for the hills, she needed to be sure she could get clean away. Trying to find somewhere to hide in a small town on a small island – a place she'd never been to before and didn't know her way around – was never going to work.

Her room was big, light and airy and had lovely Georgian windows overlooking the harbour. She thought back to her days at GCHQ when travelling on the firm meant a low budget hotel, economy airfares and third class on the railway, not luxury hotels and private jets.

Despite what she perceived to be the constant and imminent threat to her life she was actually starting to enjoy herself which was, she concluded, slightly worrying. Climbing into the big comfortable double bed, she then slept for a solid sixteen hours.

-o0o-

Early next morning at breakfast, she sat on her own in the hotel's dining room feeling much more refreshed and more like her normal self. The scab on her nose had fallen off in the night leaving a slight red mark which had improved her appearance considerably, and her eyes were now a matching pair in both size and colour.

Mario looked typically Italian and effortlessly stylish in casual shirt and slacks and carrying a cross over satchel. He sat opposite her and just ordered coffee.

'There's nothing we can find to suggest where the vault might be. De Ronson is not happy and has suggested that you look again at the text you read in the journal to see if there are any further clues to its whereabouts.'

He opened the satchel and took out a small laptop and a mains charger and lead and passed them to her.

'Everything you need is on there. We can talk later today about your progress.'

Natasha decided to work in her room where there would be fewer distractions than if she sat in one of the lounges. She had no idea where Mario had gone if she needed to ask him anything. She assumed he was staying in the same hotel but wasn't certain, but she knew he would be able to find her. The laptop was a different computer to the Apple she'd been using back in Rome but contained a duplicate of all maps and other data she'd prepared, including her version of what she had started mentally calling 'the Himmler text' and her translation of it. She immediately began her research, employing the usual search engines.

Just like anyone who searches the Internet, she quickly got side-tracked and distracted from her core search, although she rationalised that she was just gathering background information about Guernsey, information that should assist her in the search.

She hadn't realised how hard it had been for the Channel Islanders under Nazi rule, nor appreciated the scale of the engineering feats they'd achieved. The Germans' attention to detail and precision were legendary and this was borne out by the size and condition of the structures still standing like silent sentinels on the island, visible memorials to the determination of the Nazis to fortify and leave their mark on the Channel Islands, the only part of the United Kingdom they had ever occupied.

Natasha started by using a map to locate the precise location of the coordinates she'd deduced – and hoped – to be correct. She didn't input those details into the laptop, just in case it was bugged.

The map suggested the location was directly in the middle of the German Underground Hospital at a central point where six tunnels radiated in different directions. Though it was nothing to do with her search, she also realised the name of St Peter Port seemed peculiarly apposite given what was now going on, with the Catholic Church and the Vatican directing the operation to scour the island.

Natasha knew she would have to go and physically inspect the intersection for clues before she gave the new set of coordinates to Mario or de Ronson, just to see it for herself. But there was something she needed to do first.

Mario had given her a few hundred euros in Krakow so she decided to go shopping, guessing that buying with euros wouldn't be a problem on Guernsey. She found a couple of local shops and bought a complete new outfit, everything from underwear to a warm coat and a woollen hat, then returned to the hotel. If de Ronson or somebody had bugged her clothing, she would need to wear her new outfit when she finally tried to either hide or escape. It was just an insurance policy. She hoped.

Then she walked out of the hotel and made her way to the German Underground Hospital.

Chapter Fifty-Four

Bailiwick of Guernsey, Channel Islands

Just over five hours later Leon arrived in St Peter Port, about a day behind his target. The delay had been entirely predictable and expected, because of the time taken to discover the destination of Natasha Black's aircraft.

Following an aircraft is nothing like following a car and he'd had to wait for GCHQ to confirm the Cessna's flight-planned route. Until he'd known that, Leon had been unable to order the Phenom to follow, and then the crew had had to get to the airport and do the usual pre-flight checks on the aircraft and file a flight plan before it could depart. But he knew he had time in hand, because the one thing he was certain about was that Black wouldn't reach her destination and immediately gain access to wherever the vault was located. She'd have to search for it and then the people with her would have to find a way to get inside. It would take hours at the very least, more probably days or even weeks. It all depended on where it was and how well it was protected.

Once he'd arrived at Guernsey Airport and walked unchallenged through customs and immigration control on the strength of his diplomatic passport, he'd called the RAF pilot's mobile phone and released the aircraft. If he needed another flight anywhere he could charter an aircraft on the island or call his masters and arrange a short-notice flight. That would be easy enough to do on Guernsey but next to impossible in Poland, which was why he had ordered the RAF aircrew and the Phenom to remain at Krakow and on alert.

Leon had never been to the Channel Islands before and decided it looked quite pleasant. He wondered if this was where he would finally make his home in the company of all the other resident tax exiles, once he was very, very rich.

He already knew something about the history of Guernsey and the tunnels and bunkers that the Germans had built under the island and which he presumed was where Black would be heading. Leon's plan, such as it was, was to wander around and simply look for her because it was, after all, only a small island. Once he'd found her, he'd tail her, and let her do all the work to find the vault. He didn't have even the first clue about where he would start if he was running the search, so he would have to depend on Black doing the legwork and actually locating the vault. But as soon as it had been discovered he would move in for the kill, quite literally.

His masters had sent a picture of Natasha Black to his smart phone. In the image she appeared to be scowling at the camera but was undoubtably attractive. And no sooner had he sat down outside a harbour café than she walked right past him. If she'd been looking, she would have seen him staring at her, the habits of his years of covert surveillance training undone by the sheer surprise of seeing her right in front of him at that moment.

He placed a five pound note under the ashtray and left before his coffee and pastry had even arrived, making sure he kept a reasonable distance behind her.

-o0o-

In the event, Natasha was too deep in her own thoughts to have noticed the staring man outside the cafe or that the same man was now following her.

She queued up with a line of tourists at the entrance to the tunnels, then paid her entrance fee, walked into the foyer and glanced casually at the information notices as if looking for directions. In fact, she already had a good idea of the layout and knew where she needed to get to.

So as not to look too obvious to anyone watching her she wandered the tunnels and eventually ended up in a round chamber with six tunnels leading off it in different directions. She looked up at the arched ceiling and down at her feet, looking for any concealed entrance or other indications of where the vault might lie.

But there was nothing. Nothing but a ceiling constructed of bricks above her and solid concrete below her feet.

She blew out her cheeks and started to think hard, letting her trained analytical brain chew over the problem. But she gained no immediate insights and decided her mind wasn't functioning properly. She wondered if a trip to the seashore, to just look at the sea, might help relax her and help to clear her brain fog.

A few minutes later, sitting totally relaxed on the edge of the harbour wall, the random motions of the waves and the sound of the wind started to produce a calming effect. The complete change of scene seemed to somehow relax and almost empty her mind, and then provided her with a sudden sense of clarity. She had an inkling of what she'd missed. That turned into a possible hypothesis and the more she mentally challenged it, the more it seemed to make sense.

She walked slowly up towards the hotel, her mind racing as she probed and prodded at the conclusion she'd reached, looking for flaws. Almost all her thoughts were focused inwards, and she was barely aware of her surroundings, only paying attention to the extent that she knew where she was going and managed to avoid walking into any pedestrians.

She was completely unaware that at that moment she was the focus of two different pairs of eyes. Leon was acting as her distant shadow, trailing along about a hundred yards behind her, and de Ronson was standing on the pavement outside the hotel talking to two of his men and spotted her as she approached.

Natasha immediately went up to her bedroom and changed out of her new clothes and put on what she'd been wearing before. She didn't want Mario or de Ronson noticing that she was wearing a different outfit, in case they decided to bug that as well. Assuming they'd bugged the other clothes, of course. Or was she just being ridiculously paranoid?

She gave a mental shrug, then walked down the stairs and into the lounge, where she spotted Mario sitting by himself. She crashed down on the leather sofa next to him and smiled.

'You have news?' he asked, looking miserable.

'I need to do some more research but I think I now know where the vault is. The only thing I don't know is where the entrance is located, I think it's all quite complicated and until I can check it, it's still only a theory.'

'We'd better hear it then, Ms Black,' de Ronson said. Somewhat unnervingly he had crept into the room unnoticed by either of them, and the two men he'd been with outside had followed him inside. They took up positions either side of the lounge door.

'Right,' Natasha said, sounding slightly startled. 'First, I need to get the laptop, otherwise what I'm going to tell you won't make much sense.' She looked at de Ronson and then at Mario, then stood up when both men nodded.

She walked back into the lounge about five minutes later and resumed her seat on the sofa. She took a deep breath and opened up the laptop.

'Well, here goes. If I'm right, the coordinates point to an exact location in the old German Underground Hospital. That spot is known as Six Ways, and I've just come back from visiting it. It's a kind of circular space from which six tunnels radiate in different directions. There's nothing obvious to see there. The ceiling is curved and made from bricks and above it, as far as I know, is solid earth all the way up to the surface. Below it is a solid concrete floor that looks as if it might have been laid after the war. When I spoke with one of the tour guides he seemed to think at some point there had been a 'good luck' well on that spot. You know, one of those wells people toss coins into and make a wish.'

Both Mario and de Ronson looked interested, but Natasha shook her head.

'Before you get too excited I think that well is unlikely to have been the entrance to the vault. I've also looked at some of the online archives about the hospital and I have a feeling the opening had another purpose, not as extreme as the death pit we found but not too dissimilar.'

She paused. Mario and de Ronson were still listening intently.

'Go on,' de Ronson said.

'The rest is theory, as I said, but using a hospital as cover would make it easy to ship in treasure and also ideal as a working laboratory for human experimentation. I believe both are within this site. Think about it. Hospitals receive supplies all the time, and nobody watching would know if a bunch of crates or boxes contained medical equipment or bars of gold or silver bullion. And far fewer patients ever leave a hospital than are admitted to it because some of them die, so there would be a mortuary on site and probably a furnace or incinerator as well to dispose of the bodies. And I think I know the way at least some of the smaller treasure deliveries might have worked.

'I think Himmler and his teams set up the shipment of the lighter stuff, like gems and jewellery, inside dead bodies. If you open up a human torso and empty out all the squashy bits inside you're left with a quite large usable storage or transport space. Upon delivery the abdomens of the corpses would have been opened up again and emptied, and the treasure hidden away. I believe this was undertaken in the mortuary which according to the archives was located at the very bottom level of the hospital. If I'm right, the entrance to the vault is in the old mortuary which appears to be directly under the area known as Six Ways.'

'What about the well?' asked Mario. 'What was its significance?'

'The story may be apocryphal but I also read that the Germans insisted that all gold teeth removed from corpses were thrown into it for good luck. I suspect that the water level in the well wasn't very high and that the teeth were simply retrieved and taken away to be melted down. The old maps I've seen show a shallow well inside the huge vaulted chamber that's all there is to see now.'

'Very well,' said de Ronson. He stood up and strode across to where the two other men were standing. A hushed conversation took place and then he walked back to Mario and Natasha.

'My colleagues will ask for that part of the old hospital to be sealed off as soon as possible.'

'Will the authorities allow that?' Natasha asked.

'Ms Black, the name Guernsey comes from the Vikings and Old Norse, but St Peter Port derives from the time when the first Romans landed on the island as Christianity reached Italy. The Church to this day still owns a lot of this island, though not the site of the German Underground Hospital. That is privately owned but we have considerable influence and I do not anticipate any difficulty achieving this.'

'Oh,' Natasha replied, more questions lining up in her mind.

'We can do nothing today,' de Ronson said, 'so make sure you're ready when Mario calls for you tomorrow.'

Twenty minutes later, sitting again at the cafe overlooking the harbour, she wondered how the next day or so would play out and how much personal danger she was still in. She assumed that killing her anywhere in the United Kingdom – even on Guernsey – might cause more of a stir than dumping her in the relative wilds of Poland, but if the Church did want her dead she was sure de Ronson would find a way. So she was still looking for a way out, or somewhere to lose herself on the island.

-oOo-

Three tables down at the same cafe, Leon was sitting over a coffee and a cake and covertly watching her and wondering what the hell was actually going on.

He was also becoming increasingly impatient. And irritated.

Chapter Fifty-Five

Bailiwick of Guernsey, Channel Islands

Again Natasha was impressed by the speed and competence exhibited by the Church. Events moved fast with men and equipment appearing on the island and quickly disappearing into the old tunnels. Perhaps because he believed they were close to finding the vault and its potentially extremely valuable contents, de Ronson had decided to only have a small team doing the work. Obviously, the less people who were involved, the less chance there was of one of them talking about it. And, true to his word, he had had the entire area closed off with 'routine maintenance and repairs' being cited as the reason on large official looking signposts that stood at and around the main entrance to the site.

Natasha was becoming slightly bored, as was her nature when she had nothing to do, but knew she had to keep her wits about her. She spent the day exploring the town some more, half-heartedly looking for a place to hide or possibly a way out, though she knew either option would be difficult to achieve. She was still technically a fugitive and wondered whether she would ever be able to return to her home or if she would end up forever on the run.

That evening de Ronson suddenly appeared in the restaurant and interrupted her dinner. Leaving her half-eaten mushroom and truffle risotto she was ushered into the passenger seat of a waiting black van. Natasha knew better than to ask any questions and as the van pulled away on its very short journey to the tunnels Leon, who had been sitting on a bench outside the hotel waiting for her to come out again, moved his stiff legs and followed quickly on foot.

In the van de Ronson checked the view in the mirror on his side of the vehicle and nodded. Then he turned to Natasha. 'You're being followed,' he said, 'so we're driving to the tunnels to allow my friends in the back to have a quiet chat with your shadow.'

'Really?' Natasha said, totally surprised.

De Ronson smiled in his normal sinister way and she heard the unmistakable sound of the two men in the back of the van simultaneously cocking their pistols.

At the tunnels Natasha followed de Ronson down the stairs. All the lights were burning and they went immediately to the junction called Six Ways where the old well had allegedly been located. A big hole had already been dug in the floor but looking into it Natasha could see nothing but cracked and broken concrete, the damage obviously caused by the pneumatic drills lying beside the opening.

'Our surveyors estimate there are at least another ten feet of concrete and then a layer of solid steel beneath this,' de Ronson explained. 'There also appear to be pockets of explosive material positioned at various points to prevent any drilling. We have established where the old mortuary was located and you were right. It sits at the same depth as the vault below.'

'There is a vault then?' said Natasha.

'Indeed there is, Ms Black, although the foundations of the hospital were designed and constructed to camouflage its existence. It is unlikely we would have found it unless we had known exactly where to look, so that is to your credit.'

That was as near to a compliment that she imagined de Ronson would ever be capable of uttering and again the excitement she felt started to surpass her fear.

-oOo-

Outside the tunnel the sun was starting to set rapidly and the shadows were becoming longer. Leon had watched the van stop, but had been too far away to see who got out of it, though he assumed the Black woman was now somewhere in the tunnel system. He slowly approached the main entrance to the tunnels. As he got nearer he drew his pistol and attached its suppressor.

With years of training and hard combat experience, his sixth sense was on high alert and he somehow felt the presence of the two men before he saw them. They were some yards behind and clearly stalking him. As he reached the entrance to the structure he stopped, reversed his course and concealed himself behind a pillar. Then he simply waited.

Whether the men were inexperienced or overconfident, Leon would never know. He stepped out from behind the pillar as they passed, aimed his weapon and fired a single round into the back of the nearest man's head. The black-clad figure instantly collapsed to the ground, and as the second man turned towards him Leon fired again, hitting him in the chest, a centre mass killing shot.

He knew the thuds of the suppressed rounds wouldn't be audible much deeper in the tunnel system, but for a few seconds he just stood there, listening intently for any sound of approaching footsteps. But he heard nothing.

Dragging the bodies into an alcove opposite was both harder and noisier than he had expected. He quickly searched both of the corpses. Each man had been carrying a Glock 19 pistol fitted with a suppressor, which to Leon was justification enough for what he'd done: the men had clearly been intending to kill him. It was just that he had been able to pull his trigger first.

He smiled coldly as he hid the bodies as well as he could. Then, breathing deeply, he moved slowly forward, confident he hadn't been heard.

Chapter Fifty-Six

Bailiwick of Guernsey, Channel Islands

The old mortuary was cold and Natasha immediately felt a sense of depression, though she couldn't work out why she was experiencing this sensation. Perhaps it was because they were so far below ground, or maybe it was the hard grey granite stone walls or just her imagination reliving what had happened here in the past.

As before, when they had found the death pit in Poland, men dressed in black were busy with all sorts of equipment scanning and examining the walls, floor and ceiling.

Natasha counted at least thirty stone blocks laid out in rows, blocks that she assumed the dead bodies would have been laid on to allow post-mortem examinations – or any other procedures – to be conducted. Any storage containers and mortuary equipment had obviously been moved decades before. The huge room was barren and sterile with no hint of where an entrance would have been to any vault.

She slowly walked around with de Ronson to where Mario and a technician were examining a second adjacent room that was almost circular in shape and housed what looked like an enormous steel boiler or furnace.

'This is where the bodies were disposed of,' Mario said, crossing himself.

Natasha looked up. She could see a wide chimney made of steel and bricks that led upwards and presumably vented into the open air somewhere above the chamber. She peered inside the furnace itself, which was coated with layers of old carbon, and noticed a number of rectangular shapes indented into its base.

'What are these indentations for?'

De Ronson grimaced, or perhaps it was a smile.

'It looks as if this boiler had more than one function. We think it was built not only to cremate dead bodies but also to operate at much higher temperatures than normal to smelt any valuable metals hidden within them. That would have been a faster and more efficient process than your suggestion of manually removing valuables hidden inside their body cavities and then cremating the corpses. What was left after the burning process would have run down into these metal moulds and was probably gold mixed with ash and bone. When the furnace had cooled down the ingots could be removed and then fired again at a later time in this same furnace at much higher temperatures to extract the pure gold.

'We know this to be true as we have already done a basic sample analysis on the carbon inside the boiler which confirms that it contains traces of bone and other organic debris. Again, Ms Black, you have been correct. But what we don't know is where it went from here. Gold is heavy and I do not believe the ingots would have been transported by hand but we can see no other exits, no evidence of tram lines, just this concrete floor that has been laid since the war.'

'Can't you scan the walls for flaws, cavities and the like?' asked Natasha.

'We have, and there seem to be cavities and spaces all around us, which I don't understand. We simply don't know which section of wall we need to demolish, and we don't know which of these cavities is the hidden vault.' In an instant his mood visibly changed. Jabbing his finger aggressively at her, he snarled: 'Find the answer. If you don't, you're no more use to me.'

As he strode away, Natasha had a sinking feeling. De Ronson was the worst sort of bully, placing all responsibility on her, which allowed him to vent his fury on someone else – her, in this case – when things went wrong.

She also guessed from the way that he had spoken to her that his intentions were already clear: his plan was that she would die down here. The only question, with an uncertain answer, was when.

Turning to Mario she asked: 'Any ideas?'

'None, I'm afraid, Natasha. My boss is not behaving rationally. He seems agitated and that makes him dangerous. Let's work together and try to find the answer.'

Natasha was dumbstruck. This was the first time Mario had spoken to her properly using her first name, rather than just telling her what to do or where to go. Unfortunately what he'd said just reinforced her belief that de Ronson was looking for a reason to direct his anger issues at someone. He needed somebody to blame, and at that moment she was right in his cross hairs.

'Thank you, Mario,' Natasha said, looking around the chamber again. 'The only idea I've had is that we know the Nazis employed engineering efficiency in all things and the gold ingots would have been really heavy to move. I mean, even when they were killing the Jews in the death camps they set up what amounted to a factory production line to do it. So I don't believe they wouldn't have had some kind of transport system, trolleys on rails or something similar, to move the gold to the vault.'

She paused and looked around again, then settled her gaze on the concrete floor they were standing on. What she said next made no sense to Mario.

'I once screeded my cottage floor with concrete and after it had set I noticed that it wasn't completely flat. It had adapted by only about a millimetre when it settled to what was underneath, but it was visible.'

Mario looked at her blankly. 'I do not know what this word 'screeding' means. Nor do I know how you could possibly have detected that it wasn't flat. How can you see something that's only a millimetre in size?'

'Screeding is an English word for laying down concrete and I've got excellent eyesight. More importantly, I have the type of brain that notices anomalies. Even very, very small anomalies.'

Mario nodded at her and smiled.

'So let's see, shall we? I'll call the technicians in to do a scan of the floor to check for a one hundred per cent spirit level flatness and then either print it out or show it to us on a computer screen.'

About five minutes after a humourlessly glum-looking technician had completed the scan he called them over.

'*Ecco qui,*' he said in Italian, which Natasha didn't need Mario to translate as the meaning was self-evident.

They watched as the technician used the mouse to display a three-dimensional model on his computer screen.

'I am good, aren't I?' Natasha exclaimed.

Mario again nodded and smiled at her.

Showing clearly on the screen was a faint pair of parallel lines, probably about three feet apart judging by the scale, that ran straight across the mortuary from one side to the other.

Natasha looked at the image for a moment, then shifted her attention to the two opposite walls where the lines terminated.

'I think the mortuary was probably the centre of the complex,' she said. 'We don't know that for certain, but it does make sense. So the vault is most probably behind one of these walls, where the trolley line ends.'

'And behind the other wall?' Mario asked.

'I don't know. Maybe a reception area where they removed bodies from coffins before moving them into the mortuary.' She paused for a few moments, her mind suddenly filled with another possibility. 'Unless,' she added hesitantly, 'unless we've got this sightly wrong and right now we're standing between the vault and the laboratory of nightmares. Maybe the Nazis put them both in the same place, which would make a certain amount of warped sense. Only one building project, only one team of workers, that kind of thing.'

'So you think the laboratory would have used the trolley rails to send bodies that they'd finished with to be destroyed in the furnace, and behind one of these walls we'll find the vault and behind the opposite wall the laboratory?'

Natasha nodded and looked from one featureless concrete and brick wall to the other, and shivered slightly. Despite the bland surroundings, she knew she was in the presence of old and implacable evil.

Mario followed her glances then suddenly looked distraught and crossed himself again.

'What in the name of God did they do in here?' he muttered.

'I don't think God had very much to do with it,' Natasha responded.

They walked over to the wall where they knew one end of the pair of rails had originally entered another chamber, either the vault or perhaps the laboratory if Natasha was right. Mario was again his usual calm self and quickly summoned four large men carrying cutting gear and sledgehammers. Handing her a mask, Mario and Natasha then both stood back as the men began to attack the wall.

Presumably having heard the sound of the demolition, de Ronson manifested silently beside them. For one irreverent moment, Natasha wondered if he was actually a vampire as he seemed able to appear at will and, to her, he always seemed to be enveloped in an aura of darkness.

As the concrete, bricks and dust started to fall away, an archway that enclosed two rotting but heavy wooden doors appeared. The doors splintered and crumbled as the workers swung their sledgehammers and then they fell backwards into the black chasm that yawned behind them.

De Ronson lunged forward almost manically to see what lay beyond.

Ignoring the dust and clambering over the debris and past the workmen he disappeared from sight into the void of darkness.

Chapter Fifty-Seven

Bailiwick of Guernsey, Channel Islands

Leon had watched all of this with interest.

He had nearly been spotted earlier by the man they called de
Ronson as he'd stormed through the tunnels in some sort of rage,
and he knew his time was limited because sooner or later either
de Ronson or somebody else would find the two men he'd killed
at the tunnel entrance and then the search would start.

Leon had followed the sound of voices all the way down to
and then into the old mortuary. Once inside, he'd hidden behind
the large portable heavy-duty generator that was providing
electricity for the team from the Vatican. Unless it ran out of fuel
or broke down there would be no reason for anyone to look at
where he was hiding.

As he sat there listening to the two Italians and the woman,
wondering what the demolition of the wall would reveal, he
assumed that any treasure would almost certainly have been
gold, silver or gems because nothing else would have had certain
durability and longevity in its value for the Nazis. If it was gold,
simply carrying it out of the underground workings might be a
problem, simply because of its bulk and weight.

And he knew he'd have to move fast because of the other
niggling problem, the fact that the British intelligence
community, who were still his paymasters, most likely knew
where he and the Black woman now were and might already

have a clean-up team en route to the Channel Islands. Or maybe not. The group from the Church had come in discreetly by air from Poland or perhaps from somewhere else, and he himself was operating off the grid. Maybe his masters didn't yet know exactly where he was. But he knew it was only a matter of time before he was traced, if they didn't already have him under surveillance.

Realistically he suspected that they, like him, would be intending to wait until the last moment and then swoop in to pick up all the spoils.

With his realisation about the probable nature of the treasure and the possibly restricted timescale he had, Leon's game plan changed and became more realistic. He would focus on any gems, fill his rucksack, and simply run. If he could kill a few people on the way, including the irritating Natasha Black, that would be a bonus.

No one seemed to be following de Ronson into the tunnel entrance they had uncovered, and Leon decided now was not the moment to make any appearance. He would be patient and just watch and wait.

-o0o-

Natasha and Mario stood there in silence as the other men gathered round them, all staring into the archway. After a minute or so a couple of the workmen moved one of the arc lights to point into the tunnel so that the beam could cut through the darkness.

Natasha thought the vault itself could only be about seventy feet away but the exposed tunnel's curvature to the left prevented the light showing anything other than the tunnel itself, the walls streaked with dirt, damp and mould and with two rusty railway lines running along its centre.

'Do you think he's all right?' asked one of the men.

'The question should be: is anything safe that bumps into him,' Natasha said, quite pleased with her quick reply.

With unconscious and ironic timing, de Ronson could be heard charging back down the tunnel towards them. When he stepped into the glare of the arc light, they could see he was covered in ash-like dust and clutching a gold ingot in each hand, about the size of a large chocolate bar.

Standing silhouetted against the brilliant white of the arc lamp he looked almost demonic. He threw the small but still heavy ingots at Mario and Natasha who both ducked and moved sideways to avoid them. For whatever reason de Ronson looked so furious he could hardly speak.

And, indeed, he didn't speak because two silenced bullets suddenly slammed into his chest. He dropped slowly to his knees and fell headfirst into the pile of rubble.

Everybody looked around and saw Leon standing up at the back of the chamber with a big smile on his face.

'Thank you for your efforts, everyone. Now, nobody moves unless I tell them to,' he said in a calm and relaxed manner. 'We've hit gold, as you might say. Or rather I have.'

He stared at Mario for a moment and, clearly recognising him as another professional killer, he aimed his pistol at him and told him to drop down onto his knees.

'You can't kill him,' Natasha pleaded.

'I'm afraid, Ms Black, I can do whatever I like, and if you irritate me you'll most definitely be next.'

Natasha had always thought quickly, especially when her life was on the line.

'If I were you,' she said, 'I would want to see what's in the vault before you start slaughtering everybody. And it was Mario and I who found all this, not him,' she said, pointing at de Ronson's motionless body. 'And there's a hidden laboratory here as well which could have much more in it for you.'

She gave Leon her best winning smile.

'Okay, you've talked me into it,' he said, then raised his gun and shot Mario in the foot.

The Italian howled in pain and tumbled to the floor.

'That's just insurance,' Leon said, 'to keep you out of my way. Nothing personal. The bullets are hard-nosed so you shouldn't lose your leg. In fact, you certainly won't lose your leg because I'll kill you before I leave this place. So you'll be dead anyway. But it's the thought that counts,' he added, chuckling.

Natasha bent down to hold Mario as he crouched on the floor, moaning in pain.

'You bastard,' she spat at Leon.

He shrugged, then leaned forward and neatly placed a second bullet into Mario's outstretched left hand on the floor.

'Double insurance,' he said, as Mario clutched at his second wound.

Spinning round, Leon pointed the gun at the workers. 'Anyone else want a go? No? Okay, all of you, face-down on the floor.'

He pulled a handful of nylon ties from his rucksack and quickly and efficiently immobilised all the workmen, lashing their wrists together, while still covering them with his pistol. It was obvious he'd done that kind of thing before, which wasn't good news as far as Natasha was concerned. For good measure he also secured the ankles of the workmen together, then looped the two bindings together into a standard military stress position which completely immobilised them.

The last person he tied up was Mario, and he didn't tie his ankles, only his bloodied wrists, presumably because he knew his wounds meant he wouldn't be able to offer any resistance. The Italian groaned almost pitifully as the tie went on and Natasha glared at Leon as he did so.

'I'm not tying you up,' he said. 'I might need somebody to carry things and you'll do. But if you try and run away I'll shoot you. Got it?'

'Got it,' she said tightly. She felt herself becoming enraged but knew that the man in front of her was a professional killer, and she also knew he wouldn't give her any chance to attack him.

'Let's go shall we?' he said casually. 'My name's Leon, by the way.'

He picked up the two gold bars de Ronson had found and put them in his rucksack. Then he picked up Mario's rucksack, took out the eight gold coins in their wooden holder and handed them to Natasha.

'Yes, before you ask, I know all about the coins,' he said to her. 'Now lead the way down that tunnel. Let's see what we can find in there.'

Natasha stumbled through the archway carrying the coins and walked around the bend in the tunnel that she presumed would lead into the secret vault. She anticipated entering a chamber filled with piles and piles of gold bars, like the ones de Ronson had been clutching.

But what they actually saw was something quite different.

Chapter Fifty-Eight

1945: Bailiwick of Guernsey, Channel Islands

Upon completion of the German Underground Hospital, Henrich Himmler had been delighted with the outcome and how his own personal project had been hidden so easily within the bigger operation, the hospital's construction, with no questions needing to be asked or answered. The transfer of dead bodies and their disposal, and the huge numbers of human prisoners available for both hard labour and the programmes of medical experimentation didn't raise any suspicions. It was all part of the Nazi occupation of the island, which the resident civilians knew better than to question.

Like all good military strategists he had put in place a contingency plan which he had activated when the British seemed likely to recapture the islands and it was clear that the German war effort was doomed.

Once the necessary concealment of both the vault and laboratory had been finished, which the natural geology of the rock had made easier, he had personally visited the site and ordered the execution of all the slave labourers involved and anybody else who had known any details, no matter how sketchy, about the vault and laboratory. Himmler's directive meant that this final death toll was substantial because all the scientists and laboratory technicians had to die as well, plus all the doctors and mortuary workers.

Himmler had ordered the imprisonment of all these people in one of the largest chambers in the hospital and had then flown in a small *Einsatzgruppen* – the word literally translated as a 'deployment group' but it was in reality a mobile execution squad more usually employed finding and executing the Jews that the Nazis couldn't transport to the death camps – to carry out all the killings. They used groups of slave labourers to load the bodies into the furnace in batches, and then shot them as well and fed their bodies to the flames. He had personally supervised this final phase of the operation.

Once the last of the bodies had been tossed into the furnace, Himmler had left St Peter Port confident that the gold keys he carried were the only way anyone would ever be able to access the secrets and the treasures needed for the triumphant establishment of the Fourth Reich.

Chapter Fifty-Nine

Bailiwick of Guernsey, Channel Islands

Natasha was fuming inside but also high on anticipation as she strode down the tunnel with Leon walking a few paces behind her. She was doing her best to show that she wasn't afraid of him but wasn't sure it was working. So she walked along briskly, her head held high.

Turning the corner, she suddenly stopped.

The arc lights back at the entrance to the tunnel only half exposed what she was looking at. In front of her was a smooth and solid black granite wall with water cascading gently down its front. On the floor in front of her was a third gold ingot that looked as if it had been discarded in a hurry.

As far as she could see, the granite wall had no markings, no indentations and seamlessly fitted into the solid rock that surrounded it. The falling water was splashing into a shallow pool in front of the wall and was then trickling away through thin cracks in the rock. There was no indication where the water was coming from.

Leon came up close behind her. He bent down to pick up the third ingot, obviously keeping her in view in case she tried to attack him.

In fact, attack was the last thing on Natasha's mind. She was bemused by what she was seeing. She had expected something like a tasteless grandiose gothic carving decorated with swastikas and a big steel door with eight slots for the coins.

'Don't bother saying it,' she snapped at Leon. 'You're going to ask me to find a way in or you'll shoot me.'

'Ms Black, I've noticed that everyone around you seems to end up dead, so for now let's just find the way in. Once I have my treasure you can assume that I'll let you live. And if you're lucky, I might even keep my word.'

'Who are you anyway?' Natasha asked, still staring at the featureless black granite. 'You're obviously not with the Catholic Church so I need to give you a warning. The Pope has blessed me in person so you'll be in really serious trouble with God if you kill me.' Leon laughed out loud, a short and – to Natasha – unpleasant bark.

'I admire your courage,' Leon responded. 'And your faith, if you really believe what you've just said. But I suspect that's just that famous British sense of humour I've heard so much about. But I can see why you managed to get under Sir Charles Martin's skin. Did you kill him, by the way?'

'Nothing to do with me,' she snapped. 'Though I wasn't exactly broken-hearted when somebody finally decided he was a total waste of space and did something about it.'

Leon didn't respond, and instead changed the subject.

'If I told you my grandfather built all of this and that what's in the vault is my birth-right, would you be surprised?' he asked.

'Not really. Almost everybody else I've met has had a vested interest in this place, so I don't see why you should be any different. So, you're the architect of the next Reich are you? Well, good luck with that one.'

Leon laughed again.

'You're wrong about that. I have no interest in my grandfather's dream, not any longer. For me, this is just about the money now, simply the money. I suppose you know that the

British Secret Intelligence Service is after you and they've offered me a bonus to capture you? Or to kill you?'

Natasha nodded.

'I wondered when you would own up. Himmler's grandson working with Sir Charles Martin, GCHQ, SIS and Her Majesty's Government. Who'd have thought it, and yet here we both are.'

Leon looked impressed and irritated by her in equal measure. 'Anyway. I'm short of time and I need your help. What I believe is in the vault is worth more to me than a modest bonus from the British Government, so help me find the treasure and you'll be of no further interest to me.'

'Only a modest bonus?' Natasha echoed. 'That's a bloody insult.'

For the next ten minutes they both searched the area for any clues that would suggest how to gain access to the vault.

The water seemed to ooze out of the top of the granite block and the hairline cracks where it drained away appeared to have been created by nothing more than erosion over time.

Natasha then remembered it had been built under the old man made well on the level above, so maybe the water was coming from nothing more dangerous a ruptured pipe somewhere above rather than what she had first feared, that it came from the sea.

She discreetly dipped her finger in the water. It didn't taste salty. That was good news, and it meant only one thing. Not that Leon needed to be told. In fact, it might be an idea to do her best to mislead him.

'Leon,' she said. 'I think it could be the sea behind this granite wall. If I'm right and the vault is the other side of it, that means it's actually flooded.'

He scowled. 'You mean we can't blow it up?' Unconsciously his hand went to the butt of his pistol. 'Maybe I should earn that bonus, then.'

Natasha again let her imagination take over. The idea of being handed over to the British Government, most likely in a body bag for Leon's convenience, didn't appeal at all.

'But there's something else,' she went on. 'There's no sign of any mechanism here. No way to get that granite shifted or anywhere to insert the gold coins. So I think the coins probably open the door to the laboratory and maybe inside that chamber we'll find the mechanism that operates this vault. There is literally nothing here we can use to gain access and it's been bugging me that there was only one set of coins for two valuable chambers.'

Leon didn't look happy with her conclusion but nodded.

'Right,' he said. 'Let's get on with it, shall we?'

He turned and walked back up the tunnel letting Natasha follow behind him, still carrying the eight gold coins. He clearly didn't see her as a threat any longer, which she found slightly insulting.

Chapter Sixty

Bailiwick of Guernsey, Channel Islands

Back in the old mortuary, Leon bent down and used a knife to slice through the plastic ties he'd put on two of the men who had been operating the machinery. While they recovered and gathered up their tools under the silent threat of his pistol, Leon glanced at Natasha.

'I started with big plans when I came after you but now, honestly, I'd just be happy to get enough money to disappear and retire for good. This is turning into a nightmare.'

It was clear that Leon was very stressed, and Natasha started to suspect there was a chemical or something in the air that was affecting him, as de Ronson had certainly been almost manic before Leon had shot him. Perhaps she was also being affected, but then who could tell, she mused.

Bending down to Mario, she could see he was unconscious but breathing. His hand was more of a mess than his foot but neither appeared to be pumping blood and the wounds were already starting to coagulate. She made him as comfortable as she could, leaving the wounds open rather than risk wrapping them in anything that would fill the wounds with dirt and whatever else was present in the old mortuary.

She put on her face mask again and waited with a sense of déjà vu for the wall opposite to be opened up.

Like the entrance on the other wall, this one had obviously been sealed in the same way, by making it look as if there was no entrance there at all. But this time, as the heavy sledgehammers wielded by the two Italians made short work of the bricks and mortar and turned the concrete to rubble, Natasha and Leon were greeted by an ornate archway with a large engraved swastika capstone and carved skulls like gargoyles running down its arches.

'That's more like it,' she said. 'Your grandfather and his lot certainly had their own sense of style.'

Leon ignored her but she immediately knew her flippant comment might have been a mistake. She needed to stay focussed and remember that Leon was a cold-blooded killer who had not only been trained to carry out assassinations but most likely also had genetic influences that meant he would enjoy killing and torturing people, given his Nazi heritage.

As the dust cleared, they could see a set of solid steel doors inside the archway. They were inset about six feet into the entrance of a tunnel and as part of its design the left-hand door had a thick protruding tray with eight numbered slots set in it, each clearly designed to accept something the size and dimensions of one of the gold coins Natasha was carrying.

That all seemed a bit too straight forward to her. She suspected that the entrance could be booby trapped, possibly with discreet pockets of explosive, like they had detected under the well, or maybe doing the wrong thing could trigger the release of a gas or nerve agent.

Leon came over to her and took the tray of coins from her hand. 'I'm not sure I need you any more, Ms Black. I found you amusing but perhaps our brief relationship is now at an end.'

'You still don't get it, do you?' she snapped, knowing that her life was once again on the line. She was scared but she certainly wasn't going to show it. 'What if it's booby trapped? What if you need my unique brain to figure out how to get inside? Right now you've only got three small gold ingots and they're probably full of ash and human debris from the furnace so they're not worth as much as you think they are. I reckon that on balance I'm worth keeping alive.'

Leon looked at her, clearly weighing his options.

'Good point,' he said. 'You've earned yourself a few more minutes of life.'

Waving over the two men who'd used the hammers over he handed one of them the set of coins.

'Place these in the order they are in this wooden tray in those slots on the door,' he ordered.

The man looked at him, apparently bemused.

Leon didn't hesitate, just raised his pistol and shot the second man in the forehead. The copper-jacketed bullet blew a hole straight through his skull and the man's brains exploded out of the back of his cranium as he fell backwards.

Natasha looked away.

Suddenly the other man was over at the door slotting in the coins as fast as he could. Once he had done that he stood back. The three of them waited.

But nothing happened.

Natasha had guessed there would be some kind of sequence required: the problem was she had no idea what it would be.

Leon turned to her. 'You need to tell me right now how this works or I'll shoot you. No second chances.'

'How would I ….' she paused.

He glared at her, his pistol raised. 'Your job is code-breaking and all that cyber shit so it should be easy for you to break an eight-digit combination, right?'

'No,' she replied, getting angry again and running a series of rapid calculations in her mind. 'This is my field, so shut up and listen. You might even learn something.

'You probably don't understand the mathematics of it but there are 40,320 different possible combinations for what we're looking at here. That's eight factorial, if you're interested. If it took you five minutes to try each possible combination it would take you 201,600 minutes, that's 3,360 hours or 280 days working twelve hours a day to try them all. And you'd need to keep accurate records to avoid duplicating the sequences you tried. My guess is that you probably don't have over nine months to stand in front of that door sticking the coins in the slots. Apart from anything else, long before you managed to crack it somebody would notice the smell from the bodies of all the people you keep killing. And then it would be all over.'

Leon stared at her, his right arm, the one holding the pistol, slowly moving to point down at the ground as the implications of what she was saying clearly sank in. That had been her intention, but what she didn't want was for him to decide it was a completely hopeless task and to simply shoot her, take the ingots and run.

'What you need to do,' she went on, 'is think of any eight-digit numbers that had relevance to your grandfather. Let's start with the obvious, things like your grandfather's date of birth, his wife's date of birth, his SS or Nazi serial number, assuming he had one, wedding date, children's dates of birth. Stuff like that.'

'Why this fascination with dates?'

'The way human beings think means that nine times out of ten anyone who's asked to choose an eight- or six-digit personal identification number or PIN will select their own date of birth or that of somebody close to them. And we can discount any date that has the same digit twice as the coins are numbered one to eight and we only have eight slots. And just as obviously we have to ignore the numerals zero and nine.'

Leon looked as if his brain was starting to hurt.

'Why is this all so bloody difficult?' he asked, clearly a rhetorical question. 'All I want to do is to grab some of the treasure my grandfather left here and drop off the grid.'

He raised his pistol in frustration and without warning shot the other man in the back of the head, spraying bone and brain matter all over the right hand side of the door.

Natasha wasn't squeamish or had any problem with dead bodies generally but Leon's casually lethal actions repulsed her and emphasised the thinness of the thread from which her own life dangled.

'You do it,' Leon ordered, pointing the gun at her head.

She knew this was no idle threat. She left her mask on, not just because she suspected there might be toxins in the air, but also to try to reduce the smell of blood from the two slaughtered bodies lying on the ground beside her.

'If your grandfather died before he could access the vault,' she asked, 'who did he expect to pick up the challenge?'

'My father,' Leon replied.

'Your father's date of birth, please.' Natasha said more softly.

'Christmas Day 1936, which doesn't work, does it?' Leon said nastily, 'because there are two number ones and two number twos in it.'

Moving over to the slots where the eight gold coins or keys were still inserted, Natasha removed each one of them carefully. As she did so, she suddenly realised what had been niggling at her all along, why something hadn't been right with the coins.

Each of them had a very slight tremor, more of a tingle, that she could feel when she held them, and she suspected they had some natural power source built into them.

And as she read the inscription on the rim of one of the coins her theory suddenly fell into place as a reality.

'There are two coins that look the same,' she said. 'The figure two in this italic script could easily be confused for a four. That man –' she pointed at the body of the second man Leon had shot '– obviously didn't look closely enough at the coins as he was inserting them. He'd put coin number two in the fourth slot and vice versa.'

With that Natasha placed the first seven coins in their correct slots and then, holding the last one, turned to Leon. 'Do you want to hide somewhere just in case there's a monster? Or more likely a few sticks of dynamite rigged up as a booby trap?'

Leon hesitated. He clearly didn't want to look weak in front of the woman who again appeared to be taunting him.

'Go on,' he growled, but took a couple of steps back when Natasha turned away to insert the last coin.

Chapter Sixty-One

Bailiwick of Guernsey, Channel Islands

Mario came round slowly, the numbness in his foot and the sharp pain in his hand making him feel sick. He knew all the anti-interrogation techniques used for blocking pain, but it didn't seem to make it any easier now, when he was trying to use it for real. His entire training had been about inflicting pain, not suffering it, and acting as a covert assassin. Never before had he been wounded in any assignment.

He looked around for anything he could use to free himself. This place was truly the devil's palace, he thought.

The shots to his foot and hand had been precise and accurate. Begrudgingly he knew the man who had inflicted them was a professional like himself, and he respected his skill.

Leon had not tied Mario's feet which was a mistake. Once upright he saw that the technicians were also tied and two of them had been executed next to a second new arched entrance on the opposite side of the chamber. An entrance that he assumed led to what he had mentally labelled the Laboratory of Hell.

He staggered over to the generator and began rubbing the plastic ties around his wrist against the edge of one of the steel panels on the machine, and they eventually snapped.

He put on his mask and hobbled towards the way out. He knew he needed some bandages and more importantly a weapon.

Until he got that, he was in no position to fight anything, either people of flesh and blood or his own demons.

-o0o-

At the same time as Mario was stumbling out, Leon and Natasha stepped into a surprisingly small room where the air smelt stale and musty. They had entered the chamber through the steel doors about five minutes before.

The doors had swung open inwards easily and without sound the moment she had inserted the eighth coin. There had even been a light switch that had worked but the three bulbs that had illuminated were so dirty the dim light seemed to create more of a gloomy feel.

This was compensated for by the walls, roof and floor which were all brilliant white and appeared to be covered in a coating of a type of plastic material.

Anticipating Leon's likely reaction and to prevent him having an explosive tantrum after they had briefly searched the room, she explained what she thought they were seeing.

'Don't panic, Leon. This is more or less what I expected. What we're in is a shell within a much bigger room. I think this was done to preserve the laboratory. When we remove this white boarding, everything should be as it was left by your grandfather, including an entrance to the treasure vault.'

He calmed down and took a deep breath. Like de Ronson he was starting to look a bit demonic, she thought.

Ignoring her he tucked his pistol in his belt and started to kick and tear at the panels to pull them down.

Natasha waited by the entrance wondering whether to take the chance to flee, but the temptation to just stay a moment longer and see what was hidden behind the false walls was simply too great to ignore.

Chapter Sixty-Two

Bailiwick of Guernsey, Channel Islands

Thick metal tubing held the protective white boards in place and once Leon had broken through one panel, he managed to make a gap large enough for them both to look through.

Luckily he had a torch and swung the beam around inside the opening. This revealed a much larger room that had a roof like a cathedral and row after row of bookcases and alcoves, all of them covered in thick layers of dust.

Leon stepped forward into the hole but Natasha decided she would stay put. As soon as he had disappeared, she just turned and ran, not daring to look back. Searching for Mario as she sped through the old mortuary, she saw a trail of blood leading towards the exit and assumed he had somehow already escaped.

She didn't stop running until she was at the top of the stairs and heading for the daylight of the entrance. She couldn't hear Leon coming after her and the blood trail from Mario was still fresh and heading towards the outside.

Bursting through and out into the sunshine, she saw the Italian lying on the ground in a heap. He was again unconscious, probably through the pain and exertion in getting that far. She manhandled him as quickly as she could around the corner and behind an ornate bush, so he would be hidden from Leon.

As she was about to run back to the hotel, she realised she really had nowhere to go and no one to ask for help. The police would arrest her, the British Secret Intelligence Service would most likely kill her, and the Vatican would never let her talk to the Pope. That last option had sounded really crazy, she thought.

There was also the small matter that de Ronson had appeared to report to no one and that some members of the Church team were still alive and tied up down in the mortuary. She would have been prepared to hand herself in to the police or tried to stay on the run but the thought of leaving those men to die in the underground chamber would, she knew, haunt her for ever.

She reluctantly turned and started to walk slowly and carefully back down the tunnel again towards the old mortuary. She hadn't really got a plan, except to just sneak in and try to release the men.

Chapter Sixty-Three

Bailiwick of Guernsey, Channel Islands

Whatever Natasha had planned didn't actually happen.

The moment she walked back into the old mortuary, Leon came storming through waving his pistol, his timing impeccable.

'Trying to escape, were you?' he demanded, pointing the gun straight at her head.

'If I had been trying to escape,' Natasha said, giving him her winning smile and applying what she hoped was irrefutable logic, 'why would I have come back down here? I just felt a bit faint with the dusty air in there, and I also thought you might appreciate some personal time, me not intruding on your grandfather's legacy and all that.

'Anyway,' she added, walking confidently around him and back into the laboratory, 'we need to find you your treasure so we can all go home.'

Whether Leon believed any of what she was saying Natasha had no idea, but the fact that she hadn't run off – or rather she had but had then come back – might make him less likely to kill her out of hand.

Leon had started to destroy the internal walls and it looked like a tent half collapsing in on itself, only far more dangerous given the weight of the tubing and boarding.

They both manoeuvred through the mess and walked on into the much bigger hidden room.

'Wow,' Natasha said.

The room wasn't big: it was massive and wasn't really a room, more a vast chamber the size of a small aircraft hangar. Rows and rows of corridors lined with doors led off in every direction and there were bookcases and display cases everywhere. The white room or antechamber they had first entered was tiny by comparison.

Natasha noticed the whole area was illuminated with the same dirty light bulbs, stretching in lines like fairy lights almost as far as she could see. She assumed that with clean bulbs the illumination would have been adequate, but the light being emitted was quite dim because of the dust on the bulbs, and none of the light strings above the centre of the space were working. As a result the darkness, especially in the centre of the huge chamber, appeared impenetrable.

'How are we going to find the lever or door or whatever?' she asked, pointing at the vastness of the room. 'It could be anywhere.'

'There must be a control centre or hub or something in here, so we just need to find it. We'll split up. I'll work round from the left, you from the right. If you try and escape, I'll kill you. I'm not stupid so please don't treat me as if I was.'

Touched a nerve there somewhere, Natasha thought but said nothing.

Without the benefit of a torch and relying only on the dim and gloomy ceiling lights, searching through cabinets and cupboards and desks holding old and dusty medical records and whatever else was there was not very pleasant. Most of the walls were lined with old-fashioned glass-fronted wooden bookcases, some of them floor to ceiling, or to where the ceiling would have been in a room of more normal dimensions. Mobile library steps on wheels were placed at intervals but Natasha had no desire to inspect any more of the contents than she had to.

She thought Leon was right. The important stuff would all be in one place and no doubt there would be safeguards they would need to overcome.

The laboratory was oval shaped and seemed never ending. Natasha could see it had been built inside a natural rock chasm, which might have been why it would not have shown up any sonar or ground-penetrating radar searches as anything other than a natural feature.

The air she was breathing now seemed fresher than it had before, which suggested some sort of ventilation system was in place and working. She decided to keep her mask on anyway, just in case. What she still couldn't work out was where the lights and anything else electrical were getting their power from because the only generator she could hear running was the one de Ronson's men had installed in the old mortuary. But that was a minor anomaly, and she had more important stuff to concentrate on.

As she worked her way around the complex she passed seemingly endless bookcases and unmarked locked doors, behind which she suspected all sorts of horrors might lie. After about fifteen minutes she saw Leon's flashlight working its way round from the other side.

'Only bloody books and locked doors,' he murmured as he approached her.

'It must be somewhere in the middle of this place, like the bridge of a galactic starship,' Natasha suggested.

They both turned and walked towards where the centre of the complex should be, Leon's torch picking out mysterious shapes, some covered in sheets of fabric like dust covers.

Suddenly, out of the gloom a very large steel capsule that did actually look like an alien spaceship on long raised metal supports loomed above them.

'Blimey,' Natasha said. 'I was only joking.'

Leon seemed to be too focussed to even hear her.

There was a wide metal staircase that spiralled up and around to the back of the large capsule, which now appeared to be what Leon had described, a kind of central control station.

Clambering up the stairs, his boots echoed in the stillness. Natasha followed behind him. Reaching the top, they both stopped and stood looking at the door that led into the capsule.

But that wasn't what had stopped them both in their tracks.

What had shocked them both was that the entrance door was already slightly ajar and, looking down at the dust on the landing there appeared to be a set of fresh footprints leading inside the capsule.

Leon motioned for Natasha to step back.

Switching his torch off, he started pushing the door slowly inwards, his pistol raised and ready.

Chapter Sixty-Four

Bailiwick of Guernsey, Channel Islands

The capsule was not large but had windows on every side. There were three chairs placed in a line like thrones with a complex-looking control panel in front of each of them and on one side there was what looked like an old-fashioned French cage elevator that presumably allowed access down to the ground below the capsule. Or maybe even to lower levels below that.

There was obviously no one in the room so Leon switched on his torch and looked again at the footprints. They appeared to be a man's and had a military style tread pattern.

'Not an alien then,' Natasha whispered, not sure if that was a good thing or a bad thing.

The prints led across to the lift, which was empty.

'Whoever it is,' Leon said, 'is trapped now.'

Taking out his silenced pistol, he fired two bullets into the fuse box just to the right of the elevator's door. The double impact caused a flash as the circuit shorted out.

Then he started looking around for any levers or buttons that might open the door to the vault, which Natasha assumed was behind the granite wall. But he apparently found nothing that looked likely.

Natasha was way ahead of him but decided not to tell him because that might provoke him into some form of hasty action, like shooting her.

Then it also clearly dawned on Leon that the most likely place to find a control for the vault door could be wherever the lift went down to, and he started swearing in fluent German. Natasha understood every word.

Having finally stopped his tirade he shone his torch again on the prints and they both saw that there were specks of blood on the floor. Then Natasha knew exactly who was down there.

'Your handsome Italian friend is more resourceful than I thought,' Leon said, now sounding more cheerful.

'He's not my friend. And, let's be honest, the Church wants me dead, the British Secret Intelligence Service wants me dead and you want me dead. I have *no* friends. And no future, come to that.'

She crossed her arms and turned her back on him.

Leon left her alone and looked around the capsule again, apparently seeking inspiration.

Almost reluctantly, Natasha did the same thing.

The capsule was designed something like an elevated boat and that sparked another train of thought. Suppose she'd been wrong about the water running down the front of the granite block coming from a leaking pipe? Suppose it came from a hidden reservoir and was part of a last-ditch defence mechanism? Maybe the lever or button or whatever that opened the vault door also quite literally opened the flood gates to release the water, which would then flood in from above the vault killing anyone in the tunnel and laboratory and in the morgue. The water would then dissipate and the key to surviving the flood would be to be inside the capsule. That was probably why it was elevated and shaped the way it was.

There seemed no way forward. The broken lift controls meant the shaft was blocked so either Leon climbing down it or Mario climbing up was as good as impossible.

Leon shouted down the shaft.

'I know you're down there, and that's where you're staying. The girl and I are leaving.'

Leon turned to her. 'We're going,' he said in a loud voice and promptly left the room.

Natasha followed behind him. There was nothing she could do for Mario at that moment and if he was trapped under the laboratory at least that was one less person likely to try to kill her.

Leaving the huge chamber and walking back through the inner white room they went through to the old morgue, where Leon started to climb the stairs towards the tunnel entrance.

'What are you doing? Surely you're not just leaving?' Natasha asked.

'For someone so clever you're really not that bright, are you?' Leon said. 'In order to escape from whatever is down at the bottom of the lift shaft, your *friend* will need to pull levers or push buttons or whatever controls are down there. The only way he can escape is to find another way out, so he'll have to try anything. The mechanism for opening the vault is down there, I'm sure. You saw the water leaking from above that granite block. I think that will all be released once he activates the lever or presses the button. I give him ten minutes before this whole area is flooded, which is why we need to leave. As I see it the only risk is if the flood water doesn't drain away as I predict.'

'What would be the point of all that?' Natasha asked.

'It's a clever trap,' he snapped back at her.

Natasha decided not to push her luck and changed the subject, pointing at the two surviving workmen. 'What about these two? We can't leave them here to drown. We need to take them up with us.'

'They're just excess baggage,' Leon said dismissively. He raised his gun and casually fired one bullet through each man's head. 'And not a problem any longer.'

Incandescent with rage at what he had just done, Natasha finally lost it and went ballistic. She launched herself at Leon and tried to dig her sharpened titanium nails into his face. But he was too fast and too well trained for her to succeed and smashed a perfectly timed left hook into her body.

She crumpled and fell to the ground. She felt unable to breathe and almost certainly had a couple of broken ribs. If not something worse.

Leon leaned down. 'The only reason you're not already dead is because I might need someone to help me carry the treasure, so get up. Or just lie there and drown. I really don't care much either way.'

It took Natasha a couple of minutes to find the strength to stand up and follow Leon up the stairs. Knowing that at any minute Mario could activate the release to the vault door incentivised her to act through the pain

Wincing and clutching her side, she made it to the top of the stairs and along the passageway to the main entrance. She noticed that Mario had left a distinctive trail of blood both on his journey out and then when he'd come back in again.

Leon looked at her unpleasantly as she gasped for breath but said nothing.

They waited but nothing happened for several minutes.

'He can't really be that clever or stupid, can he?' Leon murmured.

Natasha, for her part, had the fleeting thought that Mario might have actually died down there. And that made her feel sad, because despite the career he'd chosen, she knew she liked him. A lot.

But at that moment they both heard a whooshing sound from deep in the underground complex below them.

Leon waited until the noise had subsided. Then he gave Natasha a push and made her lead the way down the stairs to see what awaited them.

Chapter Sixty-Five

Bailiwick of Guernsey, Channel Islands

As they approached the old morgue the dirty water appeared to be only a couple of feet deep and lapped halfway up the morgue body blocks. Two of the dead workmen were floating face down in the middle of the room. There seemed to be so little water that Natasha wondered if she'd been right in her first guess that the water hadn't been part of an elaborate trap but was either from a ruptured pipe or maybe what was left of the water supply for the old well. The water level was already falling rapidly as it ran down and covered the floor of the laboratory area.

She had discarded her mask outside and was starting to regret doing so as the water smelt rancid and clearly had been festering somewhere above them for a long time.

Leon couldn't have cared less about any of this. He rushed through the now ankle-deep water to the tunnel that led to the vault. Natasha, clutching her side which didn't then feel quite as bad as it had at first, followed him in.

The arc light was still working albeit with a slight flicker, casting sinister shadows down the tunnel.

The granite slab in front of them had opened, swinging upwards presumably using some type of counterbalance device.

Inside was what looked like a traditional steel bank vault, about the size of a tennis court, with rows of metal shelves and boxes scattered in disarray. Lying on the floor were six more small gold ingots and three silver ingots along with several loose pieces of jewellery.

But what there wasn't was a huge Nazi treasure hoard. As far as Natasha could tell, the contents had clearly already been removed and it looked like it had been done in a hurry.

Leon stared all around him and Natasha had no idea what he was thinking. Or what he was going to do. And whether it was worth trying to hide because she ached too much to run very far.

Leon completely ignored her. He strode rapidly around the room and started filling his rucksack with the leftovers.

Natasha was now really worried because time had run out for her and she couldn't think of any good reason why Leon shouldn't kill her. As far as she could see there was no weapon she could possibly use against him, so that really only left her with a single option.

While Leon was occupied with collecting what was left of his inheritance, Natasha ran away for the second time. She splashed her way through the morgue and straight into the laboratory. She knew she couldn't make it outside the underground complex before Leon caught or shot her, so that was her only option. In that vast and cluttered space she knew she could find somewhere to hide.

Leon's first shot missed her by yards, but the second bullet slammed into the steel pillar just behind her. A ricocheting sliver of the copper jacket clipped her head, opening up a shallow wound that immediately began to bleed. She screamed but didn't stop. The rush of adrenaline helped mask the pain of the injury to her scalp.

She ran as far as she could into the chamber and then huddled down under one of the desks that were set in a ragged line on one side of the huge open space. She heard the sound of Leon's footsteps getting closer and then he suddenly appeared about twenty feet away, his pistol in one hand and his torch in the other. He started to slowly walk towards her hiding place, chuckling to himself as he waved his torch around, trying to seek her out with the beam of light.

'I will find you,' he shouted. 'I will. If you give yourself up, I promise it will be quick and painless. If you make me look for you, I'll really make you suffer. And that's something I'm very good at, making people suffer. Believe me.'

Natasha believed him absolutely and curled herself into the tiniest ball she could and waited. She tried to breathe as silently and shallowly as possible and to make no noise at all.

She had no other option. Her head and ribs hurt and her battered and aching body meant she would never be able to outrun Leon.

He'd stopped talking, or rather he'd stopped taunting her, but she could still roughly estimate his position in the chamber by the sound of his footsteps. She heard him cut across the room to continue his search, again moving closer to her. He was probably assuming, rightly, that she would only have been able to get a fairly short distance into the room before he reached the entrance and would have seen where she went.

He was now just twenty feet away, then fifteen, ten.

Natasha knew was going to die and she braced herself for a final and probably futile attack. She wasn't going to just crouch in the darkness and wait for a bullet. The moment he found her, she was going to leap up and go for his throat and hope her titanium nails would be enough to do the job.

Like a devil in the darkness, she could hear his breathing, coming closer and closer.

Suddenly he turned away. Whether he had heard something or was just spooked by the room she would never know. He ran rapidly away towards the entrance, and moments later she heard the unmistakable sound of the heavy doors swinging shut and then the echoing thud as they closed. Natasha knew she was trapped, and very likely so was Mario if he was still alive, within the complex. And that was where they would die.

She let out a deep breath.

She stood up, immediately feeling very dizzy, and looked around. She hoped, desperately, that it would be possible to release the doors from inside. But this hope was quashed when she quickly walked over to look at the backs of the doors. They were completely smooth but for some faded yellow warning signs.

No levers, no handles, no buttons. No way out.

She needed to see if Mario was alive and she also ought to try to tend to her head. She was scared of what she might find and hadn't dared touch it. The wound stung like crazy but the blood was no longer trickling down her face so she figured that it must be clotting. That meant the wound couldn't be all that bad, she rationalised. And she was still alive so that meant the wound could wait. At least for a while.

Climbing up to the capsule again, using the handrail for support, she made it inside and started yelling down the lift shaft for Mario. But there was no answer.

Sitting down on one of the throne-like chairs, Natasha would have normally made some glib remark but she was too bruised and battered both mentally and physically for that. She looked around the strange structure, shook her head and closed her eyes.

She woke up about an hour later with a thumping headache and for a moment had no idea where she was. She got back on her feet and walked around the capsule. Like the chamber below, she found there were many bookcases filled with records but nothing that looked as if it would be any use to her. She wasn't looking for paperwork: she needed to find a way out, which meant a button or a lever or something, and as far as she could see there was nothing like that.

She looked around again. One of these cases looked more important than the others as it was grander in style and only had three quite slim leather-bound books inside it.

Natasha couldn't get out because the laboratory doors were closed and she had nothing else to do but wait for a rescue, hopefully before she died of thirst or hunger. A rescue that she knew deep in her soul would probably never come. She called down the lift shaft for Mario but again received no response.

So she resumed her seat on the throne and started to read the first book.

Chapter Sixty-Six

Bailiwick of Guernsey, Channel Islands

As well as having an eidetic memory, Natasha could also speed read and quickly absorbed the entirety of the first book, utterly mesmerised by its contents. The first part had been written by Himmler and the remainder was a kind of scientific treatise. Had the contents of that section been known they would changed the whole history and development of computing and artificial intelligence. She wondered how different the world would have been today if any of this had become public knowledge sooner.

It had all started, Himmler had written, when he and Hitler found they were both obsessed with the occult, with the concept of black magic and how the power of religion and sacred relics could be used to influence the masses.

They had spent many hours simply talking through all the possibilities, engaging specialist scholars and experienced practitioners to speak with them at private dinners. And as the Nazi empire grew any interesting books or relics on these subjects were automatically acquired and sent to them.

Many believed that Hitler in particular had been obsessed with Jesus Christ and the various relics mentioned in the bible or which had biblical connections. Things like the Spear of Longinus, alleged to be the spear that pierced the side of Christ while he was on the cross. That, along with other relics, had been seized by the Nazis when Germany annexed Austria during the *Anschluss* in March 1938, but later scientific examination of the spear showed that it was no older than the eighth century.

Most other early Christian relics had also been discredited in recent years. One estimate suggested that there were enough fragments of the 'true cross' held in places of worship to assemble several full-size crucifixes, and the multiplicity of authenticated body parts from several saints suggest that when alive they were particularly well-endowed with, typically, fingers, but sometimes even with heads.

Though widely held, this belief in Hitler's obsession was not strictly true, but what the Fuhrer did believe was that fact mingled with fantasy was a particularly powerful combination for influencing the thoughts and beliefs of people. The Nazi use of the swastika was the obvious example. Historically, it was a very ancient religious symbol from Eurasia and the Far East where it supposedly brought good luck. This history had helped convince people from the outset that at its core Nazism couldn't be evil and had some kind of provenance because of the symbol's benevolent meaning and ancient past.

In fact, Hitler was more obsessed with the idea of God and creation. His belief in selective genetic breeding – eugenics – and the employment of genocide as ways of removing imperfections from the human race was merely, he believed, a way of accelerating Darwin's theory of evolution and the survival of the fittest.

It was during these discussions with Himmler that they agreed that humans were impure as a species and that functionality was the most important, and in fact the only, characteristic needed. Of course, this led to agreement that a race or sub-set of humans who had the very finest brains would need to sit at the very top of the human evolutionary tree like gods.

No surprise for guessing who that would have been, thought Natasha.

It had all started with genetic experiments and breeding programmes to make fitter, stronger soldiers and whilst some man-made drugs had been developed that would increase endurance or strength, there was no short cut, certainly not within a few generations, to achieve this.

Experiments had then been undertaken at the laboratory where scientists and doctors had removed arms, legs, eyes, and in fact most body parts, from their victims and experimented with replacing them with robotic or artificial equivalents. The numbers involved ran into the thousands and the book made it clear that both the Nazis and Catholic Church had worked together to supply the scientists with the most important raw material they needed: living bodies. A constant supply of fit and healthy men and women to be subjected to mutilation and vivisection in the underground chambers on Guernsey in the name of creating a master race.

Natasha closed the book at that point and for a few seconds just sat there in the semi-darkness, her mind trying to comprehend the agonies suffered by the unwilling 'volunteers' who had lived – briefly and probably in unbearable pain – in the rooms around her before dying from the procedures or simply being killed because the experiment had failed. She felt utter disgust mingled with a massive wave of sorrow at the inhumanity of the alleged doctors – in fact nothing more than deluded animals – employed by the Third Reich.

The most interesting organ to both Hitler and Himmler was the brain and, especially, whether or not this could be replicated. Rather than worry about the enormous biological complexity of this organ Hitler had suggested that his dog's brain, as a simple example, was driven purely by instinct and not by an ability to think. He set the scientists a challenge: they were to create an artificial dog brain that would respond to commands with bodily actions.

Apparently, they had achieved this with a series of binary electronic responses in a substance that had allowed power to be stored in it like a battery. Grotesquely, the scientists had then inserted the artificial brain into the body of a dead dog, with a microphone in each ear and a speaker in its mouth. They had also strapped thin rods to the limbs like a rudimentary exoskeleton to allow the composite creature to perform actions like sitting, begging and wagging its tail.

Hitler had been delighted with the Frankenstein-inspired result, particularly when his other dogs became hostile to the new visitor.

Himmler, on the other hand, had begun exploring the entire concept of God or a supreme being and, more specifically, whether the power that God allegedly had to create Man could be assumed by Man himself. Whether, in short, men could create artificial thinking beings: robots, in fact. The key was how a brain could be constructed to respond to stimuli, to think in a way similar to human thought, to show reactions and, ultimately, to undertake tasks.

The material the scientists eventually fabricated was made from a series of elements that when combined had the structure and properties of a magnet and incorporated an inbuilt power source based on the internal repulsion of the magnetic poles. It also included a tiny circuit of binary switches. What they had designed was virtually a much earlier version of the first integrated circuit, the so-called silicon chip, which wasn't developed for almost two decades, in 1958. In fact, she realised, in some ways the Nazi device was even better and more sophisticated, using a hybrid of germanium and other materials with electromagnetic properties.

Horrified, Natasha read how this substance had then been built to create an artificial brain that was placed inside a living human being and connected to the spinal cord to take over the body's functionality.

This and other similar experiments had failed, predictably enough, but these artificial brains were then placed on mechanical frameworks fitted with wheels and mechanical limbs. The idea being that on receiving a verbal command or a radio signal, the brain would react in a certain way using a pre-determined set of commands or form of 'instinct' built in to direct its response.

There was a huge section of appendices at the back of the book, bursting with experiment results.

Shutting the book, Natasha shouted down the shaft once more but again received no reply.

She had to assume that by now Mario was dead.

The second book she picked up was full of drawings, plans, data and results covering the construction of a super robot soldier that would think and act and react on its own. This had been ordered by Hitler as the tide of war started to turn against the Nazis as campaign after campaign failed with huge losses of German manpower.

Realising that eventually Germany would simply run out of men to send to the war, the possibility of creating an infinite number of artificial soldiers on a production line, soldiers who would have their training and tactical knowledge hard-wired into their fabricated brains, was more than just a good idea. In fact, Hitler had known it was the only possible way for the Third Reich to survive in the face of the Allied advances and increasingly frequent and alarming victories.

Utterly terrifying, Natasha thought, especially if it had worked. But she didn't need to read the book to know that the concept had failed: the fact that the final and futile defence of Berlin had relied upon the *Volkssturm*, the 'people's storm,' made up of conscripted children and old men, was proof enough of that.

The third book was far more interesting. It described how the Catholic Church and the Nazis would collaborate scientifically together to work out both where life began biologically and how it could be recreated artificially. The ultimate aim had been to reduce the world's population and the inevitable drain on natural resources, particularly in the Third World, and replace these other nations of *Untermenschen* with artificially bred and racially perfect Aryans. Tables of population statistics, food yields and distributed wealth had carefully been worked out.

The utterly devastating intention of this horrendous plan was that only selected Catholics, the chosen Germans, and a tiny, tightly controlled and monitored number of enslaved peoples would eventually have been left in the world. Machines using artificial brains would provide global labour and maintain physical control of the small human gene pool that might still be needed for genetic research, pharmaceutical testing or as a living supply resource for organ donation. The Germans would continue with the eradication of what they perceived to be the weakest and most undesirable members of the human race, as they had done their best to achieve with the Jews and the Slavs, and the church would both help fund the scheme and provide global stability through its revised teachings.

Times, dates and attendees of all meetings between the two parties were recorded as well as details of the original deed signed by the Pope and Himmler.

No wonder the Church was desperate to get its hands on all this.

Natasha gently took out a paper tucked in a pocket at the back of the book and found she was holding the original deed signed between 'Hitler's Pope,' Pius XII and Himmler. She folded it twice and put it in her zipped coat pocket.

Sitting there she assumed that inside each of the locked doors was an individual laboratory where some of these human experiments would have taken place. There were so many lost souls in this place that it really was no wonder that Mario had been spooked.

At that moment she heard a wail of pain from the shaft and ran across to shout down to him.

'Are you okay, Mario?'

'No I'm not. I've lost a lot of blood and I keep passing out. And I can't climb up the elevator shaft or see any other way out of here,' he said weakly.

With no way of physically helping him, all she could do was tell him that help would eventually arrive, something she didn't even believe herself. And then she told him how Leon had locked her in the laboratory and, after debating the wisdom of doing so, she told him what she had discovered in the books she'd read.

Mario was clearly horrified when she'd finished and was silent for several minutes. When he spoke again he articulated his words very clearly.

'Natasha, I am not a good person and have done many bad things. I always thought that I was doing God's will but I now realise I have been misled and used by others. I can never be forgiven even by Him for some of my actions, and now it is time for me to face my maker.'

Natasha didn't like the sound of that at all.

'What do you mean?' she asked.

'This place is an abomination, and for the good of the Mother Church what you have found must never be revealed. Everything here must be utterly destroyed.' He paused for a few seconds, then asked her a question. 'Do you know what *Zerstoren* means?'

She didn't like that question either.

'Yes,' she said. 'It translates as destruction or annihilation.'

'Good. There are three large levers down here. The first one I operated opened the vault door, which I hoped would provide a way out for me, but it didn't. The second opens the door to the laboratory and the third one will destroy both, if you're right about the meaning of *Zerstoren*. I intend to pull the second lever which will allow you to escape, and then I'll start the destruction sequence.'

'Please don't do that, Mario. I can't leave you down there no matter how bad you've been or what you've done. Just wait a few more minutes and I'm sure help will arrive.'

She wasn't entirely sure how or why anyone would enter the underground complex any time soon because as far as she knew apart from Mario, Leon and herself, almost everybody else involved was dead. But she also knew that to keep him alive she would have to try to keep up his spirits and persuade him not to do anything stupid. That was not to be, as his next words clearly showed her that his mind was already made up.

'Natasha, I'm perfectly calm and for the first time in my life I truly know exactly what I need to do. No amount of pleading will change this so please listen to me and do as I say. And you must remember that it was never within your control to alter what is going to happen.

'I am going to open the door to the laboratory now, and you must escape. I will then pull the lever to destroy this pit of hell and at least try and redeem both myself and the poor souls that I know are trapped in here with me.'

'No Mario, you can't,' Natasha said, even though she knew deep down that this was how it was going to end.

'Natasha, this isn't what I want to do, but it's what I need to do. I would love to be able to climb out of here and sit in the sun with you one last time, but that is never going to happen. To save my immortal soul I have to do this, and I have to do it now, while I still can and before anyone else enters this place to try to help us and forfeits their life.

'I think I've worked out that the explosive pockets we found below the well weren't to keep people out. They were there to ensure its destruction. I've just pulled the first lever. Run for your life and may God now be with you.'

The laboratory doors started to swing open and Natasha knew she had no choice.

'Thank you, Mario,' she yelled, and ran as fast as she could towards the opening doors and safety.

Chapter Sixty-Seven

Bailiwick of Guernsey, Channel Islands

She was barely halfway across the laboratory from the capsule to the steel doors when the first explosion shook the chamber and the two doors stopped and then started to close. The detonation sequence had started far more quickly than she had expected. She immediately guessed that both the vault and the laboratory doors were programmed to shut automatically as part of the sequence, to keep everybody inside and to maximise the destruction.

Natasha was nimble and fast, despite what she'd suffered, and without assessing the risks she simply raced forward and slid sideways through the thin gap as the doors slammed closed. Close shave didn't even come close to describing it.

She collapsed on the floor and drew some deep breaths. Her ribs were burning with pain and her head again thumping like a drum from her injuries.

The explosions seemed to be coming in a series rather than all at once and she knew she had to move quickly. Rocks, dirt and debris were already falling all around her.

She tripped over a prostrate body. She looked down to see Leon lying there, his eyes dull and glazed looking up at her and quite clearly dead. His rucksack of treasures wasn't with him, she noticed.

Even as the mortuary walls started to shake, she still took the time to give him a good hard kick to the side of his head. She wrenched the torch out of his hand, just in case she needed light. Then she headed for the stairs.

But Natasha's hopes were dashed when her world suddenly went dark as all the lights failed. There was a huge explosion as rocks and boulders cascaded down the stairs and a billowing cloud of dust filled the space. She thanked her lucky stars that she'd picked up the torch. But in its faint light the one thing she could see for certain was that the rock fall had completely blocked the stairs.

There was no escape that way. She was trapped.

To avoid the choking dust and any other falling rocks she swung round and ran into the furnace room.

She'd ingested some of the dust and gave great hacking coughs to try to clear her throat, which magnified the pain in her ribs and didn't do her headache any favours either.

Natasha stared around, desperately looking for inspiration and found it in the most unlikely of places: the furnace. She saw particles of dust blowing around rather than just sinking slowly to the floor. There was obviously moving air in or near the furnace itself.

She ran over to it and stuck her head right inside. She couldn't see an opening but she could feel moving air. Looking up there was no sign of daylight but she could definitely feel a very slight breeze coming from the wide chimney.

Presumably because of the horrific purpose for which the furnace had been designed, the chimney had been built wide enough for a worker to climb up inside, probably to allow it to be cleaned or maintained. She shone the torch and saw a line of steel rungs built into the side of the structure that disappeared upwards into the gloom.

Natasha realised that the air was cleaner up the chimney, even with its coating of cremation ash, than the dusty air she was currently breathing. And there was a distinct draft which had to mean there was an opening somewhere above her, which was of course obvious because without an open top to the chimney the furnace wouldn't have worked.

She started to climb up the line of rungs, every step hurting her ribs and head, but whatever lay below was certainly far, far worse. Matters weren't helped by the violent explosions that kept shaking the base of the chimney even though it was built into solid rock.

Looking up she could still see nothing but the black vertical tube. Below her the dust, driven by the force of the explosions, was quickly rising up towards her. She closed her eyes and her mouth, forcing herself to breathe through her nose. Relying only on touch, she carried on up the chimney as fast as she could.

As the dust ball hit her from below, she took one last deep breath and clamped her eyes tightly shut to avoid being blinded by the fast-moving dust cloud. And because the dust ball had been driven up the chimney by the force of the explosions below, it started to get hotter.

Her hands were starting to slip on the dust-covered steel rungs, and she exhaled involuntarily. She opened her eyes and then shut them quickly as the dust stung them like bits of grit. It felt like her face had just been sandblasted.

Natasha had no choice. She had to take a breath of the dust-laden air and again started to cough violently. She felt her left hand slip off the rung and in a panic grabbed it again, wrapping her fingers around the old rusty steel as tightly as she could. But as the dust swirled and pulsed around her she knew she was mere seconds away from losing her grip completely and tumbling backwards down the chimney and back into the furnace.

She'd tried, but it hadn't been enough. Nowhere near enough.

She felt a sudden blow as something hit her left shoulder and then a second impact on her right.

Her lungs again filled with the dust-choked air. Her oxygen levels plummeting, she felt her fingers release their death grip on the rung.

A sudden gust of wind blew across her face, but it was far too little and much too late.

With a feeling of inevitability and something almost like relief, she relaxed her body. Her consciousness fled as she waited for the crushing impact that she knew would kill her.

Chapter Sixty-Eight

Bailiwick of Guernsey, Channel Islands

Natasha opened her eyes. She was lying on her back on a grassy slope and looking up at a clear blue sky dotted with fluffy white clouds that her natural pareidolia was busy forming into all sorts of familiar, albeit unlikely, shapes in her mind.

'Ms Black,' a voice said cheerfully. 'I see you're back in the land of the living. Jolly good!'

She turned her head and looked at the speaker. He was a tall dark-haired man with a trim moustache who appeared to be dressed as an old-fashioned sailor. She looked at him for a couple of seconds, then laid her head down again.

'I've died, haven't I?' she said, coughing what felt like pounds of dust from her throat, 'and this must be my phase in purgatory. Otherwise I have no clue why I'm being talked down to by some idiot from the Foreign Office dressed as a pirate.'

The man appeared unfazed by her response and continued addressing her in the same jolly vein.

'No, my dear, you are indeed alive, luckily. And on this occasion you were particularly lucky because your tracker was still working, and we –'

'Tracker?' Natasha demanded. 'What tracker?'

'Ah. I gather your former colleagues had installed tracking devices in most of the clothes they gave you. We persuaded them to let us use one of their monitoring units while we tried to locate you.'

That just confirmed her previous suspicions, and she had put on the jacket de Ronson himself had provided for her, so no doubt that was where the tracker had been concealed.

'Anyway,' the man continued, 'we were able to detect the signal once you climbed up towards the top of that chimney. We managed to dig out the grass covering and dropped one of my team down the chimney on a harness so he could descend to your location as fast as the constraints of the structure and the harness permitted. He managed to reach you just as you lost your grip and wrapped his arms round you. And then we pulled you out *tout suite*.'

'You are from the Foreign Office,' Natasha said. 'I knew it. Nobody else I've ever met talks that way.'

'You're correct. My name is Geoffrey Willard-Smith and I do indeed work at King Charles Street in London. But I must correct you about one misapprehension. I'm not dressed as a pirate. I'm actually dressed as a sailor in period costume because I was called away to tend to you from a splendid armada festival being held here on the island.'

'Ah, yes,' Natasha said slowly. 'I'd have thought a bit of historical dress up and sword waving was right up your street.'

Willard-Smith's smile slipped slightly, but he recovered immediately.

'Sorry – it's been a hard day,' Natasha said tiredly, sitting up and looking around. The hilltop, which she guessed was directly above the underground complex, appeared to be deserted apart from Willard-Smith and herself. 'And the Catholic Church?' she asked.

'That's a bit above my pay grade but I understand they've long gone. Those that were left, I mean. I gather there was a fairly high attrition rate down below in those tunnels.'

'That's one way of putting it.'

'I understand that the Pope's office, no less, and Number Ten have already spoken about this unfortunate incident.'

'And their decision was?'

'It is to be quietly forgotten, and the damage inside the underground hospital is to be rectified, so the closed signs are going to be in evidence for quite a few weeks or even months. The damage is going to be blamed on an undiscovered cache of German explosives accidentally being detonated during repair work, followed by a flood.'

Natasha stared at him.

'I didn't mean the bloody hospital,' she snapped. 'That was always going to be a cover-up, no matter what actually happened down there. I meant are you here to arrest me or shoot me or what?'

Willard-Smith looked slightly shocked at her remark.

'Certainly not. My orders are that you are to be looked after, flown back to the UK and you are then resume your work on full pay. Those are the orders I was given.'

'Good,' Natasha said, standing up. 'You can start by taking me back to the hotel so I can have a long bath and get out of these filthy clothes.'

'Yes. We did notice that the bill hadn't been paid, and I am authorised to cover your food and accommodation costs, but only for one further night. Budgets and all that. I'm sure you understand.'

Natasha glared at him and slowly stood up.

She immediately noticed two things. First, she must have been unconscious for much longer than she'd thought because her head wound had been cleaned and stitched up. And, second, the folded signed original deed she had found in the book she'd read in the underground laboratory was no longer in her pocket.

Sneaky and untrustworthy were the two words that sprung to her mind whenever she even thought about HMG, and what was happening to her right then only served to reinforce her opinion.

-o0o-

Willard-Smith visited her that evening accompanied by a doctor to check her head wound. Once the quack had done his stuff, Willard-Smith explained that the tunnels were to be closed for at least a year for public safety because one had collapsed. He didn't ask her any questions, and she assumed that she would be debriefed properly once she got back to Cheltenham. Or maybe not.

Even later that evening a new passport in her name and an envelope containing two hundred pounds in cash was dropped off at reception for her, along with a plane ticket for a flight the next morning and confirmation of a taxi pick up from the hotel at what looked to her like just minutes after dawn was due to break.

She was even less than impressed when she checked the itinerary. The airline – which she'd never heard of – managed to schedule its take-off from Guernsey at nine in the morning but wouldn't actually land at Bristol until half past two in the afternoon, mainly because the aircraft would be spending most of the day parked somewhere at the airport on Jersey, for no reason that made any sense to her. That meant a five and a half hour journey to cover a little under 120 nautical miles.

'For God's sake,' she muttered as she looked at the figures again, not having quite believed it the first time she read them. 'I could almost get from London to New York in the time it takes these idiots to do that short hop.'

-o0o-

In the event, the journey was uneventful, though very long and boring. She spent the four hours at Jersey sitting in a corner of the lounge reading a bad novel, growling at anyone who tried to invade her domain and working her way through the minimal selection of soft drinks and snacks on offer from the bar.

She picked up a taxi at Bristol Airport for the journey to her cottage, and it dropped her off after about an hour on the road. Everything was just as she remembered it, which wasn't entirely surprising as it was only about a week since the whole thing had kicked off.

It was as if nothing had happened.

As she walked up the garden path to her cottage, she realised she had never been so pleased to be home.

Epilogue

Vatican City

The Pope entered the room beneath the Vatican as he had done so many times before.

The discovery and destruction of the laboratory had come at a heavy price. He had been told that the British government now held the original agreement signed by both the then Pope and Heinrich Himmler, but all the other evidence had been destroyed by the explosions and the flooding of the chambers. At least, that was what he devoutly hoped but as yet he could not confirm. Both Pierre de Ronson and Mario had perished, but that was merely another example of God's will, he believed, because in his estimation both men had been inherently evil.

He looked around the room, which was full of gold and silver ingots and huge boxes of treasures. What no one outside the Vatican knew was that 'Himmler's' vault had been emptied years earlier when a team of architects and workmen employed by the Church had discovered it when removing the well. They'd removed a part of a solid floor that turned out to be a section of the roof of the vault, some distance behind the granite slab. They'd known they'd stumbled on a major Nazi treasure vault but they hadn't known it was the one that had been created by Himmler. They'd emptied the vault as fast as they could and then rebuilt the floor to cover their traces. His predecessor on the throne of St Peter had then overseen the covert transfer of the contents of the vault into the Vatican's secure storerooms.

But that earlier expedition hadn't found the laboratory, mainly because they'd had no idea that it was located just yards away. Even if they'd guessed that they'd found Himmler's almost legendary treasure vault, probably the last thing they would have expected was for the vault and the laboratory to be situated in virtually the same place. The Pope wished they had found the laboratory, because then the incriminating books and especially the signed deed could have been removed at the same time, or simply destroyed. That would have saved him a great deal of trouble and lot of heartache and doubt.

Each year a little of the treasure was discreetly sold and the proceeds used to help keep the church's coffers topped up.

There had been no written records in the Vatican describing even the general location of either the vault or the laboratory, and nobody had had any idea the structures had been so close to each other. Himmler, trusting nobody, had made sure of that. Nor had the Pope known what the gold coins had actually been intended to do.

Natasha Black had managed to achieve what so many before her hadn't and he admired her not just for her intellect but for what he saw as her courage and moral strength of character. She had asked for nothing in return for her – granted co-opted – help, and it was for that reason he had sent a message to the United Kingdom government thanking them for her assistance.

He had also, rather more in hope than expectation, pledged a large donation for the return of any wartime documents to the Vatican Museum, should any be found. He was keenly aware that Himmler's books and the research material hadn't been recovered from the ruins of the underground hospital. He hoped it had been either blown to pieces by the explosions or destroyed in the flood waters, but until he was certain it would never surface again the Pope expected to suffer a series of sleepless nights.

For his own peace of mind he had already decided to station a team of surveillance specialists on Guernsey until the repair work in the underground complex had been completed, with instructions to take possession of any such relics that were discovered, using whatever method or force was required to do so.

GCHQ Cheltenham, Gloucestershire, England

The Pope's message to the British government had ensured that back at GCHQ and in Whitehall almost everything that had happened involving Natasha Black – or at least the illegal bits – had conveniently been forgotten.

She was invited to a well-being session conducted by the Human Resources Department to see what she needed in order for her to return to work after the tragic 'suicide' of her boss. Natasha had been happy to comply because she knew that the people employed in the HR Department wouldn't get out of her face until they'd ticked all the necessary boxes on their rafts of complex and confusing forms. So she'd told them what she thought they wanted her to say and then confirmed that she was quite happy to return to work.

It had all been, she had to admit, very exciting and the prospect of returning to the dull work of an analyst wasn't likely to be a good substitute. It would, on the other hand, be a whole lot safer than dodging bullets, explosions, floods and homicidal neo-Nazis intent on killing her in a secret laboratory deep underground in Guernsey.

As she entered GCHQ through the big glass doors, she fiddled with the gold coin in her pocket. She'd taken it from Leon's hand shortly before she'd kicked him in the head. Willard-Smith and his people had obviously missed it, stuffed inside her sock, but then the document, the signed deed, tucked into her pocket had probably been the real prize for them.

She wouldn't be working that day, as far as she knew, because she'd been asked to attend a full debriefing session covering the events in which she'd been involved.

When she entered the room she saw it was clearly going to be a long haul as serious looking men and woman kept entering the room she had been asked to report to.

She touched the wound on her head and the shaved area around it and reflected that she was lucky to be there. Maybe she should have given Leon a few more kicks for good measure.

Nice, France

At virtually the same time, a man with a newish beard and small round glasses that made him look like faintly like an academic stepped out of a jeweller's shop in a shady backstreet in Nice in the south of France. He was carrying a heavy rucksack slung over his shoulder.

Pierre de Ronson had a new identity and was for the moment living in his personal safe house in Nice. In the mortuary in Guernsey he'd taken two shots to his body armour from the man he now knew had been Leon Himmler, and had pretended to be dead, not a difficult trick in the gloom of the complex.

He had seen Mario shot, then escape and return, and he'd nearly been caught by his former protégé walking around the morgue. Mario had then disappeared into what he assumed was the secret laboratory and had not appeared again.

But he'd had his revenge on Leon about an hour later when he'd shot the German dead and then stolen his rucksack. De Ronson had decided there and then that the time had come for him to finally escape from the Catholic Church and retire in style.

But as he walked along in the sunshine his plan was slowly beginning to unravel. He'd been trying to sell the ingots, but they were not pure because they all contained at least a percentage of bone and ash, which raised obvious questions about where the ingots had come from. Reputable jewellers wouldn't touch them so he was having to try the back street shops and dealers, but any price he was offered was only for a fraction of their true value simply because of the level of impurities and the lack of provenance. Any shop that did buy them would have to factor in the cost of discreetly melting them down and somehow getting them assayed, essential before they could be sold.

The jewellery he'd found in Leon's rucksack was valuable but was without provenance and was, virtually by definition, stolen property. Most likely stolen from some of the Jews who'd ended up in the ovens at Auschwitz or Treblinka or one of the other Nazi death camps, which obviously made it even more difficult to sell. Again, brokering it through dodgy shops like the one he'd just been in meant he'd only receive a small fraction of the true value of the jewellery.

Pierre de Ronson was glad to still be alive and hoped that he might have escaped the clutches of the Church for good, but he was a long way from being a happy man.

GCHQ Cheltenham, Gloucestershire, England

Her lengthy debriefing almost over, Natasha found herself sitting in front of just two rather dull looking men. She poured herself another glass of water from a carafe on the table and waited patiently.

She'd done this kind of thing before and knew that the best way to handle it was to answer every question as simply and concisely as possible and ideally truthfully, though that rather depended on the circumstances, and to never volunteer any information that she hadn't been specifically asked to provide.

In fact, the Dull Brothers had finished with their questions. One of them slid over a document that Natasha recognised immediately: one of the British Government's most effective, efficient and most-used blunt instruments, the Official Secrets Act.

'Just sign that, please, Ms Black, and ensure that you understand what it means and the implications if you disobey the rules.'

Natasha just nodded and signed where the man indicated. She'd already signed an identical document at least twice before because it was a prerequisite for working in GCHQ, but there was no point in even mentioning that. The men would already have known exactly when and how many times she'd appended her signature to a copy. She guessed getting her to sign it again was just a way of getting her attention. Or maybe it was a power thing.

A few minutes after they'd left the room, there was a single tap at the door and Geoffrey Willard-Smith walked in. He'd shed both his sailor suit and the casual clothes he'd been wearing when he'd visited her at the hotel on Guernsey, and this time he was dressed in a clearly expensive handmade suit, but again had a big silly smile on his face.

'Really?' Natasha asked.

'I think I may have misled you slightly the last time we met, Natasha, because I no longer work for the Foreign Office. In fact, I left my last post several weeks ago and I have a new job, right here in Cheltenham.'

'Oh, wonderful. And that interests me how?'

The smile stayed on Willard-Smith's face despite her obvious lack of immediate enthusiasm.

'Because we'll be able to see a lot more of each other. My new official title is Director of Advanced Research here at GCHQ, and that's a brand-new department. Come with me please. I have something to show you, and then something I want to ask you to do,' he said.

Somewhat wearily Natasha followed him along the corridor. As they approached the stairs leading down to the basement area, she had a niggling feeling that Room 23 was involved. Sensing her hesitation, he stopped.

'Apologies for my insensitivity, Natasha. Are you all right going into Room 23 again?'

She nodded. 'As long as it doesn't end up like it did the last time,' she replied.

The door to Room 23 was wide open and the interior was well lit. Standing side by side they both looked at the broken golden ball. Willard-Smith nodded at it slightly.

'I'm guessing you've worked out that this was recovered from Germany just after the war ended. What intrigues us even today is what it is made of, at the atomic level. One day we'll get it properly analysed. Anyway, it proves that what we suspected was correct, that the Germans invented both a form of machine learning and developed what we now call artificial intelligence to a level that wasn't matched properly until the 1960's.'

He paused, then added: 'Did you know Hitler called its capability the God Code because some of the protype devices they built could supposedly speak and even follow and perform simple actions?'

Natasha sensed she was being tested and decided to play dumb. She also noticed that Willard-Smith had dropped the somewhat affected manner of speech he'd used on Guernsey and sounded almost like a real human being rather than a Government flunky.

'That all sounds a bit too far-fetched to be true, don't you think?' she replied.

Apparently happy with her answer, Willard-Smith continued. 'The reason I wanted to speak to you, Natasha, is that within my new research department we come across all manner of really peculiar stuff, things that you wouldn't believe existed. What I need to find is someone with an open and enquiring mind to tell me what they actually think, not what they think I want to hear. So not the kind of answers you gave to the HR people. That sort of thing is no use to me.'

Natasha could only presume that he'd read her personal file, and briefly regretted some of the obvious platitudes she'd uttered during her HR interviews.

'The only way to deal with the idiots from human resources,' she said defensively, 'is to give them exactly what they think they want, otherwise they'll never shut up and you'll never get rid of them.'

'You're absolutely right, and I do exactly the same thing. But this is serious.'

'Are you offering me a transfer?'

'Exactly,' Willard-Smith replied. 'But only if you want to accept. I can promise that it'll be a lot more interesting than trying to analyse codes or work on IT systems'

Natasha made up her mind immediately.

'I accept. I like the sound of being in your new department for funny peculiar stuff and that you want me to speak my mind unhindered. That sort of sums me up perfectly don't you think?' she asked.

'It does, Natasha, as I know only too well. Welcome to the team.'

'How many people work for you by the way?' she asked.

'Just you, so far,' Willard-Smith said, with a broad smile. 'It's a very small department.'

'Right,' Natasha said, somewhat taken aback. 'You asked me to speak my mind, so let me tell you right now that I'm not making tea or coffee for you.'

'Understood and no need. There's a complicated-looking machine in the office that spits out quite agreeable coffee if you talk to it properly. And there's a kettle and some bags for the tea.'

He looked at her appraisingly.

'Now, one last thing, Natasha. The gold coin in your pocket needs to be destroyed, I'm afraid. Orders from above.'

Was there anything he didn't know? she thought.

She produced the coin and placed it on a heat-proof shield on the table where Willard-Smith indicated.

He handed her a pair of clear safety glasses, then picked up a torch burner that stood on the table, turned it on and handed it to her. His intention didn't need to be explained.

Natasha nodded, leaned forward and played the flame on the surface of the coin, reducing it to a pile of white ash in just a few seconds.

The thing was a bad omen anyway, she decided, switching off the burner and taking off the safety glasses. Its story and its legacy were inextricably intertwined with evil.

'Is that it?' she asked.

Willard-Smith shook his head and pointed at the flakes of ash.

'Not quite. Just wait a few minutes,' he replied. 'And watch.'

Natasha had no idea what he was talking about. But, about five minutes later she saw exactly what he meant.

In complete silence, the white flakes of ash on the heat-proof shield quietly started to vibrate, and then began to move very slowly towards each other, drawn together like metal filaments to a magnet.

'I don't believe it,' Natasha said. 'What the hell is that thing? How did the Nazis do it?'

'That's two questions,' Willard-Smith replied, 'but the answer to both of them is exactly the same: we have no idea. It normally takes the flakes about twenty minutes to reform into the shape of the original gold coin, and within an hour it will start re-acquiring its golden tinge. In two hours it will be as good as new.'

'You've done this before?'

'Several times, always with the same result. We have no idea how, but over three quarters of a century ago, the Nazi scientists somehow managed to create a type of integrated electronic circuit that incorporated a revolutionary power system and the ability to self-repair.

'And working out how they did that, Natasha, will be your first task when you start working in my funny peculiar department.'

She switched her glance from the slowly re-assembling white flakes and stared at her new head of department for a long moment.

'I told you that working for me would be interesting,' Willard-Smith said, opening the door of Room 23 and stepping out into the corridor a couple of paces behind Natasha. He finished the sentence as they headed back towards the staircase.

'But I never said it would be easy.'

Authors' note

GCHQ: The Doughnut

From the start, the GCHQ management had intended their new building to become as famous and internationally known as the Pentagon, hence the unusual circular design of the structure. Whether or not it makes any kind of sense to situate the most important intelligence gathering organisation in the United Kingdom inside a building that is instantly recognisable both from the ground and from a distance of about ten miles from the air is not an aspect that appears to have been discussed. On the other hand, trying to hide it away somewhere would probably not have worked. It's worth remembering that in the days before the Secret Intelligence Service, incorrectly known as MI6, had moved to the structure commonly known as Legoland on the Thames at Vauxhall Cross, its previous headquarters building, Century House, was actually included on some escorted tourist routes around London and was routinely referred to by cab drivers as Spook Central, so despite being the home of the Secret Intelligence Service, where it lived wasn't exactly a secret.

Work started on the site in Cheltenham in 2000 and the structure was completed in 2003. The construction costs ran way over the original estimate and eventually topped out at £337 million but that, as it turned out, was the cheap bit. The biggest expense was the cost of moving the computers and the operations into the new building while still continuing the unit's essential intelligence-gathering operations. The cost of the move was estimated at £41 million but in fact took two years to complete and the cost ballooned to over £450 million, while the total cost of the entire project reached a staggering £1.2 billion.

Staff began moving in during 2003 and the building was inaugurated and opened the following year but it wasn't until 2011, eight years later, that the last staff from Oakley – one of the two sites and some fifty buildings that had housed the previous GCHQ operations – finally made the move.

And, perhaps predictably, although the Doughnut was intended to be a single building that would house all of GCHQ's staff and equipment, almost as soon as it was completed it was found to be far too small for this purpose and so a significant number of staff, primarily contractors working on certain technical aspects of operations, are now accommodated in a second building in an undisclosed location elsewhere in Gloucestershire. So despite the expenditure of well over £1 billion, GCHQ still operates from two separate sites in Gloucestershire exactly as it did before the Doughnut was constructed.

As the French say: 'plus ça change.' So the more it changes, the more it stays the same.

The authors have taken certain liberties with the geography and social strata of Cheltenham, and particularly with the functioning, layout and procedures in place at GCHQ on the reasonable basis that if they had stuck too closely to the truth, not only would they have been arrested and shot, but also every reader of the book would have suffered the same fate. It was felt this would have had a negative impact upon potential sales.

The Three Smurfs

For whatever reason, the people who work at GCHQ appear to have a weakness for coming up with silly names for quite serious, even disturbing, activities and operations. The Three Smurfs suite is a fairly typical example.

These are three programs or applications developed by GCHQ specifically to target smartphones. They're individually referred to by the innocuous-sounding names Dreamy, Nosey and Tracker, but what they do is anything but innocuous.

Dreamy Smurf allows GCHQ staff to activate a targeted mobile when it has been turned off by its user, without that fact being apparent. Nosey Smurf goes one step further, as it's a 'hot mic' application, meaning it switches on the phone's microphone to allow GCHQ staff to monitor and record any conversations within audible range of the device.

But Tracker Smurf is the boss, the full-house option. Once activated, this application suite can do more or less anything GCHQ decides it wants it to do. As the name suggests, it can track the smartphone's location, but that's just for openers. It can also analyse, read and retrieve almost everything the user has ever done with the phone, including call records, the browsing history, SMS messages, emails, the contacts list, calendar and notes. So not only would GCHQ know your – or at least your phone's – location, and very probably exactly where you had been with it for whatever period they decided to select, but pretty much anything you've ever done with the device could be analysed and recorded for whatever purpose the officials at GCHQ deemed to be appropriate and necessary.

And, of course, it's all perfectly legal and approved by the UK government.

Bletchley Park

This is a fascinating place to visit and the museum is a real eye-opener for all sorts of reasons, but to the best of the authors' knowledge, there are no hidden underground chambers quite like those described in this novel.

However, there are numerous legends about hidden tunnels linking the local pub and the railway station to the mansion or its grounds, apparently to allow Churchill to nip over to the pub for a swift half and permit other personnel to arrive and depart without being seen, but various survey teams investigating these stories have so far failed to find any trace of them. Having said that, back in 2009 a volunteer who was moving equipment in a building on the site did discover a tunnel entrance, which was duly investigated but was apparently only a disused and long-forgotten underground service tunnel.

Fritz X

Also known as the FX 1400, the PC 1400X, the Ruhrstahl SD 1400X (after Ruhrstahl, the company that manufactured it) and the Kramer X-1 (after its designer, Max Kramer), this unusual weapon was a modified version of the PC 1400, the *Panzersprengbombe Cylindrisch* armour-piercing bomb, which weighed 1400 kilograms, hence its name. This earlier bomb had first acquired the nickname Fritz.

Hitting even a slow-moving target like a ship was difficult with unguided iron bombs, and the Fritz X was designed to combat this problem. It was essentially an aerodynamic guided weapon intended to glide to, rather than drop vertically down on, the intended target, and was fitted with spoilers that could be adjusted using a radio link, allowing it to be aimed in flight. Its design and weight, its armour-piercing 320 kilogram warhead and its maximum 767 miles per hour impact speed – Mach 1 – made it an effective penetration weapon against the heavily armoured capital ships of the day. It was designed to be launched from a minimum altitude of 13,000 feet, and ideally from 18,000 feet, and had a maximum range of just under three nautical miles.

In some ways the most novel and effective feature of the bomb – being guided to the target – was also its main weakness because the bombardier in the launch aircraft had to use his Kehl radio transmitter to link to the Fritz X's Straßburg receiver in order to control the weapon. That meant he had to be able to see both the target and the gliding bomb at all times in order to accurately direct the attack, and to assist him the Fritz X had a flare mounted on its tail.

The further obvious disadvantage was that after launch, the bomber had to fly towards the target on a steady bearing, which made it an easier target for anti-aircraft fire or for a defending fighter aircraft to engage it. During the launch, the bomber had to climb slightly before release and then descend towards the target to keep the weapon in view.

The Italian battleship *Roma* was hit by two such weapons on 9 September 1943 and sank with the loss of nearly 1400 lives after the detonations of the Fritz X devices caused explosions in her main magazines. And in the same month both British and American warships were badly damaged by Fritz X bombs during Operation Avalanche, the codename for the Allied landings at Salerno.

The other obvious potential weakness of the Nazi system was the radio link and Allied scientists worked quickly to develop electronic counter-measures and jamming devices. In the first few months of 1944 the United Kingdom deployed its Type 650 transmitters which successfully jammed and defeated the Fritz X's receiver. By the time of the Normandy landings in June 1944, the use of ship-mounted Type 650 jammers and Allied control of the skies ensured that the weapon was no longer a significant threat.

Horten Ho 229

This advanced prototype aircraft had been designed to try to satisfy the requirement issued by Hermann Göring for what he described as a '3 x 1000 project' aircraft. This slightly odd brief was for a high-speed light bomber that would be able to carry a payload of 1000 kilograms for a distance of 1000 kilometres at a speed of 1000 kilometres per hour. It looked good in the metric system, rather less so in imperial units, where it would be 2200 pounds for a distance of 620 miles at a speed of 620 mph.

The specified speed requirement meant that the aircraft would have to be powered by jet engines but this then impacted the range because jet engines of this era consumed prodigious quantities of fuel. The Horten brothers – Reimar and Walter – were pilots rather than engineers but since about 1930 they'd been designing gliders based upon a flying wing concept in which the pilot lay prone rather than sitting at the controls as in a conventional aircraft. To them, the only solution likely to work was to follow the same route: to create a flying wing aircraft with few conventional control surfaces like a tailplane and rudder in order to reduce drag. And that design would also provide large enough fuel tanks for the two jet engines. Göring approved the design and work started.

But it was really a case of much too little and far too late for the Nazi war effort. The first flight didn't take place until March 1944, and this was only a test of the airframe, essentially an unpowered glider. Development continued for the rest of the year and the first two test flights of the powered aircraft took place in February 1945, culminating in a third flight on 18 February when one of the two Jumo turbojet engines caught fire, resulting in the total destruction of the aircraft and the subsequent death of the pilot. Although by then it was clear to everybody that the war was almost over, the Nazis continued trying to develop the aircraft and to rush it into production, but without success.

The Americans got involved with this project as part of Operation Paperclip, the highly successful attempt by the United States to recruit German scientists and recover what they could of the Nazis' advanced weapon technology, especially the rocketry, in part for their own purposes but equally importantly to avoid the Russians getting their hands on it. As a part of this effort they recovered both a Horten flying wing glider and the V3 version of the Ho 229, then in the final stages of its assembly. Both airframes ended up in America for evaluation purposes under the auspices of Operation Seahorse and the sole surviving Ho 229 V3 prototype is now on display at the Smithsonian National Air and Space Museum in Washington DC.

Both the Horten brothers survived the war, Walter becoming an officer in the post-war German air force while Reimar, like an astonishing number of former Nazis, emigrated to Argentina. Once established there, he continued his design work and constructed numerous gliders as well as planning a supersonic delta wing aircraft and building a powered flying wing craft with four engines known as the IA 38 Naranjero, the latter part of the name providing a clue to its purpose: it was designed to carry oranges from local farms and plantations to Buenos Aires. Only a prototype was built by the DINFIA, an Argentinian state-owned conglomerate of factories manufacturing aircraft, and was test-flown but was found to be severely underpowered. It was eventually scrapped.

Interestingly, as the number of sightings of UFOs proliferated after the end of the Second World War, the American Air Force opened Project Sign, the first of several investigations into what are today often referred to as UAPs, unidentified aerial phenomena. Late in that decade, Project Sign investigators gave serious consideration to the idea that at least some of the sightings might have been of Russian aircraft, developed in secret and based upon the flying wing designs pioneered by the Horten brothers.

Z3

In 1941 a German inventor and engineer named Konrad Zuse designed and built a device he called the Z3, a brief and uninformative name for what was actually the world's first functioning and programmable digital computer. But what might be gleaned from the name is that it was not the first such machine he had produced.

Zuse had constructed the Z1 version between 1935 and 1938, but this was an entirely mechanical device and could only operate for short periods of time. It was followed shortly afterwards by the Z2 which operated using relays. In 1940 Zuse had two strokes of luck: first, he was able to demonstrate the machine to representatives of the German Laboratory for Aviation, the Deutsche Versuchsanstalt für Luftfahrt or DVL and, second, that was one of the very few occasions when the Z2 functioned as it was intended to. The successful demonstration enabled him to secure partial financing of the succeeding design from the DVL, and the following year he was able to present the working Z3 model to the organisation. Like the Z2, it functioned using relays – 2600 of them – but was infinitely more reliable than its predecessor.

The problem Zuse had was that nobody, not even Zuse himself, realised the importance of the machine he had built, so his request to the German government for funding to be provided to construct the Z4 version with electronic switches instead of relays was rejected on the grounds that the device was not important to the war effort.

Despite what has been depicted in this novel, the Z3 did not survive the war, being blown to pieces on 21 December 1943 during one of the Allied bombardments of Berlin. But in 1961 an accurate working replica of the machine was constructed by Zuse's company, Zuse KG, and this can be seen on permanent display at the Deutsches Museum in Munich.

Balkan 176 vodka

This is a triple-distilled spirit that's colourless, tasteless and odourless and, at 88% alcohol, it's one of the strongest drinks in the world. The bottle carries no less than thirteen different warning labels because of the number of people who have died of alcoholic poisoning through drinking far too much of it, far too quickly.

Hitler's Pope

Eugenio Maria Giuseppe Giovanni Pacelli was born on 2 March 1876 and reigned as Pope Pius XII from 2 March 1939 – his sixty-third birthday – until his death on 9 October 1958, guiding the papacy through the horrors and confusion of the Second World War. Along the way, he became known as Hitler's Pope because although in 1942 he and the Vatican were presented with clear and unambiguous evidence of the mass slaughter of Jews during what became known as the Holocaust, he refused to condemn either what was happening in the concentration camps dotted around Europe or the activities of the Nazi party itself.

In all, including sub-camps, there were more than one thousand concentration and extermination camps in Germany and Nazi-controlled territory. The first was opened by Heinrich Himmler on 22 March 1933, immediately after Adolf Hitler assumed the role of Chancellor of Germany, and was one of the most notorious: Dachau. It was built on the site of a disused munitions factory in Dachau, the town located roughly 10 miles to the north-west of Munich, initially to hold political prisoners. Famously – or notoriously – the gate through which prisoners entered carried the ironic legend *Arbeit macht frei,* which translates more or less as 'work shall set you free.'

This became the blueprint for the construction and operation of every one of the SS-organised concentration camps that followed and was where around 41,000 victims were murdered. These weren't only Jews, but various other groups of 'undesirables,' including Catholic priests, Communists, criminals, homosexuals, Jehovah's Witnesses, Poles, political prisoners and Romani or gypsies. The final death toll of Jews during the Holocaust was around 6 million.

In an attempt to counter criticism of the conduct of Pope Pius XII, between 1965 and 1981 the Vatican released eleven volumes of documents relating to the wartime period, but these were condemned by a researcher as both 'selective and insufficient' in that certain documents known to exist and also known to contain anti-Semitic statements were excluded.

It does seem somewhat bizarre that a religion allegedly based upon the life and sayings of a Jewish man who lived a couple of millennia ago should harbour anti-Semitic views and attitudes …

The rat lines

Researchers who have studied the immediate post-war period have claimed that as many as 10,000 former Nazis managed to escape justice and ended up in South America, and particularly in Argentina, including some of the most notorious war criminals.

Whatever the true figure, it is indisputable that the Vatican and the Catholic Church were instrumental in facilitating the escape of many of these fugitives from justice. And it is also established fact that the Catholic Church was riddled with vocal and outspoken Nazi sympathisers, people like Alois Hudal, an Austrian Catholic bishop, who presumably thought that ridding the world of the Jewish nation, the nation that had produced the man who had effectively founded their religion and in whose name they prayed and preached, was for some reason a good thing.

Heinrich Himmler

In reality, there is no reason to doubt the official version of the circumstances surrounding the death of Heinrich Luitpold Himmler. The architect of the 'final solution' was a coward all his life and on 23 May 1945, as described in this novel, he died by his own hand at Lüneburg rather than face the consequences of his actions. The location of the unmarked grave where his corpse was dumped is still unknown.

Roberto Calvi

At about 0730 on Friday 18 June 1982 a commuter spotted the body of Roberto Calvi dangling by his neck at the end of a rope from the scaffolding under Blackfriars Bridge in London, which at least solved one minor mystery: where the banker had gone.

The previous day he had been officially but in absentia sacked as chairman of the failed Italian bank Banco Ambrosiano, an event that coincided with his private secretary, Graziella Corrocher, falling to her death from the bank's headquarters building. She had left a note accusing Calvi of ruining the bank – which was not really in dispute – but despite the official verdict that she had committed suicide there were suspicions that she had been 'assisted' out of the fifth-floor window, because the bank's collapse had far wider implications than the failure of a major financial institution and had annoyed rather a lot of very dangerous people who had lost substantial amounts of money. One likely such group was the Cosa Nostra or Mafia, which was widely believed to have used the services of the Banco Ambrosiano as a convenient conduit for laundering vast amounts of money.

Calvi himself had walked out of his apartment in Rome eight days earlier, disappearing from view for reasons that quickly became obvious, and made his way out of Italy using a fake passport in the name Gian Roberto Calvini. He first travelled to Venice, where he chartered a private aircraft to fly him to Zurich and then on to Britain. When his body was cut down the authorities reported his pockets were stuffed with bricks and he had three separate wads of cash in different currencies, the combined value amounting to about US$15,000. It appeared to be a clear case of suicide but, as with so much about Roberto Calvi, all was not as it seemed.

The collapse of the Banco Ambrosiano had happened because it had somehow 'mislaid' just under $1.3 billion (roughly $3.5 billion today) but that, really, was simply the end-game. Four years earlier an investigation by the Bank of Italy had discovered the bank had illegally exported several billion lire, actions which resulted in criminal prosecutions. Calvi was given a four-year suspended sentence for illegally sending the equivalent of $27 million out of Italy and was also fined just under $20 million. Bizarrely, but not too surprising to people familiar with Italian bureaucracy, he kept his job at the bank.

He had acquired the nickname 'God's banker' – the *Banchiere de Dio* – because of his, and the Banco Ambrosiano's, close personal and financial links with the Vatican. Calvi certainly knew the bank's failure was imminent because on 5 June 1982 he wrote a personal letter to Pope John Paul II warning him of the consequences of the collapse. Correspondence between the Vatican and Calvi showed that not only were illegal transactions taking place between and on behalf of the two entities, but that this was common knowledge. It also became clear that significant amounts of the 'mislaid' funds had been channelled from Banco Ambrosiano through the *Istituto per le Opere di Religione*, the Institute for the Works of Religion, better known as the Vatican Bank.

The latter's involvement was tacitly acknowledged two years later when some 120 of the creditors of Banco Ambrosiano received a total of around $225 million in payment for what was described as the 'moral involvement' of the Vatican Bank. No liability was ever admitted by the Catholic Church about the matter, and no definitive proof of its involvement in the financial fraud was ever found. However, bearing in mind the importance of the Vatican and the Catholic Church to Italy, it could certainly be argued that the investigators were not encouraged to look very hard …

Calvi wasn't just an arguably incompetent and corrupt banker. He was also a senior member of the covert and illegal masonic lodge known as P2, *Propaganda Due*, run by the crooked financier Licio Gelli. Gelli's villa in Arezzo was raided by the police in March 1981 and led to the discovery of a P2 membership list of 962 people, which included very senior civil servants and military officers, not to mention the directors of all three Italian secret intelligence services and a man named Silvio Berlusconi who would later achieve wide notoriety.

A fact that would later become significant was that the members of P2 often used the expression *frati neri* or 'black friars' when they referred to themselves.

The first coroner's inquest in London into Calvi's death returned a verdict of suicide in July 1982, but this satisfied nobody, and certainly not his family, who were convinced he'd been murdered. A second inquest a year later recorded an open verdict. Almost a decade after that, in 1992, Home Office forensic scientists proved that the suicide verdict could not be sustained because there was neither rust nor paint on Calvi's shoes so he could not have walked across the scaffolding below the bridge to reach the point where his body was found. No action was taken by the British authorities in response.

In 1998 Calvi's corpse was exhumed for further examination by a German forensic team. The results of the tests were published in 2002 and confirmed this conclusion, further proving that Calvi had not handled the bricks found in his pockets and that the injuries to his neck had not been caused by hanging. The most obvious and logical conclusion was that he had been murdered, probably by being strangled, and his body had then been taken by boat to Blackfriars Bridge and suspended there from the scaffolding, obviously to make a point.

Various culprits have been suggested as his killers, including the Mafia, though the way he died is usually considered to be far too subtle for a Cosa Nostra assassination, that organisation generally preferring to use a bomb or a bullet. Another obvious suspect was the P2 lodge, and especially because of where his body was found. Quite possibly the 'black friars,' the *frati neri*, of P2 had murdered Calvi as retribution for the failure of the Banco Ambrosiano.

But there is another possibility. When the various inquisitions began operating in Europe from the twelfth century onwards, torturing and executing anyone who was not a devout Catholic – and quite probably some people who were – the enforcement arm, so to speak, of the Church was the *Ordo Praedicatorum*, the Order of Preachers. Also known as the Dominicans after the order's founder, Saint Dominic, they were additionally referred to as the *Domini Canes*, the 'hounds of God,' but also as the 'Black Friars' because their traditional robes were white habits covered in a black cloak or *cappa*. These Black Friars became the Church's inquisitors, the Pope's torturers and executioners and, eventually and to some extent, the Pope's guards and protectors.

Bearing mind that as a result of Roberto Calvi's colossal failure the Vatican Bank was out of pocket to the tune of an absolute minimum of $225 million because of the repayment made to the Banco Ambrosiano's creditors, plus whatever other losses it sustained as a direct or indirect result of the collapse, it would actually be somewhat surprising if the Vatican had not wished to make its displeasure known.

And a very obvious and visual method of ensuring that Roberto Calvi paid the ultimate price, and that people in the know would be acutely aware of who or what had ordered his execution, was to leave his corpse suspended below the bridge in London that was actually named after the Dominican order.

Himmler's son

Heinrich Himmler married Margarete Boden in 1928 and she bore him a daughter, Gudrun Margarete Elfriede Emma Anna, in 1929. She was forced to testify at the Nuremburg trials but remained unswerving in her support of her father and what he had done, remaining a supporter of the ideology of the Nazi Party. She also worked with various Neo-Nazi organisations and particularly those that supported former members of the entity shaped by her father, the SS. She married a man named Wulf

Dieter Burwitz who worked for the National Democratic Party of Germany, the Nationaldemokratische Partei Deutschlands or NPD, a Neo-Nazi and very far right political party.

The couple also acted as foster parents to the orphaned son of an SS officer, a boy named Gerhard von Ahe.

In 1936 a woman named Hedwig Potthast was appointed as Himmler's secretary and within three years she had become his mistress, leaving her official post at the Gestapo headquarters in Berlin on Prinz-Albrecht-Strasse in 1941. They subsequently had two illegitimate children, a boy and a girl. The son, Helge, was born in 1942 and their daughter, Nanette Dorothea, was born at Berchtesgaden two years later.

Both Himmler's illegitimate son Hans, and his grandson Leon, the man whose actions are described in this novel, are figments of the authors' fevered imaginations.

German Underground Hospital, Guernsey

The authors have also taken considerable liberties with the layout of the German Underground Hospital, which does not in reality contain an incinerator or some of the other structures described in this novel.

Swastika

This very old symbol or icon is utilised in several Eurasian and Indian religions, often being used to indicate divinity or a high degree of spirituality or enlightenment, and with different meanings depending upon whether it faced left or right, and it was also used as a symbol in the ancient pagan religions of Greece and Rome. The word swastika itself is derived from Sanskrit and in that language it meant conducive to well-being or health, while the right-facing symbol, as appropriated by the Nazis, symbolised good luck. In the West it was also regarded as a good luck charm, at least until the rise of the Nazi Party in the 1930s.

Under the Nazis the swastika became the symbol of the 'perfect' Aryan race, as well as being the most common emblem of the Nazi movement, but is now reviled and effectively a banned antisemitic symbol throughout the Western world because of the Holocaust and the atrocities committed by the German nation under Hitler in the Second World War. However, in Middle and Far Eastern nations from China to India and Mongolia it is still regarded as representing prosperity and good fortune and is commonly seen.

Feedback

If you enjoyed this book, please remember to leave a review on Amazon! We always appreciate reviews, good because they make us feel better or bad so we can try to fix what you don't like, and it only takes a minute to do.

Natasha Black will be back soon in Black Ops: Red Death.

Check the website www.JamesBarrington.com *for details of this and other new publications, and you can download a free book there as well.*

Other books by the same authors

James Barrington and Richard Benham

Cyberstrike: London

Cyberstrike: DC

Richard Benham leads a simpler writing life than I do because he has only one name. For a number of dull and largely irrelevant reasons I've ended up with several noms de plume, though mainly James Barrington and James Becker. The full back-catalogue is listed below, but if you don't want to bother wading through it, you can see details of all the books on the website www.JamesBarrington.com. While you're there, don't forget to download your free book.

Max Adams (Writing for Macmillan & Canelo – WW2 thrillers)

To Do or Die

Right and Glory

Operation XD

James Barrington (Writing for Penguin UK)

Joint Force Harrier (non-fiction)

James Barrington (Writing for Macmillan & Canelo – thrillers)

Overkill

Pandemic

Foxbat

Timebomb

Payback

Manhunt

Retribution (novella)

Insurrection

Understrike

Bioweapon

James Barrington (Writing for Canelo – non-fiction)

Falklands: Voyage to War

HMS Illustrious

John Browning: Man and Gun Maker

James Becker (Writing for Transworld – historical mystery thrillers)

The First Apostle

The Moses Stone

The Messiah Secret

The Nosferatu Scroll

Echo of the Reich

The Lost Testament

The Templar Heresy

James Becker (Writing for Penguin USA & Canelo – Knights Templar trilogy)

The Lost Treasure of the Templars

The Templar Archive

The Templar Brotherhood

James Becker (Writing for Canelo – historical mystery thrillers)

The Last Secret of the Ark

James Becker (Writing for Canelo – thrillers with a sci-fi twist)

Trade Off

Cold Kill

Jack Steel (Writing for Simon & Schuster & Canelo – conspiracy thrillers)

The Titanic Secret

The Ripper Secret

The Dante Secret (novella)

Peter Lee (Writing for PostScript Editions – non-fiction)

The French Property Nightmare

MH 370: By Accident or Design

Cruise Control

Peter Stuart Smith (Writing for PostScript Editions – non-fiction)

Inspiration, Perspiration, Publication

Thomas Payne (Writing for PostScript Editions)

The Dietaholic's Diet

That's the lot for the moment!

Don't forget to download your free book from www.JamesBarrington.com

Printed in Great Britain
by Amazon

76514114R00203